The Glowing Cow Boy

'I love kind, clever Albi, who's come to help save the world.
His amazing, magical story will open kids' eyes to the possibility
of a greener, happier future. Georgia magnificently captures the
imagination of this calf on his journey through the world. This
is something to really inspire us to stop eating animals and take
care of our precious planet. A great book for our time by the
talented Georgia Byng.' MARY McCARTNEY

'Prepare to have your heart stolen, your imagination fired,
and your mind blown by the adorable Albi, a small cow
with a big message!' BEN MILLER

Also available by the author:

The Sock Monsters
Jack's Tree
The Ramsbottom Rumble
The Girl With No Nose
Molly Moon's Incredible Book of Hypnotism
Molly Moon Stops the World
Molly Moon's Hypnotic Time-Travel Adventure
Molly Moon, Micky Minus and the Mind Machine
Molly Moon and the Morphing Mystery
Molly Moon and the Monster Music

GEORGIA BYNG

ALBI

The Glowing Cow Boy

Cover illustration by LEVI PINFOLD
Interior illustrations by ANGELA COGO

uclanpublishing

**Eating mushrooms found in the wild can be dangerous.
Never eat a wild mushroom unless an adult has
told you it is safe to do so.**

Albi: The Glowing Cow Boy is a uclanpublishing book

First published in Great Britain in 2023 by
uclanpublishing
University of Central Lancashire
Preston, PR1 2HE, UK

978-1-915235-13-8

1 3 5 7 9 10 8 6 4 2

Set in 10/16pt Kingfisher by Becky Chilcott.

A CIP catalogue record for this book is available from the British Library.

Printed and bound in Great Britain by Clays Ltd, Elcograf S.p.A.

For wonderful Guy

Snow-white winter,
When spring shoots come
May they be glowing and good.
May the people of today and tomorrow,
Have the strength and kindness and magic in them
To help make the world a great place to live,
For every person,
Every animal,
Everything,
Everywhere.

WINTER

Chapter One

THE BEGINNING
OF THE MAGIC

It was freezing and frosty, that January night. The sky was slate-black and sprinkled with stars. A milky moon hung from the heavens, stroking the sleeping hills and the snow-covered land. A cloud in the shape of a cow drifted towards the full moon, then seemed to jump over it. At the same time a comet shot overhead, and it began to snow.

It wasn't ordinary snow, though. This stuff was more silver than white and it glowed. Down it tumbled, buffeted by the winter wind. It landed on the crusted ground and disappeared.

Any animal close enough to see would have noticed how the silver flakes hit the frozen earth and slid quickly into it, and then how the icy soil pulsated with light – like a blanket with a torch underneath, switching on and off, on then off.

More of the powdery droplets fell, for miles around and further afield, in counties and countries beyond, in places where it was raining and others where it was dry. The glowing stuff fell north, south, east and west. But few seeing the falling silver would have known this.

Some of it floated down through a crack in a barn roof, drifting through cold air to land on a small white calf who lay curled up beside his sleeping mother. He shivered, tickled by the bright bits as they touched him. His eyes fluttered but didn't open, so he didn't see his fur shine and glow before dulling to plain white again. He snuggled into himself and breathed a contented sigh.

Eleven wide hills away, a twelve-year-old boy lay asleep in his bed, his red hair feathered across his pillow. In his hand was a bird. Not a toy one, a real one, and a dead one at that; a stuffed white dove. His window was open and a silver flake drifted in. As though searching, it floated about and hovered over the boy. Dropping down, it settled on his forehead. Its kiss of light twinkled there, then coursed into him. For a moment his red hair flickered with a fiery light.

A few hours later, the sun rose. It warmed and thawed the fields. And here and there where the silver snow had fallen, white milk mushrooms began to sprout.

Rufus Chumley crouched in the grass beside a fire that he'd made. Warmed by its heat, he felt drowsy. He gazed at the trunks of the trees in the woods nearby. He blew at the hot embers of his fire's burning logs and their flames grew, licking the underside of a

chicken that was cooking on a spit – his breakfast. He'd meant to shoot a rabbit but as usual, they'd all been too fast for him. So, to make up for it, he'd stolen the chicken from his parents' fridge. Its flesh glistened and spat hot fat.

'Ten minutes and you'll be done,' he told it.

He picked up his air rifle and put it to his shoulder. He twisted as he swept it from left to right, looking for something to take a pot shot at. He spotted some fat white mushrooms under an oak. He aimed and pulled the trigger. *BANG*. The flesh of the mushrooms splattered on the tree's trunk.

'Shot!' Chumley congratulated himself.

'RUFUS!' A screeching, more like a car's brake than a human voice, came from the house. Rufus turned. 'Don't you *dare*!' his mother shouted. 'Don't you point that thing at me, you idiot!'

Rufus dropped his gun. He wished he had his pea shooter with him. He would have loved to shoot a hard pea at his mother, to clip her earlobe and make her diamond earrings jangle. Or to hit her neck. That would sting. Or to hit one of her soft, ring-encrusted hands. She'd go mad. He could imagine her screaming and hopping about. And how satisfying that would be. He watched her as she tottered over the grass towards him, the stiletto heels of her sparkly shoes sinking in the mud. She was dressed up as lavishly as someone at a Hollywood party. In her hand was a tulip-shaped cocktail glass with clear liquid and an olive in it. He wondered why she was coming to talk to him. She usually avoided him.

'I've told you before. Fires here blow smoke into the kitchen,' she complained. Her dark-ringed eyes darted around as they absorbed the sight in front of her. 'Is that blood on your hands?'

Chumley looked at his fingers. 'Yes. Had to get the giblets out of the chicken.'

His mother grimaced at the mound of chicken innards on the ground. 'Didn't it strike you that you might wash your hands? You're a filthy animal, Rufus Chumley.' She began to cough as a wind caught some of the fire's smoke and blew it in her face. She scowled. 'Like a dirty, feral child.'

'I *am* a child,' her son reminded her.

'Could have fooled me,' she slurred. 'Look at the size of you, you great galumphing upstart. You're not a child.' She wagged her red-nailed finger at him. 'You fit in your father's clothes. Your shoes are the size of a lumberjack's. Don't you lie to me, young man. Now go to work! School.' She hiccupped. 'Wherever it is you go.'

She tripped a little as she made her way back to the house. Rufus Chumley didn't bother to explain to her that there was a staff training day happening at his school, and so he had a day off.

'Your father wants to see you later,' she called back, now remembering what she'd come out to say. 'He's got a job for you.'

Chumley watched her walk towards the ugly grey-brick house that he had to call home. By the time she closed its back door she would have forgotten she'd spoken to him. She seemed to only think about him when he was irritating her. And then, when she communicated, the icing on the conversation was always an insult. Usually telling him how stupid he was. She definitely did not like him. She never had. If he had been smaller, might she have liked him more? he wondered. He looked down at his huge feet and at his long legs, and at his big hands. He looked like a sixteen year old, even though he was only twelve. When he was born, he'd been regular-sized. But he had soon grown twice the size of other babies. Twice the size! This was because he had a growing condition. His parents had taken him to lots of doctors but no medicine could stop him growing. Now he was huge. His mother, disgusted, had given him to mean nannies to be looked after. Now he was old enough to look after himself, she'd said. And so, he did.

He was hungry. The chicken was done. Chumley took it off the fire and waved the meat on its stick in the cold air to cool it down. It smelt delicious. A pheasant squawked in the wood, as though reminding him that he preferred eating pheasant to chicken. He could live off wild pheasant, he thought. He might have to if he left home. He'd considered leaving home countless times, and, every time his horrible mother reminded him of how little she cared for him, how repulsive she found his largeness, the idea of running away became more attractive.

A church bell sounded eleven o'clock, its chime thrown out across the Salisbury countryside over hilly fields full of snowdrops and crocuses. A blackbird chirruped as it found a safe place to sit. And on a hillside, in a shed, under a corrugated roof, a mother spoke to her son.

'Albi, that's a spider. Careful, keep your hoof off it. Don't tread on it. It didn't do you any harm.'

Albi, her young calf, wobbled as he held his hoof aloft and the small creature scuttled away over the straw, past his mother's front hooves to the side of the shed, to safety. Albi sniffed after it.

'It's gone to weave a web to catch some flies,' his mother said.

'What for?'

'To eat.' A fly buzzed about Albi's mother's udders and she flicked her tail to shoo it.

'To eat?'

'Yes, spiders are carnivorous. That spider eats nothing but meat, the meat of flies and bugs. It knows no other way.'

'Carnivorous.' Albi practised the word.

Just then, the shed door creaked open. Morning light flooded in. Albi stepped behind his mother and stared past her white legs at a big human outside. The man opened the shed door wide, revealing a view of the yard, then he climbed back over the metal bars of its enclosure fence and was gone.

Albi had never been outside the shed before. He'd felt sunlight on his fur, but it had only been through a small crack in the shed roof.

'Is today the day?'

'Yes, Albi. It's warm enough now. Don't be scared.' His mother put her head behind his rump and nudged him.

Timidly, Albi stepped out. Strong shafts of warm sunlight hit his back. He blinked as his eyes adjusted to the day's brightness. Under his feet, instead of straw there was glistening hard ground, dark and wet like the end of his own nose. Albi stood still. He breathed in the cool, fresh smells of the farmland nearby – grass, mud, soil with bulbs in it, and hellebore flowers, whose subtle scent was carried on a cold breeze all the way from the pine-smelling woods where the fir trees were. His mother had told him about these things. She'd already taught him a lot and it had all sunk in.

Like the other calves of the herd, Albi was much more advanced in his thinking and understanding than he looked. He was inexperienced, but he had soaked up his mother's lessons and he was ready to learn more about the world for himself.

As he shut his eyes and breathed in deeply, someone sniffed beside him. Albi looked to the left and jolted with surprise. A tawny calf stood there. This calf jumped with surprise too. Albi darted back into his shed.

'Mum, there's another calf next door! And it's got *blue* eyes.'

'That's normal,' his mum said, her pink eyes smiling. 'Other cows and calves have blue or black or brown eyes.'

'Are my eyes blue?'

'No. You're like me, Albi. White as snow with pink eyes. We're albinos.' She nudged her calf out again. 'Now go and make friends.'

Chapter Two

HENGE FARM,
THE SHAPES AND
THE HUNTERS

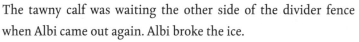

The tawny calf was waiting the other side of the divider fence when Albi came out again. Albi broke the ice.

'Hello. I'm Albert. Albi for short. What's your name?'

The younger calf blinked and looked down shyly. 'Er-Er-Ernie.'

Albi smiled encouragingly. 'Is this your first day out?'

'Y-yes. Scary, isn't it?'

Albi considered this. 'A bit. But exciting too.'

Ernie nodded, but his eyes kept checking behind him, to see if his mother was still there.

'Mum says I've got to get some fresh air.'

'Don't worry, you're all right.'

Cautiously, Ernie stepped closer to Albi and they looked about. Their sheds were surrounded by lots of other sheds and pens.

'It's so big, isn't it?' Albi said, glad to have Ernie as a companion. 'My mother says there's twenty-two calves here.'

'I th-think I've had enough air for now,' Ernie stuttered and he trotted back inside.

Albi stood where he was, and studied the world about him. At the end of the row was a flat white block with a set of shapes on it. They looked like this:

HENGE
FARM

The man walked under the block. He began to work his way up the row, opening all the other shed doors. One by one, calves poked their heads out at the world. A grey calf in the shed to the right side of Albi's came bursting out. The man made some angry noises.

WHOOOOOAAAAAWHOABOY!

Albi shrank back, but the stocky grey bull calf didn't seem to notice the man's rough tone at all. He pushed past and stuck his head out through the bars of his pen to have a good look about. When the man had gone, he turned his big head, crowned with scruffy curls, towards Albi and smiled.

'Hello Albi. Very white, ain't ya?' He paused to chew something that was already in his mouth as he sized Albi up. Then he added, 'I'm Bodge.'

'Hello Bodge. What are you chewing?'

'Feed,' Bodge said, matter-of-factly.

'Feed?' Albi was astonished. 'What, you mean *nuggets*? But I thought we weren't old enough for nuggets yet.'

Bodge raised his eyebrows and nodded.

'Don't you like milk?' Albi asked.

'Naah, not much. Trying to give it up. Mum says it's best to. Maybe the milk's why you're so white.'

'Well,' corrected Albi, 'actually, I'm an al—'

'— bino.' Bodge finished Albi's sentence. 'My mum knows your mum. Says she's all right. My mum's much older than your mum. Bigger, too.'

'Yes,' said Albi, remembering. 'Yes, your mother's important.'

'Yup, you got it,' said Bodge, puffing up proudly. 'My mum always walks in the centre of the herd or at the front. She's the dom . . . domino, no, dom . . . dominant – yeah, that's it – she's the dominant cow.'

'Oh, I see,' said Albi, impressed.

Bodge chewed some more feed, though from his face Albi wasn't quite sure he was enjoying it.

'I'd like to see the fields,' Bodge said with a sigh. 'And I'd like to meet Dad.'

Albi hadn't thought about seeing the fields for himself, or about meeting the bull. The bull, their father. Father to all the calves here.

'He's massive,' said Bodge, spitting out his mushed-up nugget. 'He doesn't let anyone push him about. He's the king.'

Albi suddenly felt very small. Bodge seemed to know so much already. Maybe there was something special in those nuggets he was chewing. Albi decided to try one. He sniffed at the trough.

'Go on,' urged Bodge. 'They won't poison ya.'

The nuggets had a sweet, earthy smell. Albi picked one up in his mouth and broke it with his teeth. It was crumbly, but quite hard too. It wasn't delicious like his mother's milk. It tasted like the smell of hay. Bodge caught his eye and winked.

'Good, Albi,' he said, chewing away. 'You and me are gonna grow really big. These nuggets will make ya clever. So clever you'll be able to do ya pats without making a mess.'

Albi couldn't help noticing that Bodge's behind was very brown and messy.

'I haven't got the hang of patting yet, Bodge admitted. Albi smiled. Bodge took this as a cue to go further. 'Mind you, my mum's not got the hang of patting, neither. Her tail end is a right old mess. The other mother cows aren't much better. Nor is the bull!' he whispered.

Albi laughed.

'*Splat, splat!*' Bodge raised one of his eyebrows.

'Bodge!' came his mother's voice from inside. 'I heard that! You come inside at once!'

'I'm in for it now.' Bodge turned sheepishly. Before going in, he smiled at Albi. 'Eat up your nuggets, mate! You and me have got to grow big. The bigger, the better.'

Rufus Chumley sat in his den, eating his second breakfast. He loved to eat. He was always hungry. A massive TV set filled the whole of the wall in front of him. Trees were on the screen so the room felt like it was the woods. A stag appeared, then a camouflaged man and child, hiding in the bushes.

'*The hunters lie in wait*,' the narrator of the programme explained. '*Look at the size of this deer. A shot to the heart will do it.*'

Rufus took a bite of his bacon sandwich and ketchup dribbled down his chin. The boy on the screen reminded him of himself. He munched and studied the people on the TV, still as statues, and he thought back to when he'd first got the hunting bug. It had been a long time ago, on the school playground, when he was six. As usual, he'd been playing on his own. Talking to himself. Then there had been a thud; a white squirrel had fallen out of a tree near him. He'd picked up the hurt creature to take to the teacher. On the way to the staff room, some older kids had come to see what he was holding. They'd crowded round him. At that very moment, the squirrel had twitched and died.

'Cool!' the big kids had cried. 'Chumley's killed a squirrel! And it's a weird white one!' The kids had congratulated him and patted him on the back. It had felt good, especially as the squirrel was a rare albino type. This had made Chumley feel extra-good.

That was when it had started. Chumley had begun to kill things after that. He started with insects, swatting them, squashing them, then he moved on to the creatures that lived in the village pond. He liked to fire small stones from his pea shooter at the frogs. He wasn't a very good aim and so, rarely hit them, but he still enjoyed it.

He asked for a catapult. His parents happily bought him one. They were pleased he was out of the house and away from them. So, the seven-year-old Rufus spent whole days in the woods and fields, stalking rabbits and pheasants, trying to get close enough to kill them with a slingshot stone. He still missed most of the time but he liked the wild world where he tracked animals.

He felt free. In his mind, he'd pretend to be a prehistoric hunter or, at other times, a boy on a desert island, trying to survive.

By the time he was eight, he'd moved on to hunting knives. For a while, they were his best possessions. They made him feel powerful. He kept them out of sight because he didn't want some grown-up confiscating them. He liked to do target practice on an old tree stump in the woods. His problem was that his bigness made him clumsy, so he frightened away the rabbits and birds he was after with his noise. But this didn't stop him lying to the children at school. He liked to watch their amazed faces when he lied and told them what he'd hunted down, from rats to foxes to deer. He liked it when they listened to him. It made him feel popular.

A few kids started to come over to his house. He took them to the woods and taught them how to use a catapult. They never hit anything, but they liked trying. He showed off his survival skills, building dens for them to relax in and camp fires to sit beside. It seemed to him the kids liked him. The truth was, they didn't really. They thought he was a freakish person who they talked *about* and only talked *to* sometimes; a person who they never actually played with. But eight-year-old Rufus had thought they considered him interesting and special, and so his hunting obsession continued. After the knives came the bow and arrow, and the air rifle and finally, when he was eleven, his prize possession – the shotgun. His parents didn't bat an eye when he asked for that.

Chumley slurped at his hot chocolate and admired the hunter on the TV as he raised his gun.

'*He fires,*' the narrator announced.

BANG!

'Good shot!' Chumley exclaimed.

Suddenly, the TV froze. Chumley looked up. There was his mother again, this time pointing the TV controller at him as though she would like to vaporise him. Rufus wasn't shocked by the hateful look in her eyes but he was very surprised that she had come to see him again – normally, she didn't speak to him for days at a time.

'You!' she said fiercely. 'Look at you. Eating like a pig. And this room is filthy. Stinks like a sty. I don't know what I've done wrong to deserve you.' She stepped towards him and looked at him as though he was a cup of mould. Her nose flared. 'Revolting. If I was the kids at your school,' she added meanly, 'I wouldn't want to spend time with you, either.'

Chumley tried not to think about the playground at school, about watching the other kids playing tag or hopscotch or football, about none of them ever asking him to join in.

His mother shook her head disgustedly. 'Your father has got some plans for you, young man.'

'I know, you already told me. And I'm not a man, I'm only twelve,' Chumley reminded her for the umpteenth time.

She ignored him. 'Time for you to leave home. College, anything to get you away.' She locked her eyes on his and narrowed them nastily. 'I think my real child was separated from me at its birth. There was some sort of mistake and *you* were put in its place.' She laughed. Her phone rang. She answered it. 'Hello . . . Yes, Rebecca Chumley here . . . No, I'll take all five pairs. The snakeskin boots, yes. All five colours, yes. Yes. Oh, and while you're on the phone, I want to talk to you about that mink fur I bought off you. It's wonderfully warm and I need to order another . . .'

Mrs. Chumley drifted out of the room, dropping the TV controller like a toy she was bored with.

Rufus had trained himself not to dwell on any of the horrible things his mother said to him. As soon as she'd gone, keen to not think about her, he switched the programme back on. Now, the man and his son were standing behind the dead stag, smiling and holding up its horned head to the camera. The interviewer stepped towards them with a microphone.

'*That was quite some tracking to get that shot,*' he said, thrusting an orange microphone towards the man.

'*Yes,*' the man answered. '*Over hill and dale. Tense. But it was worth it.*'

'*Quite some kill.*'

'*Yes, my hunting association will be impressed!*'

'*That means a lot to you?*'

'*I'd say,*' the hunter replied. '*My hunting association is like family to me. I'm gonna make 'em proud.*'

'*You'll be entering it for the big-game competition?*'

'*Oh yes. This monster is a winner.*'

'*And what will you spend the prize money on if you come first?*'

'*A trip to Africa!*' the boy shouted. '*To shoot us one of the Big Five! We wanna get us a lion!*'

Now the hunter and his son and the interviewer stuck their hands at the camera as though they were guns. '*Happy hunting!*' they shouted into Chumley's den. The credits began to roll. Rufus Chumley read them eagerly. The Worldwide Hunting Association was the name of the club that the man belonged to. Rufus wanted to be a member, too. He liked the idea of a hunting competition. He imagined himself holding a dead tiger up to the camera. That would show his parents. And the Worldwide Hunting Association would be so impressed. Suddenly, everything looked brighter.

'Mum says she's very br-bright. Her name's L-L-Lily,' Ernie said. He'd come out of his shed again and was telling Albi about the girl calf to the left of his stall.

'Bright?'

'Clever, like she's got a l-l-light inside her head. She's completely black with a small white flower mark on her forehead. She says we're half-Highland cattle – that's why some of us are so f-f-furry – and we're half–another kind of cow called Dexter, which is why we're so small as well. Some of us are black, some grey, some o-orangey like me, and you're al-albino. She said that very, very big, ancient cows used to live on the plains near here. They helped the humans build a big circle out of b-big, big stones. A long time ago. She knows a lot.'

Albi nodded as he absorbed all this information. He knew so little about the world. Far less than Bodge or Lily. He wondered if he would ever stop feeling that way.

Bodge returned. There was a clank as the man came back, too. The calves all stuck their heads out of their pens to watch him. He took his black top off and tied it around his waist.

'My mum says the humans have different second and third skins,' said Albi. 'The mother and girl humans have the brightest skins and smell sweeter than the bull humans.'

'Yeah,' Bodge agreed, 'and the mother humans keep their udders under their second skins.' The farmer's wife now walked past. Unlike the drably dressed man, she wore a red spotted dress, a blue coat and had green boots. 'See those lumps on her front? Those are her udders.'

'Do they have horns?' asked Ernie.

'Yeah,' said Bodge. 'Hidden under all that hair on their heads.'

'They've got ears too,' said Albi. 'Small ones, see hers? No hair on them.'

'My mum thinks,' a voice said, 'that the humans are big walking worms, because when they take their top skins off, they're smooth as worms underneath. And the second and third skins are called "clothes".'

The three bull calves turned their noses towards a black girl calf standing in the pen next to Ernie's.

'My name's Lily,' the girl calf said. 'Hello again, Ernie, and hello, Bodge and Albi.' Albi and Bodge nodded in the friendly way their mothers had taught them.

The mother cows had now come out of the sheds, too. They started to talk to each other through the bars. Albi heard Bodge's mother congratulating his mum on her first calf – him, Albi. Albi's mum admired Bodge, saying how strong he was.

As Albi watched them, he thought how lovely this was – to be surrounded by the mother cows and all his half-brothers and half-sisters. His mother called him in for a drink. She seemed worried.

'Glad to see you've made friends with your brothers and sisters, Albi.'

She licked him in that nice way she did, with her warm, rough tongue brushing the top of his head. It comforted him and made him feel safe.

And then, all at once, the peace was shattered. An ear-piercing, clanging noise rang outside and Albi could hear Lily and her mother both mooing. There was the sound of hooves on concrete.

CUMONNOWMOVEITYASTUPIDANIMAL! the man shouted.

Albi heard more clanging, more mooing. This time from Ernie and his mother. Albi sensed his own mother's fear.

'What's happening?' he asked her.

'Get behind me, Albi.'

The metal gate of their pen swung open. The man came into their shed. Albi had never seen his mother like this before. She was puffed up and making a very fierce, growling moo. Albi didn't like it at all. The man was making scary noises,

WHOOOOAAAGALCUMONOOOWWHOOOAAAGAL.

Albi's mother stepped threateningly towards him. But as she stood there, the man, sly as a fox, threw a rope around Albi's neck and pulled; pulled him past her. She managed to block Albi for a moment. Tears filled her eyes. She licked his head, only to have him roughly pulled away.

'*Maaaaa moooooo!*' Albi cried.

'Be brave, Albi!'

With that, he was pulled out of the pen. And the gate shut behind him with a hollow bang.

Chapter Three

SEPARATION

The next few chaotic moments were a blurred memory to Albi, afterwards. The fear of all the calves, the noise of their crying moos and the harsh voices of the two men who were pushing them about frightened him so much that he could hardly think.

The lasso was taken off his neck and Albi was pushed towards Ernie, Lily and some other calves he hadn't met. Ernie was making a scared, bleating moo, and Ernie's mother was mooing from her stall as if her heart might break. Albi looked desperately for his own mother. Then he saw her whiteness. She was standing in the pen, craning her neck to see him. He stuck his muzzle towards her. Her big pink eyes were locked on to his, almost talking to him. *You'll be all right Albi, be brave,* was what they seemed to be saying. Albi felt small and powerless. He was jostled sideways.

Now Lily was beside him, the other calves too. They were all being moved along, away from the pens. Twenty-two calves. Past the last pen, through a gate. And out to the world outside, the world under the big sky.

Clouds hid the sun. The men behind hurried the calves along, hitting the gate with sticks to make them move. Most of the calves were crying. All of them were scared. Their mothers mooed for them to be brought back. But the humans didn't pay any attention. The calves were urged on, down a fenced road further and further from the yard and the pens. On and on. Albi saw his first field but he wasn't excited, just bewildered and frightened. All the calves looked lost and confused and sad, except . . . except Bodge.

Albi had to talk to him. He pushed over to Bodge, who was in the middle of the calf herd.

Bodge looked up and winked. He gave Albi a tender nudge with his shoulder.

'Bodge . . . What's happening? Where are they taking us?'

'Off. Away.'

'Will our mums come to join us soon?'

Bodge sighed. 'Nope, Alb.' For a moment, Bodge looked as if he was missing his mother too. Then he bit his lip and snapped out of it. 'This is usually the way, Albi. It happened to all our mothers when they were calves. It happened to all my mum's other calves. It's the way. My mum said the best thing to do is to tough up as soon as possible. Mum says we'll get over it soon. Just like when you bump your head; it only hurts for a bit, then it stops hurting. You mustn't think of baby things, or of how you miss them, never. That's the way to get through it all.'

Bodge looked about him at the other calves. Some had a stunned look on their faces from the shock of what had happened. Other calves were shaking and still bleating tearful moos.

'And you're going to have to tough up quick, 'cos I can't be the only brave one in this herd. Help me look after the others.'

Albi took a deep breath. He wanted to tell Bodge that he couldn't be tough, that he wasn't that sort of calf, but, as if reading his mind, Bodge insisted, 'You can do it. My mum says the more you care about others, the stronger you get.'

And so, as the calves were driven along a covered way, Albi checked on the calves nearest to him and tried to console them. By the time they arrived at the big shed at the passage end, all the calves were calmer.

The man waved his big stick, shouting, GOOINTHAR!

The calves trotted into the shed's pen. It had a concrete floor. Troughs were fixed all round its edges and bottle feeders were tied to these. The man shut the gate and lots of the calves sank down, huddling near other calves with their heads on their front hooves, utterly miserable.

'C'mon, you lot,' said Bodge, trying to buck them up, 'it's not so bad. Hey, what do you call the time of day that cows get up?' Nobody answered. 'The moooorning!'

Bodge delivered his punchline, expecting at least a few smiles but all the calves stared glumly at the ground. He tried again.

'I say, I say, I say, why do humans live in big pods?' Again, nobody answered. 'Because they are human beans!'

Albi tried to turn his mouth upwards.

'Ah-ha! We're getting somewhere,' said Bodge, noticing. 'How about this one . . .' Then all at once Bodge saw something that made him start. 'It's HIM!' he shouted, and he rushed over to the edge of the pen. He stopped and stared out at something through a gap in the wall, his head rigid with interest. 'It's him!' he said again in awe.

Lily, Albi and Ernie joined Bodge and looked through the gap.

'Look at him,' yelped Bodge in excitement. 'He's magnis . . . magnisifent.'

'Yes, he is magnificent,' Lily agreed.

An enormous animal stood with his back to them in the field a little distance away.

'Just look at his muscles,' Bodge said and sighed.

All the other calves had come to the fence by now and were craning their necks to see.

'I'd love to see his face,' said Bodge. 'Let's call him.'

'No, don't,' said Lily. 'He's busy.'

'No, he isn't,' Bodge replied obstinately, and he began to moo. 'Hey! Dad! DAAAAAAD!'

The big bull didn't react for a moment. Then he turned his massive head. He saw the young calves and he nodded. A ring glinted in his nose. 'All right, kids?' he mooed, his voice deep and rumbly.

'Yes! We're all right, Dad!' Bodge mooed back.

'Good. Good for you,' said the bull. He nodded again and then he moved away from the gate to his field and was gone.

'Why is that ring in his nose?' Albi asked.

'He wears that because he's the king,' Bodge said, sighing again.

'The king,' whispered Lily. 'Our dad, the king!'

'Everything's going to be fine now,' Bodge said with conviction. And all the calves were filled with courage. It was comforting to know that their dad, the bull was so nearby.

The morning slipped into the afternoon. Bodge hovered near a gap in the wall, hoping to catch a glimpse of their father again.

'Our dad's getting older,' Lily said. 'Maybe you'll be chosen to be the next bull, Bodge.'

'Hope so,' said Bodge, rolling a nugget about in his mouth. 'I'll miss the holiday, but who cares.'

'W-what's a holiday?' asked Ernie.

'A holiday,' said Lily, 'is a trip somewhere special. Away from ordinary life. It's something that only the bull calves get to go on. 'It's not fair, really. I mean, *I'd* like to see the world, but only the bull calves get to go.'

Albi considered this. A holiday. It sounded exciting. Then a crash shook him from his daydream. The man was back again. This time with some others.

'Uh-oh!' Bodge exclaimed. 'It's decoration time.'

Albi didn't like the anxious look on Bodge's face. Nor did he like the way these surprises made him feel. He wished he knew more about the world, like Bodge and Lily.

'Is decoration time good or bad?' he asked.

'See what you think afterwards,' Bodge suggested.

Eleven hills away, Rufus Chumley sat at a desk inside a large garage where three Land Rovers were parked. His eyes were locked on to a computer screen with a picture of a burly hunter on it. The man's jacket was decorated with metal rosettes and braided badges. Behind him were silver and gold trophies, and beside him was a stuffed lion that he leant against. Underneath this picture a caption read:

The Worldwide Hunting Association's finest member.

'Wow, so cool,' Chumley said as he clicked on pictures of different members of the hunting club: photographs of men and women and sometimes young hunters too, outdoors, on hillsides, on grassy plains, in wooded places; wherever it was in the world that they had made their kills. They stood happily, beaming with pride beside recently-shot grizzly bears, holding up heavy heads of big wild mountain goats with curly horns or sitting on top of huge, dead elks. On other pages there were selfies of hunters with leopards or big cats, or cougars or lynx that they'd shot. There was even a picture of a girl with a dead giraffe.

The picture reminded Rufus of one he had taken when he was eleven, back in the time when kids still came to his house. His mind skipped back there. He remembered how he'd lied to his classmates that he'd killed a deer and a few of them had come over for the afternoon to see. Rufus had taken them to the woods and shown them four legs of lamb that he'd got out of his parents' freezer the night before and defrosted. The kids had believed that this was the meat of the deer he'd said he'd shot and were very impressed. One of the girls had wanted her picture taken with the meat. He shivered slightly as he remembered how that afternoon had panned out. It all went wrong that day. He'd taken the girl's picture, then he'd built a fire and cooked some of the meat. His classmates had eaten the lamb and had enjoyed it.

'Tasty,' one of the boys had said.

'Beats a burger,' another said.

Rufus's mistake had been to make a side dish from wild brown mushrooms that he'd foraged and a relish from red berries that he'd picked. They'd eaten these. How was Rufus to have known that the brown mushrooms with black spots on them were poisonous; that the red berries were almost deadly? He'd never been told. He'd never eaten them himself. He knew about them now.

The girl and boys had all got so sick that they'd had to be in hospital for a week. Rufus had been in big trouble and the few friendships that he thought he'd made had disappeared. Kids avoided him on the playground and no one ever wanted to come to his home now. They made excuses not to be his partner in games. No one wanted to sit next to him in class. He'd hated all mushrooms and berries ever since: the white mushrooms that people cooked at breakfast; field mushrooms that they baked; raspberries and blueberries and blackberries too. These foods reminded him too much of the terrible mistake that had made his life go wrong.

He looked at the girl with the giraffe in the photograph. She would like him, Rufus thought. He just knew she would.

'Hunting Competition Rules,' he read. He clicked the link and up came a long list as well as forms for entering the club's competitions. There were various categories – lots of animals he knew, from bear to deer, then a category called 'caribou', and another called 'Dall sheep'. He wasn't sure what either of these were. Then there were the more general categories – 'Big and Impressive', which included all big animals from rhinos to actual elephants, and another – 'Small and Rare', which had things like wild mink, white badgers and weird scaly animals. There were lots of animals to choose from. 'The kill can be made in any country but before the year ends. The deadline is 31st December.'

Chumley took a bite of his pork pie and munched as he thought.

Where was he going to find a big animal to shoot? He really needed to go to Africa or Canada if he wanted a big one. An idea began to form in his head. His parents didn't want him around. Perhaps he could persuade them to send him away to another country to train as a hunter? Then, while he was at it, he could shoot himself something impressive, and win the Worldwide Hunting Association competition and its money! Why, he could even tell them that when he won his prize, he would pay them back for the ticket and the cost of the hunting school. It was a win-win situation for them, he thought. There was no way they would turn that down.

Chapter Four

DECORATION
TIME

A grinding-metal noise made Albi look up. A small, shiny grey box on wheels had rolled into the yard. Albi wasn't sure if the box was an animal or not. After all, it moved on its own and made a mechanical, growling noise.

'That's one of the humans' moving pens,' explained Lily. 'It's a machine. A truck. My mother had a ride in a big one once.'

The back door of the truck opened and a smaller, rustier machine was rolled out of it, down a ramp. One of the men started to poke and pull at the smaller brown machine. A few flickers of orange air came out of it and in a few minutes, it was giving off a hot, smoky smell. The man picked up a stick thing with a long stalk and the shapes HF at the end of it. Albi recognised the shapes but didn't know where from. The man put it into a hole on the side of the machine. Then he came over to the edge of the pen.

WHICHUNFARST? he said to the other man.

THATUN. The farmer pointed to Bodge.

'Decoration time,' said Bodge, who was looking very serious. 'They've chosen me first because I'm the biggest. And you watch Albi, I'm not going to cry when they do it.'

'When they do what?'

'When they decorate me. My mum says it hurts for a bit. Says she saw Dad being decorated when he was a calf, and he didn't flinch.'

Albi watched as the men put a rope around Bodge's neck and led him to the smoky machine. Bodge went without a fuss. One of the men pushed him against the wall. The other man took the hard stick out of the hole in the machine. The HF-shaped end of it was changed. It was glowing orange.

'That's a pretty thing,' said Albi.

'I th-think it's a flower,' said Ernie. 'They're pretty things on the end of stalks.'

'It's not a flower,' Lily said and sighed. 'It's a decorator. Flowers smell sweet, but this thing smells bitter.'

'What does it do?' asked Ernie nervously.

'You'll see.'

The men talked amongst themselves. The orange decorator was put back in the hole in the machine. Bodge was now looking worried. When they pulled the decorator out for the second time it was bright-red in colour. And then they did it. One of the men pushed the decorator's flame-coloured end on to Bodge's rump. Bodge lurched sideways from the contact but the men held him in position. Bodge winced and his eyes watered. Smoke rose up from his hindquarters. The red-hot brander was burning his fur and searing his skin. The men took the branding iron away and thrust it into cold water. The water bubbled loudly. A new smell, an acrid, burnt smell filled the air. Bodge was led back to the large pen. He limped slightly, but had a brave face.

Albi looked at Bodge's rump. In a patch of his fur, there was now a hairless circle with the shapes HF raised in pink on his skin. Now Albi knew where he'd seen the shapes before. His mother had the raised marks of HF on a place on her rump. The HF shapes of hers were scars that had once been raw burns like Bodge's.

'What was it like?'

'Blimey, that was . . . Coooeeey, that was . . .'

'Was what?'

'Sore.'

Bodge winced again. 'My decoration.' He looked proudly at his rump.

'D-did it hurt?' asked Ernie.

'Not much,' said Bodge. Albi knew he was lying.

All the calves were branded that afternoon.

There was a lot of sniffing and crying and mooing, but at the end of the whole business, most were proud of what they had on their rumps.

'It shows we are part of the same herd,' Bodge explained. 'And the shapes stay forever, so we'll always feel together.'

Albi and Lily didn't like theirs. The men seemed to have made a mess of them. The shapes on their rumps were smudged, so didn't look the same as the others'.

'Ours just look like red moons,' Albi said. He'd seen the moon through the crack in his stable roof.

Late in the afternoon, the calves watched as the woman in the red spotted dress brought round buckets of white water. She filled up the bottle feeders in the pen. The white water that dripped out of one smelt a little like his mother's milk. Albi had a sip. It was nowhere nearly as good as his own mother's milk but he was hungry so he drank it. All the calves were glad of sustenance and comfort. Albi felt that the humans were doing the best they could. The decorations had hurt but but at least he had one. It had been sad to leave his mother but obviously it was for the best – after all, he was going to get to go on the holiday now.

As Albi stood studying the grass beyond the pen, thinking about how little he knew of the world – so much less than Bodge and Lily – he wished he knew more. He hoped there weren't any other nasty surprises ahead of him. He wondered what was beyond the farm. Then he noticed that the woman had brought her child with her. A girl child, wearing a purple-coloured skin, or 'jacket', as Lily had told him these pieces of clothing were called.

HURRYUPNOWEMMA, the mother human called.

The girl opened the gate and came into the pen. She looked at Albi, and gently held her hand out. Albi stood very still. She stroked his nose.

AAAHHHHHENTYOUSWEET, she said quietly. Albi pulled away, but when she stood there, still as a stone, he was curious to have a proper smell of her, so he put his nose up to her outheld palm and sniffed. She smelt salty and muddy and smoky and sweet, at the same time. Albi was drawn to her smell, and her nature. The warm feeling he got from her was like a light, playful wind compared with the rough storminess of the grown-up humans. Albi liked her, and she seemed to like him.

AAAAHHHENTYLIKEAPOLARBEAR.

She stroked him more. ANDLOOKATYOURPINKEYES.

Her mother made more noises at her.

BEINSIDEBEFORESIXFORSUPPERSTEAKTONIGHT.

OKAYMAM, the girl called back. This made Albi lurch backwards.

Her mother walked off. Then the girl turned away from Albi, left the pen and walked away. The gate hadn't swung shut. Albi was curious. No one was watching. Surely no one could object to him taking a little stroll?

Calmly, he took this opportunity. He stepped through the gate. When he heard it clang shut, he was already round another corner, and out of sight.

Chapter Five

MILK MUSHROOMS
AND MILKING
MACHINES

Albi knew he shouldn't be outside the pen. For a moment, he thought of going back but then he stepped off the stone path and on to the grass, where the earth was much bouncier than the concrete in the pen, and he felt excited. It wasn't just the ground that was inviting. There was something else near him that was special. He could sense it.

He sniffed at the air. There was a very lovely smell of something milky nearby. It was coming from some large white bulbous things on the ground a little way off. Albi wondered what they were. They seemed alive. They seemed to be inviting him to go to them, so he did.

Each one was as big as one of his hooves. He touched one with his muzzle. It was soft and almost furry. It wasn't an animal; it was definitely a flower or a plant or a vegetable, but it felt more alive than the grass. It felt like a big thing too, as though this was just its nose; as though there was much, much more of it under the ground. When Albi's nose touched it, he felt like it was touching him too, speaking to him in some way that he couldn't understand, as though it knew him. But how could it do this if it wasn't an animal?

Albi shook his head then lowered his muzzle again. The milk bulb smelt good. So good that this time, Albi licked it. When he did, he found it tasted just like milk but was creamier and sugarier. Albi couldn't resist taking a bite. The white plant melted in his mouth, turning to a delicious whipped liquid. He swallowed and a lovely warm feeling filled his stomach. He took another mouthful and then another, until he had polished off all six of the mushrooms. Mushrooms. That is what these things were. His mother had talked about mushrooms that grew in the woods. She hadn't told him that they tasted of milk. Nor had she told him what the milk mushrooms did.

The beaming warmth inside him felt as though it was growing. Albi shut his eyes and burped, and an effervescent, tingling sensation crept from his ears to his tail, where it swirled before diving to a ticklish place under his stomach. The fizzy feeling then shot up his neck to the dip between his ears. Here, the strange, bright whizz swirled about more, then flipped up and down his cheeks and over the bridge of his nose. Finally, it seemed to come together and dive into the place between his eyes, bringing a wonderful white light into his mind. Albi felt as though tiny stars were sparkling in his head; as though a great big moon was glowing in the centre of his thoughts. It was a marvellous sensation, one that made him feel steadier and calmer, and strong. He opened his eyes.

Albi looked about. The world seemed to have changed. For instance, the strange shapes seemed different.

HENGE FARM

Albi studied them and suddenly he noticed that one of the shapes, the E, was repeated. In a flash, another thought struck him – he recognised the shapes H and F from Bodge and Ernie's decorations. His mind sparkled and fizzed. He now saw something else too, something that he hadn't seen before. The shapes were human marks that meant something. What he *didn't* know was that just as he was sparkling on the inside, the tips of the strands of the hair on his forehead were pulsing with a tiny glowing light too.

Albi shook his head. His mind had just leapt and he felt incredibly satisfied by it. He looked at the grass where the milk mushrooms had been. He sensed that some earthy force – as strong as the wind or the sun but under neath him – was nodding in approval and he knew that this leaping feeling in his mind was something to do with the mushrooms. He licked his lips and looked at the sky. The clouds had gone and the low sun shone. It was a grand thing. Albi blinked and smiled and breathed in the fresh winter air. He looked at the bare trees and marvelled at the small animals that flew about. Birds! His mother had told him about birds. One landed on a post and trilled its song, Albi was delighted. He gave a moo of approval.

Albi turned his attention to a large grey building on the right. Machine noises were coming from it. *SSHHPPEEDIGOUGH.* Amidst that noise, Albi heard moos and he smelt mother cows. He bounded down the track towards them.

Along the side of the building were gaps in the wall. Albi could see parts of the mother cows through these. He could see their udders with strange sucking machines stuck on to them. These machines were making the *SSSSHHHPPEEDDINGOUGH* noises. Albi picked his way along the wall until he came to a cow he recognised. It was Bodge's mother. He could see her black legs and the side of her neck, though not her face, and she couldn't see him. She was busy chatting to another cow. Albi knew how important Bodge's mother was. He didn't want to interrupt her.

'I love these milking machines,' she was saying. 'After the whole day in those fields without little Bodge to lighten my load, ooh, my udders were beginning to get so heavy!'

'I miss my Ernie,' said the young mother cow beside her.

'I miss Bodge too, dear, little tyke that he is. It's best not to think about them, you'll only upset yourself. It's the way of the world.'

SSHHPEEDIGOUGH went the mysterious machines that were sucking the milk from them.

'*Aaaahmmmmoooo.* This is lovely!' Bodge's mum sighed. 'What a relief.'

'*Moooooo,*' agreed Ernie's mum.

'The boys will be going on holiday soon,' said Bodge's mum. 'And then, the girl calves will join us again. Won't it be nice to have the little heifers back?' She sighed. 'That Albertina, though.' Albi's ears pricked up when his mother was mentioned. 'Albertina is so upset about losing her boy, Albert. She says she doesn't want him going on the holiday at all. She says she wishes he could stay behind like the girls.'

'I feel the same way about Ernie. It would be nice if all the boys could stay behind like your Bodge.'

'*If* he gets chosen to be the next bull,' Bodge's mum reminded her.

'Oh, he'll definitely get chosen. He's so obviously the strongest.'

A woman started to move through the milking parlour undoing the contraptions from the cows' udders.

'Time's up,' Bodge's mum said. 'Hope the humans enjoy drinking our milk! Back to the buttercups.' Both cows moved backwards and out of their docks.

Albi stood where he was and watched through the gap as the cows were led out of the milking parlour and herded along the lane to their meadow. He went towards the end of the building and peered around it, watching longingly as they walked away. He saw his mother's albino-white form walking at the back and his heart skipped a beat. They all looked so peaceful. Albi wished he could be with them. He didn't want to go on the holiday, whatever it was. How could he stop it happening? Then, suddenly an idea struck him. He would visit his dad, the bull. If anyone would know what to do, surely he would.

Chumley was hungry again. It was only midday and he'd already had two breakfasts and some pork pies. But he was so hungry he could, as the expression went, eat a horse. Actually, he thought, he'd like to try a horse steak. He'd heard people ate that in France and Belgium and Italy too. The blade whizzing around in the plastic milkshake mixer, humming as it went, made him feel dreamy and his mind wandered. *What would horse taste like?* he wondered. And how long it would take him to eat a whole horse? Not long.

His mind skipped back to his childhood. As a toddler, he'd been able to pack away ten sausages at a time. Because of his growing condition he'd been a very big toddler; at the age of two, he'd looked like a six-year-old, at four, he'd looked like a ten-year-old. He remembered eating three whole pizzas when he was four. That had been lovely. But not everything about being big was lovely. He'd had many visits to hospital, for the doctors to try to work out why he was growing so fast. These trips involved lots of blood tests and injections, and X-rays to examine his bones. He'd been put in long, tube-like MRI machines; machines that took clever scan pictures of the insides of him, with special interest in his pituitary gland which, Rufus learnt, was inside his brain. His pituitary gland wasn't working properly and it was the reason he was so big. After a few years of expensive treatments his mother and father had decided that it was a waste of money.

'Let him get big. What does it matter?' His father had laughed. 'He can leave home earlier!'

'Good idea,' his mother had agreed.

And from that day on, Mr and Mrs Chumley had grown less and less interested in their son.

Being big had made Rufus's life very difficult. People had

always expected him to do more than he could because of his size. His teachers, the nannies who'd been employed to look after him, his parents – they always forgot his real age, always thought of him as much older than he was. One nanny had given him an encyclopaedia when he was four and he barely knew his alphabet. 'Read it, you numbskull,' she'd told him. A few years later, when he was six, parents of the other six-year-old kids in his class complained about his size, and so he'd been put into the form with the eleven-year-olds. That had been a disaster. None of the eleven-year-olds wanted to play with him. Plus, of course, being only six, he was always bottom of the class. It wasn't fair. They were eleven. He was six. But no one seemed to care about fairness.

Chumley watched a squirrel running along a branch of a tree outside. *That white playground squirrel changed things a bit*, he thought, but on the whole, things had stayed the same – bad.

As his milkshake spun and frothed, Chumley's mind fell to thinking about his father. His father paid him very little attention; he was always caught up in his own business. Rufus was dreading their meeting. He knew it wouldn't be pleasant. Useless, talentless, lazy, ugly, good for nothing. These were just some of the words his father usually threw at him.

His parents were often out. Rufus preferred it that way. They left him to get his own breakfast, and they ordered taxis to take him to and from school. Rufus cooked his own supper when he got back – usually two suppers, actually: a quick pasta first and then he'd pop a leg of lamb or side of beef with potatoes in the oven for a roast. His parents were perfectly happy leaving their twelve-year-old son at home. With his collection of weapons, they knew he'd be able to take care of himself if anyone tried to break in. They saw him as a human guard dog. They sometimes left him home alone for a week at a time.

A saucepan sat on the stove. In it was part of his parents' lunch – a meaty bolognaise sauce for pasta that their maid had prepared. Chumley's eyes wandered past it, under the many legs of ageing ham that hung from the kitchen rafters, past the single piece of tinsel that dangled sadly from the ceiling – the only decoration his mother had put up at Christmas – to outside, where some sheep were grazing in the front meadow.

He was soon in the sheep field, scooping up some of their droppings. Back inside, he crumbled these into the bolognaise. Then he washed his hands and stirred the new ingredient in.

'New invention. *Bog*onaise. For you, Mother and Father, because you are so nice. I've made it specially as a thank you.'

It felt good knowing that his spiteful mother and the old carbuncle would be getting upset stomachs that night. Goodness knows they'd upset him often enough.

'A taste of your own medicine,' Rufus Chumley said with satisfaction.

Chapter Six

THE BULL

His father. The bull. Where would he be this time of evening?

Staying in the hedgerow as much as possible, Albi cautiously began to explore the farm. He walked towards another building, this one with a shiny roof. Albi sniffed. The air had a strong, musty odour in it. To a cow who knew the world better the smell would have seemed like that of a very old tree after it has rained. Albi followed his nose. The scent got stronger and stronger. He sniffed his way along the ground, past a blue door and along a concrete passage. He turned another corner. His nose came up against iron bars.

Albi didn't dare look straight up, for in the straw in front of him were two huge, rough hooves. Above them was a pair of very hairy knees. On top of these was a mass of shaggy grey hair and up further still was a big wet nose with a ring through it. Finally, Albi's gaze made contact with two humongous eyes. His dad, the bull, stared calmly down at him. His head was four times as big as Albi's. Albi went rigid and then started shaking.

'Well, well, well,' rumbled the bull. 'And what have we here? An escaped prisoner?'

Albi gulped. For a moment, he was lost for words.

'N–not really,' he managed to stutter. 'I was j–just having a look about, sir.'

He waited to hear what his father had to say. From the serious look on the bull's face, it seemed that perhaps he didn't approve of Albi being out and about. His gaze was unnerving and, what with the size of him, he was scary. But there was a softness in him too. He nodded as he looked Albi up and down.

'And . . . ?' he asked.

Albi straightened up and admitted nervously,

'And, and I just wanted to meet you and ask you something before I go back to my pen.'

The bull sighed.

'So, what's your name? You must be Albertina's boy.'

'Yes, I am, and my name's Albi.'

'Albi. Hmmm. So, what's your question m'boy?' The bull spoke quietly. 'And keep your voice down.'

Albi had lots of questions to ask the bull, but he looked tired and Albi didn't want to stretch his patience so he got straight to the point.

'Um, D–dad,' he whispered, 'the thing is, I don't want to go on the holiday. I want to stay here with my friends and my mum and the cows, and you. I don't know much about anything and I certainly don't know how I get to stay. I thought you would know what I should do.'

The bull came close to the fence. Albi thought he was perhaps about to get a telling-off for being ungrateful to the humans. But instead, the bull replied, 'You must run away.'

'Run away?' Albi asked, incredulously.

'Yes, my little bull calf. You must run.'

'Run? But if I run, I won't go on the holiday *or* stay here.'

'If you run, little bullock, you'll be running for your life.'

'Running for my life?' Albi didn't understand.

The bull pushed his nose through the metal bars and close to Albi's. As he spoke, Albi smelt his warm breath. Grass and cud and salt.

'Listen,' he whispered, hoarsely. 'What I'm about to tell you will shock you, so prepare yourself. I've never told this to another cow, because there didn't seem to be any point, unless they could get away. You're out of the pen so you can get away and so, I'm going to tell you.'

The bull took a deep breath, as he opened the lid of a deep well of memories.

'When I was your age, I went on the holiday. When I got there, the humans realised they'd made a mistake, that I should have stayed here to be the bull, so they brought me back again. But I saw it all before they brought me back.'

'Saw what?' asked Albi.

'Saw the lie.' Albi didn't like the tone of his father's voice.

The bull hesitated, then he spoke very gravely. 'The holiday isn't a holiday, Albi. It's a lie. The humans put the young bull calves in a truck, and they take them to a place of . . .'

'A place of what?' Albi asked.

'A place of death.'

Albi didn't understand. 'What?' he said, shocked. 'Do they make us kill things like spiders and worms and birds?'

'No,' said his father. 'It's a place where the *humans* kill.'

'Kill what?'

The bull looked at his innocent son and sighed. 'Kill you.'

There was silence. Albi's nose wrinkled as he struggled to understand what his father was saying. He wasn't sure whether this was some sort of horrible joke.

'But, but why would they want to do that? Dad, are you joking?'

Albi's heart filled with fear as he waited for the bull's answer.

'No. This is deadly serious, Albi. Believe me, I'm telling you because you have a chance. A chance to run. Humans are harsh and cruel. They think they are better than all animals. They kill the bull calves because you boys don't make milk.'

Albi took a step back and turned his head away, but his father's presence was like a magnet and kept him from leaving.

'There's one more thing. It's another terrible thing. It's a secret I've kept for years, but I'm going to tell you.'

Albi was scared. The bull petrified him. He didn't want to hear any more.

'I don't want to hear,' he said.

But the bull was insistent. 'You must know, Albi.' He fixed Albi with his wise old eyes and spoke slowly. 'The humans eat . . .' The bull paused. 'They eat animal meat, Albi. They eat cow meat. They eat *us*. They take the bull calves to the fattening farm. And there they feed them until they are big and juicy, and then they kill them. For humans to eat. I'm sorry to have to tell you this. But now I've told you, and you must run. Run, because your life depends upon it. Run to the woods and stay hidden, forever.'

He's mad, thought Albi, *he's old and mad.* 'I don't believe you,' he blurted out. 'I just don't believe you.'

'Don't trust the humans,' the bull said. 'It isn't like you think it is. See this ring through my nose? It's not a crown of a thing. It's here so the men can pull me about. You're much bigger than you think. Believe me and run.'

Albi turned. 'Goodbye,' he managed to say. But inside he was thinking, *You liar! You LIAR! YOU'RE HORRIBLE!*

He lurched away and ran back down the concrete passage. Then he slowed to a trot and started to cry. How could his father say such things? It was so cruel of him. Tears fell down his furry face. His father's ideas were so violent and ugly. Why would he want to upset Albi like that? Perhaps he disliked all his calves. This idea made Albi cry more. In fact, he was so upset that he started to trot faster and then run blindly, not really seeing where he was going. It was only when he heard a tinkling sound that he came to his senses.

Albi walked towards the tinkling noise and looked in through an open window to see where it was coming from. Inside was a human room with two long green soft, lumpy things in it. The human child, the girl who Albi had met before, was sitting on one of them. The noise was coming from a strange box that she was watching. The box was very pretty because its centre was full of pictures and moving things. The noises coming out of it were a bit like bird song. Albi remembered his mother talking about something called music. She'd said it was a bit like human bird song. Suddenly, the box had a baby human crawling inside it.

'*PADZ NAPPIES ARETHEBEST!*' a voice sang out of the television.

Albi forget about his father's words. Instead, he wondered about the baby in the box. He didn't know humans could be so small. The baby human wore nothing except for a white pad about its bottom. Its skin was pinkish in colour. Another baby crawled into the box. This one's skin was dark brown. So, humans came in different colours just as cows did, Albi thought. Next, there were small cows in the box, dancing about in an extraordinary way; in a way that he had never seen cows dance. Albi felt relieved. So, the bull had been wrong. These cows were on the holiday and they were having fun.

'COUNTRYCHEESE IFYOUPLEASE! COUNTRY CHEESE FORYOUAND MEEZE!' more voices sang out from the box.

Albi looked more closely at the girl. She was holding a flat, round thing. On this were straw-coloured sticks which she dipped into red mud stuff and ate. A large, brownish slab of something was near the sticks. Albi didn't like the smoky, burnt smell of it, but still, he knew the humans weren't . . . What had his mother said that spider was? *Carnivorous.*

They eat cow meat, Albi. His father's words stung his ears again.

LARVELLYSTEAKMAAM! the little girl shouted loudly.

Albi studied the room. The ground beneath the girl's feet was black and furry. As furry as Bodge. It was as though it was cow skin. In a rush of horror, Albi saw that it *was* cow skin. Albi's heart began to beat very fast. All of a sudden, he was afraid.

Albi walked quickly away. He passed a mound of grass where a few more of the big milk mushrooms grew. He couldn't resist them so ate them up. His body tingled and his mind fizzed in the same way as it had before. This time, his mind felt even brighter. And with this brightness came a clarity about what these humans were. They *were* cow-eaters. They kept the mother ones so that they could drink their milk. They sent the young bull calves somewhere to be fattened so that they could kill them and then eat them. These humans weren't friends to the cows. They were only pretending. His father had told the truth. Albi felt dizzy from fright. He looked down at his hooves. For a moment, his fur seemed to be glowing. He supposed it must be because he was so shocked, that the scared feeling was making his eyes go funny.

Albi heard a low, cross mooing. His father came into view. He was in his field and mooing angrily. The men were in there with the bull. They were pulling him, pulling him by his nose ring.

Albi felt a rope around his neck.

Rufus Chumley and his father, Charles Chumley, stood facing each other. The veins in Charles Chumley's neck were bulging from all the rage that was pumping through them and his face was furiously red. He stood behind his leather-topped desk which he now slammed with his fist, making a silver-framed photograph of his wife fall over. The Chumley Senior leant forward and glared at his son.

'You're a useless, good-for-nothing waste of time and space. Call yourself a man? You're like a kid fresh out of nappies, still sucking your thumb, probably still playing with plastic swords and pop guns.'

'I'm not a man yet, I'm only twelve.' The familiar words tipped automatically out of Rufus Chumley's mouth. 'And I use the James Purdey gun. You bought it for me.' Rufus tried to smile, as he wanted his father to agree to the suggestion that he had for him;

of going to hunting school. But the way Mr Chumley was glaring made him stop at once.

'I don't care if you've got yourself a machine gun with bells on it. I'm just sick of you. Your mother and I both are. Your lazing about, your prowling round the woods trying to kill things. Pathetic. You need to get serious. Put on an overall! Abattoir work will sort you out.'

'But when I worked in the abattoir before, the other workers were really mean to me.'

His father ignored him and steamed on. 'You'll get some proper blood on your hands. Do some *real* killing. That'll be good for you. You'll learn the value of meat and bones. I didn't build my empire of abattoirs from killing in the fancy-pants way you do. Pah!'

'Hunting is a skill,' Rufus said, trying to stay calm.

'Rubbish!' Mr. Chumley roared. 'Load of claptrap. What's more . . .' He paused, as though filling his mouth with horrible words. Then he fired them at his son. 'What's more, you are a tap of crap! To think of the money I spent on you, on your clothes, your nannies, on the lorryfuls of food you eat. An utter disappointment. From what I put in, I deserved a mighty man, a champion, but all I got was a wet toad.' The wiry man sat down. The framed 'CHUMLEY'S, FIRST-CLASS ABATTOIRS' certificate was now visible on the wall behind him. A look of satisfaction crossed Charles Chumley's face, as though he was remembering some victory he'd had. It was certainly something that made him feel good. He chuckled to himself, then began whistling a tune and singing some words,

'And so, the end is nigh, *you'll* do it *my* way.'

Rufus Chumley didn't like what he was hearing.

His father clapped his hands together. 'Unlike you,' he spat, 'some of us have been working hard round here to find a solution.' He slapped a slim, maroon-coloured booklet on the table. 'Your passport.'

For a moment, Rufus Chumley's hopes soared. Had his father come to the same conclusion as him?

'A young man like you ought to be out in the world, making your way.'

'Yes,' Rufus agreed, eagerly.

'When I was a lad, I was slaughtering sheep at ten. Left home at fifteen. All through history, people have worked as soon as they are able – young sailors, young farmers, soldiers, labourers. The time has come for you to leave home.' Chumley frowned at his son, who looked surprisingly pleased at what he was saying. Then he hit Rufus Chumley with his plans. 'I've told the school you won't be going back. Told them that I'm going to educate you. And my way of educating you is to get you a job. I've found a placement for you in an abattoir in America.'

For a moment Rufus was speechless. 'An abattoir in America? But why would you send me to an abattoir thousands of miles away and—'

'Precisely. Nice and far away.'

'You have me work in *your* abattoir but it isn't legal. I'm definitely too young to work in Amer—'

'Nonsense,' his father butted in. 'Look at the size of you. You are what it says on this passport. Old enough to travel alone and old enough to get a job.' He gave the passport to his son.

Rufus opened the passport and found the picture page where his face peered out at him. 'But my birth date is wrong,' he said. 'This says I'm sixteen!'

'You look like a sixteen-year-old, so you are.' Mr Chumley tapped the side of his nose in the way people did to show that they had done something on the sly. 'I have my ways. Amazing what these passport services can do if you pay 'em.'

'But isn't it illegal to have a passport with the wrong details on it?' Mr Chumley slammed his fist down on the desk again.

'Don't you *isn't-it-illegal* me. You are off to America to work!'

The young Chumley saw his chance. 'But Dad.' It felt peculiar calling the old man this, but it had to be done. 'I've had a really good idea. Even better than yours. I could go to *hunting school* in America. Then I could enter the Worldwide Hunting Association's big-game competition. Did you know about it? The prizes are massive. Twenty-five thousand dollars for some kills.' His father's mouth dropped open. This was good, Rufus thought. He carried on. 'I could learn to hunt like a pro in America then go to Norway or Finland or another country and shoot a bobcat or a lynx or a snow leopard. You know how a good a tracker I am. I can make you a fortune hunting and—'

'YOU WILL DO AS YOU'RE TOLD!' his father shouted. He grabbed the passport and shoved it away in a drawer. He was fuming. Rufus wasn't quite sure what he'd done to upset him so much. Mr. Chumley didn't look up again. 'Out of my sight,' he growled. 'Sick of the sight of you.' He burped. 'Sick from that lunch too. Disgusting mess of a bolognaise.' Then, remembering his son was still in the room he added. 'And to get you right and ready for the American abattoir, tomorrow you'll work at *my* abattoir. They don't like you there. But they don't dare disobey me so you'll be going in, no matter what. And try not to lumber about like the clumsy big ox that you are.'

Chapter Seven

THE HOLIDAY BEGINS

The man hit Albi on his rump and pushed him into the pen.

GETINTHERE, he said in an irritated tone. YASTUPIDANIMAL.

The gate swung back and shut with a rusty creak and the man walked away.

'I know what you are! Let me OOOOOOUT!' Albi mooed.

DUMBBEAST! the man said snidely over his shoulder.

Albi didn't like the humans at all any more. He felt exhausted, and sick. He burped, and the taste of the milk mushrooms came into his mouth. He'd eaten a few too many of them.

'What do you mean by that, Albi? What are they?' Bodge said. 'And where have you been?'

Albi didn't want to explain the scary situation to Bodge – it would only upset him, and like the bull had said, there was no point in knowing the truth, unless you could run. So, Albi bent the truth.

'They're thieves,' he said. 'That's what they are. They take the milk from our mothers.'

'Oh, I knew that,' said Bodge. 'I know what you are TOOOOOO,' he mooed after the man, laughing. 'It's no big deal, Alb. Most of the calves will have forgotten what real milk tastes like in a few days.' He smiled. 'Great to have you back. I saw you slipping out.' He gave Albi an impressed nod. 'What did you see?'

'I saw your mum in the milking place. She seems very well. Bodge, I heard your mum saying that you're staying behind to be next bull.'

'I know.' Bodge nodded. 'I'm sorry.'

'It's not your fault that the man is choosing you, Bodge. But it got me thinking. When I get taken on the holiday, I won't see you again, not ever. I don't think anyone ever comes back from the holiday. It's a forever holiday.' Albi felt suddenly desperate and doomed. He was well and truly trapped now.

'You've got a sifnificant, signigifant, I mean, significant point there,' said Bodge. 'So, it must be really good on the holiday. That's why the bull calves never come back.'

It felt strange to Albi to suddenly be wiser than Bodge. He smiled and licked Bodge's shoulder in a friendly way.

'I'll miss you.'

'Maybe,' said Bodge, eyes lighting up. 'Maybe, Albi, you'll get chosen to be bull number two! Maybe both of us will stay.'

Albi's eyebrows lifted. Was that a possibility?

It was dark in the pen now. All the other calves were asleep. Albi settled down. He thought about his decoration. HF and the long line of shapes in HENGE FARM. Why had they chosen just the H and the F for the decoration? It was as though those two shapes were the most important ones. He thought about how Bodge's mum had been at the head of the herd when he'd seen the cows all walking back to the meadow. Just as she was the most important cow in the herd, was the H the most important in HENGE?

Albi thought hard. As he did, he felt his mind sparkle and his skin pulse and tingle and when he looked down at his legs, he saw what he'd seen before. His fur was glowing, it really was. It wasn't his eyes playing tricks on him; it was as if thinking was making him glow. Then the glowing stopped. Albi shook his head. Of course he wasn't glowing, he thought. He was either imagining it or, more probably, it was just the reflection of a yard light outside.

'Are you all right?' Bodge asked, adding, 'You know, Albi, your fur is so white it sometimes looks like it's got a light in it.' He chuckled as he shut his eyes to sleep. 'You're the glowing bull calf. You'd better learn to pat tidily because if you don't, your pats are going to make that white fur of yours a big mess. If we're going to be the bulls here, Albi, we've got to have a bit of style. I'm better at it than I was yesterday. Every day, in every way, I get better and better.'

' . . . and more Bodger,' said Albi. And they both fell asleep.

Albi slept particularly soundly that night, even though it was his first without his mother. He slept until the middle of the next day, as his body grew and changed and accepted everything that had happened to it. He was woken by the roaring sound of a machine. His friends were already up. Albi rose and, still bleary from sleep, looked over at a big truck that was in the yard.

Lily came over. 'You're off on the holiday today, Albi,' she said shyly. 'We missed you last night and now you're off.'

'Is that the h–holiday truck already? Albi asked.

'Yes. My mother said it would be the one with patterns on the side.'

Albi scrutinised the shapes.

LIVESTOCK

'I think we'd better say goodbye, then,' said Lily. 'Have a lovely time on the holiday. You are lucky. I wish I could come with you.'

'Goodbye, Lily.' The words slipped out of Albi's mouth easily but he didn't feel easy. He felt panicked. Fear bolted through him, from head to hoof. He nudged her neck. 'I'll miss you. Lily . . . if you find any big white mushrooms that smell of milk, eat them. I have a feeling they will make you cleverer.'

Lily laughed. 'You are funny.'

'I mean it. Eat them.'

'I'll miss you too, Albi,' she said. 'Look after Ernie, won't you?'

'Of course I will.'

Bodge strolled over with Ernie following closely behind.

Ernie gave Albi a lick on his shoulder. 'I'm glad you're back,' he whispered.

Just then, three men walked into the yard. One opened the back of the truck. A ramp came down with a thud. The other two humans came into the calves' pen and began to separate the bull calves from the heifer calves, like Lily. Albi held his breath in anticipation. Would he be taken or left?

Bodge knew what he was thinking. 'I've got my fringes crossed for you Alb,' he said.

The man had a glint in his eye and smelt of salt. GET ONNNN.

He roughly pushed Albi towards the truck and Albi's heart sank. Any hopes he'd had of being bull number two vanished. He resisted for a moment but the man was forceful.

'GOOOOOOOODBYE!' Lily mooed.

Then they were all surprised as the man slapped Bodge on his back legs.

YOUTOO COMEON MOVEIT.

Bodge stubbornly resisted. 'You've gOOOOot it wrong,' he mooed. 'This is a mOOOOistake. I'm noOOOt going on the . . .'

But the man paid no attention. He started to make whooping noises and he began to wave his arms.

MOVEYASELF YAGREATBIGHUNKOFASTEAK.

When Bodge refused again, the human walloped him as hard as he could.

'But, don't you understand?' Bodge mooed angrily. 'Ask the oOOOOther human, I'm staying to be the next bOOOOOull!'

However, all the man in the pen saw and heard was a noisy, stubborn bull calf, mooing.

YAAAHH! he shouted. This time his voice had fury in it, and he brought his stick down onto Bodge's rump with a hefty thwack.

Bodge lurched forward and he stumbled up the ramp and into the cattle truck. The ramp was thrown up and bolted shut. The twelve bull calves jostled to find a comfortable place to stand in the cramped space. A few strands of light came through thin slit windows high up near the ceiling of the box, but otherwise it was dark. Someone near Albi was crying. He saw Bodge's markings.

'Bodge, have you hurt yourself?' Albi asked.

'Yes . . .' Bodge sniffed. Then he came clean. 'No. I'm supposed to stay behind to be next bull. You know that.'

Albi didn't know what to say. The truck made a rough mechanical sound and started to shake a bit. Some calves started laughing. Bodge was still crying.

'Listen,' said Albi. 'I spoke to Dad on my walk. He told me that he was taken . . . to the . . . er . . . on the holiday, by mistake too.'

'Rrreally?' Bodge sniffed again.

'Yes, really,' Albi replied. 'So they'll probably realise they made a mistake when we get there.' He thought once more about what the bull had said and he felt like crying himself.

The journey was bad. The truck swung this way and that, tossing its load about. The air was thick and smelly. Albi could hardly breathe. Then, just as he thought he could take no more, the machine slowed down. It rumbled over stonier ground and it came to a halt. The back was opened. The calves tumbled and trotted out.

Chapter Eight

CHUMLEY'S

Albi looked about. The sky was heavy with billowing clouds. The calves gathered in front of a big brown building. The strange shapes, these ones red, hung above its entrance.

CHUMLEY'S
ABATTOIR

There were no meadows around the building, just other dismal-looking structures. No flower-filled fields, just jagged pine trees that swayed in the strong, cold wind. Albi thought about the shapes. They were like a tantalizing riddle. He felt his skin tingle as he thought, but before the full ticklish feeling flooded him, a stick hit him across the rump.

A man, who Albi hadn't seen before, barked, INYAAAGO!

The man had a small white stick in his mouth. He puffed at the stick then blew cloudy air out of his mouth. Gruffly and impatiently, he urged Albi into the brown building. Albi did as he was told.

The place was enormous and grim in its greyness. It was long and wide, housing scores of thin stalls. Inside each stall was a bull calf; calves that were bigger and fatter than Albi and his brothers. The new arrivals were now corralled down the central aisle.

'I-I don't like the smell of it here,' said Ernie. 'D-don't like the noise, neither.'

The walls of the building were metal, not stone, and the gusts outside made them wobble and wail in a low, quivering way.

'That's just the wind outside on the walls,' Albi told him.

Bodge frowned. 'This lot don't look very happy,' he commented, pointing his nose at a few bull calves they were passing. 'I'm glad we're not stopping here.'

'T-this doesn't look like a holiday place,' Ernie said.

'No,' Bodge agreed. 'I reckon this is where they walk us through. These calves are probably going home. That's why they're looking so sad. Hey!' he called to a bullock. 'Cheer up. The farms are nice too, you know!' The bullock glanced at Bodge and shook his head. 'Some cows are very trough half empty instead of trough half full, aren't they?' Bodge said. 'Mum told me that one. Cheer up!' he mooed to some more miserable bullocks that they were passing.

At the end of the passage was an enclosure. Albi eyed it nervously. He felt like a stone that was rolling down a hill, on and on, out of control.

'This,' Bodge told him, as they approached its gate, 'is where the humans check to make quite sure that the bull calves here are all *supposed* to be going on the holiday. This is where they'll see that that there's been a big mistake. They'll see I was supposed to stay behind and be bull.' His cheerful tone saddened. 'So, I'd better say goodbye, because this is the end of the line for me.'

A woman came up behind them noisily, clonking her metal stick on the rails of the calf pens, making the calves inside them shy away from her. Bodge turned towards the woman. He stood his ground, as though giving her a chance to see him properly, to see that he should be taken back to the farm. However, she didn't react the way he'd supposed she would.

ONYAGO! she growled.

'MOOOOOO!' Bodge replied.

The woman looked surprised. DON'TYOUMOO AT ME she said crossly. GETINTHERE!

Bodge shook his head. And stayed where he was. 'LOOOOOk! Can't you see? I'm the young bull,' he reasoned. The woman held up her baton and waved it at him but Bodge stood solid. 'I'm nOOOOOt suppOOOOOsed to gOOOOOO in there,' he mooed. 'I'm the young bOOOOull!'

GETINTHERE! the woman insisted, stamping her foot.

This made Bodge paw the ground. He dipped his head at her. The walls of the building banged as the wind hit them, as though they were giving Bodge a drum roll.

'Look, I can charge already. Just like a bull's supposed to,' he said. And he started towards her. 'I'll show you, you see, I'm supposed to be the bOOOOOOuull.'

A deep voice came from the other end of the building, OIWHAT'S HE DOING? A man joined the woman.

'I'm the BULL!' Bodge told them both.

GOTACRAZYONE HERE, the woman said, and the man began to make a *HU HU HU* noise.

STOPLAUGHING ITSNOTFUNNY the woman said. HES MAKINGMENERVOUS.

The man tapped Bodge sharply on the side of his neck.

ITSTHEWIND. MAKINGTHEM FRISKY, he said. MOOVE ON! he shouted.

Bodge backed away. Then, mad with furious frustration, he put his head down and lunged at the man.

OOOOOOOOH! cooed the woman.

'I'm the next bull,' Bodge mooed.

The man's patience snapped. He hit Bodge hard with his stick. Bodge fled to where his brothers were.

HU HA HU HAAA, went the man.

The woman swung the enclosure gate shut, hooking its metal loop over the post on the end of the fence. Then she and the man leant on the gate and inspected the bull calves.

OOOOH LOOKONE OFTHEM ISALBINO WITHPINKEYES the woman said, adding, THISWIND ISPICKINGUP WESHOULD GOHOMEEARLY LEAVE THISLOT HERETILL TOMORROW.

YOURERIGHT, the man replied. WEATHERREPORTSAID THIS STORMIS GOINGTOHAVE HURRICANEWINDS. LETS NOT HANGABOUT.

IDIOTBOY RUFUS! The woman seemed to be calling to someone else.

YEAH? A voice from the door beyond shouted.

WE'RE GOINGHOME EARLY SO GETYOURSTUFF.

OK.

HE'LL BEGLAD, the woman said. HES A LAZYSOD THAT USELESS CHUMLEYKID. COMEON! she shouted again. HURRYUP IDIOTBOY!

Albi tried to make sense of what they were saying but couldn't understand. He watched the two humans make their way out of the building. They touched something on the wall and the light went out.

SEEYOUTOMORROW.

BYE.

Bodge hung his head dejectedly, then lay down. Exhausted and upset, the other calves lay down too. Albi stood near Bodge. He was so tired that he could hardly think. But he must try to devise a plan of escape, or else this was the end. As if to show him how serious things were, a flapping door nearby was suddenly blown open and through it, Albi saw a terrifying sight.

He saw calf-sized things hanging from hooks in the back of a truck that were swinging slightly. They were calf-sized because they *were* calves, but not live calves; these were dead. *All for the humans to eat,* Albi thought, and a dense, dark fear surged through him.

An orange-haired human walked past the dead calves, hardly noticing them. The human was as big as a man, yet Albi could sense he was much younger. He wore a white overall with brown marks on it.

HURRYUP RUFUS! the woman shouted.

I'MCOMING! The red-haired boy spat on the ground.

The flappy door shut again; there was a noise of an engine starting up. It grew loud then moved away. The next time the flap opened, the truck and the nightmare vision of the dead calves had gone.

Albi began to shake. He didn't know what to do. Like his brothers around him, he shut his eyes. He was glad none of them had seen the dead calves. He took some deep breaths to calm himself. His eyes were heavy. He couldn't keep them open. He slumped on the uncomfortable concrete floor to rest and think, but was soon deeply asleep.

He dreamt about giant people with hard eyes who carried sticks. He dreamt that there were two hills behind them. On one stood his mother, bright and shining white. She called to him. *'Come back to us, Albi, you will find a way, you're bigger than you think. Come on, Albi.'* On the other hill stood his father, the bull who called to Albi more urgently. *'RUN, ALBI! Your life depends on it! RUN!'* The strange shapes – ABATTOIR FARM LIVESTOCK HENGE – swam through Albi's dream and white milk mushrooms snowed down on him. His head fizzed as the humans came closer, closer, with their sticks. Their snarling teeth flashed in the dream light. *'DUMBANIMAL!'* they barked. And Albi felt naïve and unworldly and weak. The bull spoke again, louder this time. *'You must run, Albi. The men will kill you otherwise. Come on! What are you waiting for? RUN!'* But in Albi's dream, his legs wouldn't move. He willed them to move, but they stuck to the ground.

'Please don't kill me, I don't want to die!' he screamed, and he screamed so loudly that he woke up. He opened his eyes to a ring of calves all looking down on him. The wind was thrashing against the sides of the building, hollering and howling.

'You were having a bad dream,' Bodge said.

'Is . . . is it really true? What you said in your sleep?' gasped Ernie. 'Do the humans eat . . . eat cow meat?'

'Do they?' Bodge asked.

Albi looked sadly at the other calves.

'Yes, they DOOO!' shouted a bullock from one of the other stalls.

'Yes, they do,' Albi admitted. He saw the faces of his brothers, all horrified and frightened as this truth sank in.

'H-how long do you think it'll be before they c-come for us?' Ernie stammered.

Some of the calves began to cry. The wind was whistling around the building, banging its walls as though it wanted to get in.

'They're coming to get us!' Ernie cried.

CHUMLEY'S ABATTOIR

Albi felt the fizz in his head once more as he thought about the shapes. He shut his eyes to concentrate.

'Maybe the shapes are like hoofmarks,' he said, thinking aloud. 'Cows can tell who's walking in front of them by reading hoofmarks. Maybe the shapes are like hoofmarks to the humans. Maybe the shapes tell them things.'

'What are you talking about?' Bodge said. 'You're not making sense, Albi.'

'It *is* starting to make sense,' Albi said as his mind whirred. 'It's like lights are being turned on in my head.' Then he heard the calves gasping. He opened his eyes and saw why.

'Albi, you're *glowing*!' Bodge said.

Albi looked down at his forelegs and took a sharp intake of breath. It was true; his fur was glowing again, this time as brightly as the moon. He thought back to the other times he'd been glowing. So, he really had been!

'It's because of the milk mushrooms.'

'Milk mushrooms? I'm not sure about that, Alb, but whatever the reason, you're lit up like a glow worm. It's a pity you didn't glow like that before, you might have saved your skin.'

'But what good would that have done? I would have been saved, but it wouldn't have saved you all too.'

'Holy cow pats, that's a nice thing to say, Albi.' Bodge nuzzled his friend. 'What are we going to do?'

Outside, a fresh wind was whipping up about the corrugated buildings, making moaning, ghostly noises.

'T-those are the cries of all the poor dead calves,' whispered Ernie. 'Maybe, they're what's making you glow, Albi.'

A crash outside made the building shake. The calves huddled together, trembling.

The wind whined and wuthered, making the roof above them flap and rattle. Albi studied a section of it that was bending sideways and banging down as the wind worried it. Then, with a sudden ripping noise, the wind caught the roof and tore it clean off. Moonlight poured down into the slaughterhouse. The trembling calves longingly gazed up. How they all wished they could jump out! The moon disappeared behind a cloud. Everything went dark except Albi, who, as though the moon was inside him, glowed luminously.

The wall at the edge of their pen began creaking. Albi knew that all the calves were having the same thought as him – that the humans were back! Albi's mind felt white-hot with panic.

'You lot,' he said in a fierce, urgent whisper. 'If we're going to run, we've got to charge *now*. We've got to charge them, like bulls. It's our only chance. And we have to get the others too. They will help.'

'How do we get the others?' Bodge asked.

'Like this.'

Albi had seen the humans shut the pen so he had worked out how to open it too. He put his hose under the metal loop on the gate that hooked over the post of the fence, and the gate was loose.

'Did you see how I did that?'

Bodge nodded.

'Right, let's do the same to the hooks on all the other pens.'

'All of them?'

'Yes, and teach the calves in the pens how. Then they can help. Quick!'

And so, Bodge and Albi and the braver little calves left the enclosure and began freeing the bigger calves. One, two, three, the bull calves came gladly out of their stalls. And then they helped too. Four, five, six. Once the calves knew how, it was easy to open the pens. Eight, nine, ten. Twelve, fifteen, twenty bull calves now joined Bodge and Albi. All of them were bewildered and scared. But Bodge and Albi rallied them.

'Wake up!' Bodge said. 'We're getting out. Come and help us. We are going to charge the humans, come and help!'

All the bull calves stared at the huge wall that was wobbling and juddering. It shook this way and that, as though a huge human was trying to get in.

'Don't be frightened!' Albi told them.

Then two parts of the wall flew open.

Chapter Nine

THE ESCAPE

The calves stood still, petrified, ready for some hideous thing to dive in and attack them. But nothing happened. The great wind outside blew in the darkness. Through the gash in the wall, they saw the dented moon playing hide and seek with the clouds.

Albi thought hard about what to do. He remembered the earthy force that had been under him, nodding its approval when he'd first eaten the milk mushrooms. And his instinct took over. *Something good is out there,* it told him. It was something bright and he must walk towards it. As he felt this, his tail tingled and the tickling feeling under his skin moved up his body into his head. He was glowing again.

'We have to go.' The words tipped out of his mouth. He still felt very small and unknowing but something was urging him to leave and so he took heed of it and started to move. Bodge joined him. 'You're right. I'm not having those humans eat me.'

Together, they walked towards the ripped wall. Albi turned to the other calves. 'This place has the smell of death about it,' he said. 'We must get away. Follow us.'

'Some of you stronger, bigger calves must walk at the rear,' Bodge said, 'to make sure that no one gets left behind. We've got to get away from here. Well away before the humans return in the morning or we will be eaten. So, toughen up, all of you.'

'We will follow,' mooed bull calves from one side of the pen to the other.

Bodge nodded at Albi and together they stepped out into the night with Ernie close behind them. Ahead was a field. They began to walk. The calves followed, a stream of them flowing uphill, up and out of the valley of death. The night was cold and a lashing wind whistled through the bare trees. The calves tripped and stumbled and were practically blown away but they kept walking.

They stopped at the top of the first ridge and looked back. A chink of moonlight caught the sharp metal rooftop of the abattoir, making it glint like a knife. Albi shivered but he didn't let his mind slip from the dreamy, sure state that told him where to go. He felt himself glow once more.

'This way!' he called to his companions, his moo only just audible amidst the din of the wind.

Rufus Chumley sat on his bed, comforting himself by polishing his favourite rifle. He'd hated his blood-splattered day at the abattoir and was glad to be at home with the closest things he had to friends. They hung on his bedroom walls – heads of various stuffed animals: a white rabbit, an albino stoat, a snow otter, a cloudy mink, a sickly pale piglet with grey spots, a red-eyed lamb. Each stared out into thin air with dead pink eyes.

They were all albinos, just like the albino squirrel that had inspired him to hunt. He'd had that squirrel's head stuffed, and it stared down at him too. Each one had been taxidermised; stuffed – it was an art that Rufus thought he might learn one day. He had found the other animal heads on the internet at different times, and one by one had bought them using one of his mother's credit cards. She hadn't noticed. His collection of white-furred, albino animal heads might have seemed odd to a stranger but they were important to Rufus. He liked to confide in them and spoke to them often.

He got up and went to the mirror, put a comb through his flame-coloured hair. His reflection stared unhappily back at him.

'I'm not going to work at an *abattoir*,' he told the animal heads. 'Any numbskull can stun an animal that's already been caught, and then kill it. All that hosing blood down drains! Boring. Working inside all day long too. Whereas hunting is outside in nature. And it's a proper skill. Only people with a proper, tuned instinct and a practised eye can track and shoot. I'm going to America to become a brilliant hunter. Maybe I'll get a weekday job in a taxidermy shop to earn money, then go to a hunting school at the weekends. Just because Dad has found me a job in America, doesn't mean that's the job I have to do.'

The dead animals on the wall seemed to be looking at him as though they were in agreement.

'Yes.' Rufus smiled. 'I'll run away from the American abattoir.

I'll work in a taxidermy studio. At the weekends I'll hunt and soon, I'll win that competition ...'

Just then, something fluttered at the edge of his vision, something outside on the storm-blown hillside. He stepped closer to the rattling window and peered out. An animal of some sort was catching the moonlight. It seemed to be a white deer! Rufus squinted to see better. Was it a white deer? Excitement began to course through his veins.

Wind and rain hadn't stopped him hunting before – in fact, Rufus loved the challenge of it. Making a snap decision, he swung into action. He threw on his jacket and seized his gun. He tipped a box of bullet cartridges into his pocket. He donned his waterproof hat. He tiptoed down the corridor, taking care not to wake his snoring parents. The oak stairs creaked only slightly as he hurried quietly down them. The stone floor was cold under his feet, then he found his walking boots and was soon outside.

Rain lashed him and slapped him in the face but he ignored it. He started up the steep climb to where he'd seen the lit-up animal. He turned his torch on and pointed it at the ground. There he saw a very surprising sight. For what greeted his hungry, hunting eyes were hoofmarks not of one animal, but of many. And all small hoofmarks. Calves. He glanced back at his father's abattoir. How had the calves escaped? He snorted, then he laughed. He was pleased his father had lost his calves. It served him right, Rufus thought. He wasn't going to tell him. Then, Rufus remembered an abattoir worker talking in the van when they'd left. She'd mentioned that one of the calves in the pens there had been an albino. Usually, Rufus wouldn't want to hunt a calf, but if this was an albino calf, it was a very different proposition. An albino calf

would be the perfect addition to his collection! He'd send it to the taxidermy company and they could stuff the whole thing for him, just like those huge taxidermised animals he'd seen at a museum. There was the entire weekend to go before anyone would discover the calves had escaped. The other calves would be rounded up; the missing white calf would just be a mystery. Why would it be missing? Because he, Chumley, would have shot it. They'd think it had just wandered off on its own and died in a ditch.

Chumley began trudging up the wet hill after the hoofmarks. Though fighting the gusts, he began to make good headway. Then he slipped back down the hillside, landing in a puddle.

'I'll get you tomorrow!' he shouted after the hoofprints. 'Crack of dawn, I'll be up.'

Cheered by this new challenge, pleased to have a nice distraction from the thoughts of what his father had planned for him, Rufus Chumley stumbled home.

The calves followed Albi trustingly. The January night was now doubly chilling but they plodded on, not complaining. On the procession went, through woods, along paths, over a stream. Albi and Bodge led them resolutely. Albi's hooves ached, his back hurt, his legs throbbed from exhaustion and they were moving automatically, just one step at a time, on and on because he could still feel that something good was ahead. It wasn't just instinct, it was as if the very ground was telling him so. Determined, he kept on into a wood and out to a place where the land was open and flat. It felt good here too, even though the wind was fiercer. Albi wasn't sure why it felt safe, but it did. More than this, it felt magical. For a moment, he doubted his impulses then he felt the strange pull so strongly again that it was undeniable. He put his head down and shut his eyes.

'Nearly there!' he mooed to the others.

Ahead, he could feel the strong magnetism, as though an invisible lead was tugging his whole being along. Tired as he was, he lifted his head and continued.

'There!' he mooed. 'That is where we are going!'

Ahead in the gloomy night mist was a small copse of thickly-trunked trees. Albi led the calf herd into its centre, where they were out of the storm. Still the gusts howled and still the rain fell, but they were protected now and safe in the circle of trees. Here they slept; some slept standing, some lying down. They were too tired to do anything but sleep.

Albi woke at dawn. Bird song broke through the dewy air. He leant against the big trunk beside him and rubbed his itchy nose against it. It was very cold. Cold as rock, with a different sort of roughness to ordinary bark. He could smell moss on the tree but otherwise, oddly, the tree didn't smell like a tree.

The sun began to rise. It threw its warming rays through the inky clouds. Albi saw where they were. They were not in a small wood at all. They were in the centre of a group of huge standing stones – great rocks as tall as sheds, oblong blocks that pointed up to the sky. Some had other big stones laid across them, making blunt rock arches. They were like gargantuan pebbles piled on top of each other. The simple arrangement of these stones was very beautiful. They had an ancient feel to them. The strong pull that had reeled Albi in before pulsed through him again. This place was very special.

Bodge woke up. He saw the rocks. 'Where are we?' he asked in bewilderment.

'I'm hungry,' one of the smaller calves said. 'Will you take us back to our mothers?'

Albi shut his eyes. The special feeling was fading. Where had he brought everyone? He suddenly felt ridiculous. But then, as though in answer to his question there was a loud, low grinding noise. One of the flatter rocks on the ground was beginning to move, move as though something was trying to budge it *from underneath*. What's more, it was grudgingly shifting. Juddering its way open. When it was open, it revealed a dark pit beneath it. Albi peered inside and saw there were earthen steps. These led down to a tunnel. A great waft of sweet, milky air danced out of the darkness.

'We have to go down there,' Albi said, with the same certainty that he'd had before. He felt himself glow. Bravely, he began picking his way down the steps. 'Are you coming? Bodge? Ernie?'

For a few seconds, the darkness of the tunnel swamped Albi's vision, then his eyes adjusted. The light from his fur helped him see, as did strange small lights that dotted the ground along the passageway. Albi smelt that they were the milk mushrooms. These ones were glowing.

'Is everyone following?' Albi called back to Bodge.

'Yes. Me and Ernie will make sure everyone comes down,' Bodge assured him. 'We won't leave anyone behind. But Albi, are we dreaming?'

'No,' Albi said. 'I'm awake. So you must be too. I think.'

Albi walked on nervously, round one curve, then down a slope. The passageway began opening up into a cave. He noticed a low humming noise. He stopped and listened. It wasn't frightening so he kept on. The path went downhill more; the noise got louder and louder. Albi started to feel warmer.

At the path's next turn, the hubbub became very clear. Albi's brothers caught up with him. They drank in the vision – a huge underground cave filled with cows, bulls and calves. Black, white, black and white, brown, creamy-coloured, some stocky, some puny, some very big, some hairy, some velvety. Some that were shaggy with huge horns, others thin with none. Some eating, some chewing the cud, some sleeping. They mooed, soft and low to each other. That was what the humming noise had been. Some of them were glowing.

'Holy cowpats!' Bodge said.

A few of the cows and bulls looked up and nodded at Albi, as though he'd been expected. A young glowing grey bull stepped up the slope of the cave towards them.

'You look shocked.' The bull laughed. His eyes shone. 'What are your names?'

'Albi.'

'E-E-Ernie,' Ernie bleated more than mooed.

'Bodge.'

'We have come from the death place,' Albi said, not knowing what else to say.

The bull nodded and looked at the shivering calves in front of him. 'Let's forget the introductions. No time for them now. More important things to sort out, like food and rest. You must be famished and thirsty. You'll be wanting some milk. And calves, you can relax. You don't need to worry. You are safe now.'

The bull led the exhausted calves to an enclave in the cave lit by strange luminescent bugs. Here, mother cows welcomed them.

'You poor, dear things. You look exhausted,' one of them mooed.

'Have a drink,' another said kindly. 'We may not be your real mothers, but you'll find that our milk is nearly the same.' And the calves fell upon the milk that they so desperately needed.

Albi blinked. Now he wondered whether he was dreaming. He didn't know places like this existed. He'd only heard of cows living above ground.

The bull turned to him.

'You'll be wanting the mushrooms, Albi. Most cows like the smell but hate the taste. They make 'em sick. But you, you obviously have a taste for them. Good for you. They'll make you very strong, both in your mind and in your body.' He nodded. 'You'll be the youngest glower here. Oros will make a fuss of you.'

'Oros?'

'You'll see. I will be back later. I've got to go and check the hatch is closed.'

Albi nodded. 'Thank you,' he said politely. Then, sniffing them out, he found a patch of the milk mushrooms and ate his fill. Again, his mind sparkled and fizzed and his fur glowed. Warm and satisfied, he lay down for a sleep with the other calves. Even though cows can walk great distances without tiring, calves need to rest a lot, and these calves were completely out of energy. Very soon, the bewildered escapees were all sound asleep.

Albi and his brothers slept, as stony-still as the rocks of the cave, but Albi woke before the others. He stood up. He felt refreshed, relieved and very, very curious. What was this place and who were these cows? Why were they all here without humans? Or was Oros a human? Albi thought he must be.

At one end of the cave, cows and bulls – some glowing, some not – began to line up along the wall.

Bodge and Ernie had woken now too and joined Albi to watch. What was just as marvellous as the sight of the glowing herd was what was lit up on the cave wall behind them – a picture made with dark lines on the pale cave stone, and coloured in with browns, greens, reds, white and other colours too.

The picture was of a moon, with a cow-shaped cloud jumping over it. Drawn under that were huge brown and black cows and a giant black bull with *pink* eyes. All had grand, crescent-shaped horns. They stood on a mound, majestic and proud with drawn men and women offering them gifts of flowers and food. In the picture too, behind these humans and animals, were the strange standing stones that the calves had sheltered under the night before.

'That's beautiful,' Albi whispered to Bodge.

'W-what is it?' Ernie asked. 'Are those cows real?'

'No, they are made from marking the wall,' Albi explained. 'Like hoofprints.'

'The bull's got pink eyes,' Bodge observed, 'like you, Albi.'

The real cave bulls and glowing cows in front of the picture began to moo. They left the platform and other glowing cows took their place. These were bigger cows, *much* bigger cows.

'Holy cud!' Bodge exclaimed under his breath. 'That is what I call a momstar – I mean, monster.'

Chapter Ten

STONEHENGE AND OROS

An enormous black bull emerged from behind the rock picture and walked on to the platform. Albi had never seen a bull so big, so tall. He was twice as big as their dad. The top of his head was as high as a stable door. His horns were each as wide as a pen gate. To add to the spectacle, the bull began to glow, beaming as though every hair on his body was giving out light. And his eyes, eyes that were pink, seemed to glow too. Albi felt very drawn to him, in the same way that he'd felt drawn towards the stones the night before, through the magic that Albi had sensed was under the ground.

Other huge cows and bullocks of the same enormous breed emerged from behind the tableau too. These cows were a reddish brown, or some a deep brown or black, with a white stripe running down their backs. All of them had curly blonde forehead hair. Most of them were glowing.

'They're like the b–big, ancient cows that used to live here that Lily talked about,' Ernie gasped, watching intently as the giant cows organised themselves, stepping on to the rock in front of the picture. 'She said they h–helped the humans build big stone circles.'

Albi nodded. 'You're right.' He felt very small again.

Slowly, grandly, the old bull turned his head towards the collection of other cows before him. His pink eyes shone. When he spoke, his voice was deep like the cave.

'Welcome,' he said. 'And a very special welcome to the young calves who arrived this morning.' He nodded at Albi and his friends. His glance was warm and wise. The young calves blushed and looked away. There was a hush in the room.

'Let me introduce myself. I am Oros.' He paused. 'You may be wondering what this place is, and who we are.' He gestured to the cows around him. 'This is the auroch herd.'

The giant cows, bullocks and heifers nodded to the audience. Oros continued.

'You will never have seen cows like us. That is because we are the last of the auroch – an ancient breed of cow that was almost wiped out by the humans. Long ago, auroch cattle roamed the plains and forests on the land above. To begin with, we came from a country very far away, called India. As you can see, we are huge, much bigger than cows that walk in the open air now. Humans marvelled at our speed, our size, our bravery, our intelligence. But they also feared us. For the auroch did not take to being slaves. We scorned their ropes and their lassoes and we charged them and their barriers. So, humans dug pits and caught our ancestors. They killed most of us. Eventually, the humans thought they had wiped

us out. They now think that we are extinct. Extinct like the dodo.'
Albi wondered what a dodo was.

'But we are still here and, who knows, if we are here, maybe the
dodo is too!' Oros nodded and continued. 'This picture on the wall
behind me is very ancient. It was painted thousands of years ago
by humans, when humans and cows loved one another. Long ago,
humans thought that cows, with our moon-like horns, belonged
to their moon goddess. Are you connected to the mOOOOn?'
he mooed.

Bodge laughed so loudly that Oros looked towards him and
smiled.

'In this painting, you see ancient humans offering flowers
and food to the auroch cows. This is from a time when humans
revered nature and cared for her, not like now. Behind them is
the mysterious stone circle that the auroch helped the humans
build. It is called Stonehenge. The auroch cattle pulled the stones
miles and miles to this place.' Oros's gaze moved towards the calves
once more, this time settling on Albi. Albi blinked, then quickly
looked down at his feet. Oros went on. 'Humans lost the secret of
this cave. Some of you calves came into it from under Stonehenge
this morning. We do not often use that entrance, but we felt you
there, as I think you felt us nearby. There are other entrances
further afield, where the humans tread less often. Occasionally,
we leave through these entrances to graze and get a little
moonlight. This maze of a cave runs for miles under the ground
and we have lived here secretly for hundreds of years, protected
by its spirit. We have the spring to drink from. There is algae on
the rocks to eat and recently we have had the milk mushrooms.
Cave moss cleans the air. The blue, white and green pools are

home to plankton – small water creatures that are luminescent.'

The biggest brown cow beside him now stepped forward and spoke.

'Not long ago, there was a milk moon. We left some of our entrances open and many of the mushroom spores blew in with the snow. Those who have eaten the mushrooms will know already how you glow when your mind is growing or thinking. Auroch who have eaten the mushrooms every milk moon now understand more of what human beings are saying when we hear their noises through the cracks of the cave above us. We understand more of everything. And we have dreams. Dreams about what the future holds and dreams about places we must go. In our dreams the earth tells us that now is the time we must leave this place. In our visions, we have seen humans digging under the ground near here. We must not be discovered. Our dreams have shown us *where* to go, too. The earth whispers to us for help, now, for humans are stealing from her everywhere. They bleed her of her oil; they use her soil without helping her grow it back; they put stone on her land – not ceremonial stone like here, but huge buildings of stone that cover miles and miles of land; and they take her water so that parts of her dry out. They cut her trees and destroy her wild beauty. Without her green wildness, the air will thin. The earth is asking us to help her. We don't yet know how, but we will dream it. Most of you will not be able to stomach the milk mushrooms, but if you can, please do try to eat them. They are very, very powerful. It was already clear that we must end our mole-like existence in these caves. We long for our calves to be able to run about in the fresh air and the daylight. We are going to a place where we dream there is freedom. But we're not going not alone. We want to take with us as many other breeds of cows and bulls as we can.'

'That is why you are all here,' Oros explained. 'Tonight, we start on a very long journey. So, rest as much as you can today.'

The glowing auroch left the stage, some walking behind the rock of the cave painting, others to lower parts of the cave. The tableau wall went dark. Oros stepped down into the crowd and began to speak to different cows. There was a hush as he moved through the throng. Albi watched, then realised that Oros was coming straight towards him and his friends.

'Albi, I think he's got 'is eye on you,' said Bodge.

'Or you,' said Albi.

'N-n-nope, Alb,' Ernie piped up. 'He's looking straight at you.'

Sure enough, Oros was walking purposefully towards Albi and seemed to be getting bigger and bigger as he approached. He was so huge, so imposing that Albi's knees started to knock together.

'Don't shake like that,' said Bodge, his voice quaking. 'He'll think you're frightened of him. You're not, are you . . . ? I am,' he added.

'Hello, all you young calves, and welcome,' Oros said in his deep, earthy voice. His eyes were smiling and kind. 'I am glad that you all made it here.' He turned to Albi. 'What is your name?'

Albi could hardly speak. 'A–Albi.'

'Come with me, Albi. There is a very nice patch of mushrooms that I know of. I will show them to you.'

Albi was rooted to the spot. Bodge gave him a nudge. 'Go on!'

With his friends giving him encouraging looks, Albi followed the great bull.

Cows and bulls, bullocks and heifers nodded in deference to Oros and stepped aside to let him pass. Oros led Albi along a wide cave-corridor lit by small lights and pools of bright blue water.

'Many of the caves are lit by fungi that glow, and glow worms and insects that let off light. They like it here.'

Albi nodded and kept following. He couldn't think what the great Oros wanted him for. He wondered whether he was in trouble. He was so nervous that he didn't notice the intense milky smell in the air until they turned the next corner. Suddenly, he was hit by a beautiful sight – a broad, high space with glowing white mushrooms that covered the rocks like snow.

'These ones are particularly good,' Oros said. 'They will make you strong. You won't need milk if you eat these. Try some.'

Albi smiled nervously and nibbled at one. It had an even more powerful taste than the mushrooms he'd eaten before, and his mind seemed to fill with brighter stars as he ate it.

'I felt you coming here last night,' Oros said. 'I felt you before that too, from the first time you ate the milk mushrooms. The message was passed through the earth, through the network of underground fungi and mushrooms, to the mushrooms here. And, because I am friends with the earth and its deep world, I heard the voices that told me of you. Did you feel me here?'

'Yes, I th–think I did,' Albi offered, craning his neck up. Talking to Oros was like talking to a giant.

The bull came slowly down on to his knees, bringing his vast head closer to Albi's. 'That better?' he asked.

'Yes,' Albi said, not really sure that it *was* better, as it was still a little alarming being so close to Oros's massive face.

'You, young calf,' Oros said, 'are a friend of the earth too. For only those alert to its subtle urges will be open to the pull. The earth needs you.'

Albi didn't know what to say. 'Um. OK. That sounds very nice. Thank you, sir,' he added. He liked the idea of being a friend to the earth. He noticed his front legs glowing.

Oros chuckled. 'I've heard what you did. You're a brave one.'

'Erm, not really,' Albi said, remembering how nervous he'd been leaving the abattoir and how much braver Bodge had seemed. 'I only did what I could. I led the way because I was the only one who could glow. Bodge is far braver and in any case I'm not much at all really – I don't know anything of the world, not like Lily and Bodge and I don't know how they do it but they are just so good at knowing how things work . . .' The words came tumbling out of Albi's mouth like milk from an upturned bucket.

'The milk-moon chose you, Albi; you are bigger than you think.'

Albi looked down at his tiny hooves next to Oros's that were twenty times bigger. He couldn't be much smaller, he thought.

Oros smiled and Albi saw from the old bull's deeply kind eyes that he was safe.

'So, young Albi. Tonight, when the humans are back in their nests, their houses, we will set off. I have had dreams about other caves like this under other ancient stones. They are connected to this cave by mushrooms and fungi even though they are far, far away. In my visions I have seen woods where it is safe, too. We will all leave tonight – some may not want to follow of course, for it will be dangerous. The journey will take a long time. But the dreams will show me where to go. Do you still feel the pull?'

Albi shut his eyes.

'I feel the pull of my mother,' he said suddenly. He dropped his eyes. All at once, his heart opened up. 'I feel like there's a hole inside me because I miss her so much. The other calves have these holes too.' He raised his head. 'I can feel more than the pull of my mother. I can *hear* her. She seems to be saying that I must rescue her.' Now Albi surprised himself. As wave of sureness filled him, he found himself saying, 'Oros, sir. You say that some won't want to come on your journey. I think I am one of them. I would like to go to my mother and the herd and set them free.'

The old bull stood silent then asked, 'Do you feel where your whole herd is?'

'Yes.'

'Then you are able. Do you feel they are close?

'Quite close.'

Oros nodded. He looked at Albi a while longer. 'Albi, you have the power to both rescue your herd *and* bring them to us. They can come on our big journey too. If you can feel where they are, you will find them. You will sense where we are, too, to find us again. I have a good feeling about you. You now have the strength of these cave milk mushrooms in you too. We will be walking towards where the sun rises, towards the east. We will sleep hidden by day and travel by night. If you go, you must do the same and catch up with us.' He sighed. 'Albi, you must not tell Bodge or the others. They aren't glowers yet, so they can't come with you. They would struggle. And I cannot ask any of my herd to risk their lives for you. If you go, you go alone. Once you have set off, I will let your friends know where you have gone.' Oros got onto his knees and raised his enormous body off the ground. 'We are going to a large snowdrop wood – that is where you will find us. Beware of humans. Remember, they are not to be trusted.'

'Why did you ask me to come here with you?' Albi asked.

'Because I sensed that you had something to tell me. My dreams told me you would make a journey alone tonight.'

'Did your dreams tell you that I would manage to set my herd free and get back to you?'

Oros knocked his nose against Albi's neck in a kind, encouraging way. 'The dream did not say, but I believe you can do it. Eat your fill here,' he said. 'You need all the energy you can get.' And then he walked away.

Albi ate all he could, then returned to his friends. As Oros had suggested, the cows who hadn't eaten the milk mushrooms tried them, but most found them disgusting. Bodge chewed one, spat it out and was sick afterwards; Ernie coughed up the piece he had eaten. But Albi was full of them and and tired. He lay down to sleep. He couldn't stop glowing, thinking about Oros and the auroch. He imagined his mother and Lily, and their father and all the cows at the farm, and the strong feeling came to him again. It was like a silent noise that sang that he could hear with his heart, a pulse that he could feel. He thought about the shapes he had seen. CHUMLEY'S ABATTOIR. LIVESTOCK. HENGE FARM, and his mind flashed. He thought more, and glowed more. He would definitely need to learn how to control his glow, he decided. Then drowsiness got the better of him, and he fell asleep.

It was the middle of the afternoon, but Rufus Chumley was in bed having nightmares, tossing and turning with strange visions, inspired by what he'd seen that morning.

His return to the hunt for the albino calf had gone well. He'd got up at the crack of dawn as planned and picked up the hoofprints. He'd tracked through foggy fields for a mile or two until he'd got to Stonehenge. He'd had to hide behind a bush there because of the security guard but, undeterred, Rufus Chumley had waited. Eventually, the tired man went in for a cup of tea and Chumley had crept past his office and got on to his trail again. This is where things had taken a mysterious turn, where he had discovered something very peculiar, something creepy that was giving him nightmares now. For, inside the ring of ancient stones, very, very weirdly, the hoofprints stopped. What was more, the prints suggested that the calves he was tracking had walked in one final direction, *into a giant stone.*

On closer examination, it seemed that the grass beside this low boulder had been flattened and wiped by something very heavy, as though this rock had been moved and put back again. Of course this was impossible, and yet Chumley had had a feeling that the stones *had* moved. It seemed there was something alive in the place; it felt as though something was watching him. Spooked, Chumley had turned and fled.

And so, his dreams now were of talking stones with big mouths, and to make matters worse, his mother, as ferocious as any monster, was in the dream too, with fire shooting from her mouth. Chumley shook himself awake to get away from her, only to find her in his bedroom shouting at him to wake up.

'What sort of time do you call this?' she raged. She picked up his bin and tipped the contents of it over him. Old sandwich wrappers, the remainder of a curry in a tin tray, some worn-out socks and bits of paper and plastic landed on his head.

'Your laziness is an embarrassment to the family. Look at the junk you've been eating. Perhaps,' she added nastily, 'if you ate less, you'd stop growing.' She chucked his passport onto the bed. 'Your father has bought you a one-way ticket to Texas. You're leaving tomorrow. I hope you are as excited about it as I am.' On her way out, she said under her breath, 'I can't wait to see the back of you.'

As she left, Chumley shrank under his covers.

'You've asked for it,' he whispered after her. 'Punishment time.'

When Chumley's mother was mean to him, he'd punish her in a way that he felt was fair – stealing her jewellery and her cash. She hid it all in the cupboards where she kept her fur coats, and in the drawers where her alligator handbags were stashed. She had bundles of cash that Rufus's father gave her to spend and plenty of diamond rings and necklaces and, since she shopped when she was drunk, she always forgot what she had. So, she never noticed what Rufus took from her.

Today, as he burrowed into the places where her forgotten treasure was hidden, he suddenly paused. His parents were about to put him on a one-way plane to Texas. But what about the albino calf? Rufus kicked himself now for not hunting it down and for being put off by a bit of spookiness. It occurred to him that hunting down that calf was the easiest way to impress the Worldwide Hunting Association. The fact hit him like a ton of cold water. It suddenly became very clear. He wasn't going to America, not yet.

Looking at the banknotes in his lap and thinking of the wads he already had, hidden under floorboards from previous times he'd pinched stuff, he had a huge amount of money. He climbed out of the cupboard and sat on the chair in the wardrobe room and thought more. Yes. He had loads of his mother's jewellery;

he had gold chains and precious stones. He had her credit card too, the one that she never noticed him using. He had five expensive watches and twenty gold sovereigns that he'd stolen over the years.

Today he'd taken a set of collectable gold coins that seemed to celebrate children from around the world. Rufus studied the picture of a boy and girl holding hands and dancing on one of them. It actually made him feel sad. The faces on the coin made him think how lovely it must be to have friends. Other kids seemed able to collect friends as easily as collecting apps, but he didn't have even *one*. No wonder, he thought; even his own mum and dad didn't like him. Obviously, something was wrong with him. *Or maybe not,* he thought.

'I don't fit, that's all,' Chumley said to himself. 'Maybe the old bat was right and I *was* switched at birth. Maybe my real family is somewhere else.'

Now his mind whirred and Rufus's imagination projected pictures of his *real* family on to the wardrobe cupboard doors. His real mother would have hunting clothes, he thought, not high shoes and cocktail dresses. His sister would be like the girl with the dead giraffe on the TV. Chumley knew his people were out there. With his passport and the credit card and money, with all the jewellery and gold, he could do whatever he liked, he thought. And what he wanted to do was find his people. Rufus Chumley made a decision. He wasn't going to America to work in an abattoir. He was going to disobey his mother and father. He was going to leave this place he had been calling home.

He'd kill two birds with one stone. He'd get two things he wanted with one kill! Why, he could win the Hunting Association's first prize and impress his hunting family *with the same bullet*!

All he had to do was track and shoot that albino calf.

Dusk was falling. He was much too scared to revisit Stonehenge in the dark, and anyway, he needed to pack. Chumley hatched a plan. He'd go back the next morning with provisions, weapons and a camping kit and he'd continue from there.

Chapter Eleven

THE TUNNELS

A chill wind brought every bull, cow and calf to their senses when they stepped out into it. Albi's heart surged with a mixture of trepidation and excitement as he breathed in great lungfuls of the fresh air. He stood with Bodge and Ernie, watching as the massive auroch bulls replaced the boulder on the tunnel entrance, budging it back with the weight of their great shoulders and chests. Albi felt very nervous. Was he really going to split away from this herd to try to get back to his home herd at Henge Farm? He steeled his mind.

The night walk began. The sky was still cloudy so it was mostly dark. The calves followed the bigger glowing cows and Albi tried to glow too. Cows and calves, bulls and bullocks put their heads down and walked, following Oros. Oros kept them as far away from human dwellings as possible, off the road and out of sight. He took them through woods, through fields. A few cows from these fields joined them. Oros opened their gates and they were allotted places in the line. When the moonlight burst through the clouds, Albi was amazed to see how many cows there were. All led by huge Oros at the front.

Albi felt his mother and Lily getting closer. Like a light, the feeling flashed in him, showing him the direction to go. Familiar farmyard smells came through the air. Suddenly Albi saw something that jolted him. Oros had led the procession of cows over a road and there, on a board were shapes he knew:

HENGE

Albi realised now that the country smells were familiar because he was near his home. Without wasting a moment, without saying goodbye to his friends, he slipped away.

Albi trotted towards the feeling of where his mother was. It began to rain. Doubts started to fill his mind. What if this feeling wasn't real? What if he didn't find his way home? What if he lost Oros forever? What if he, Albi, was caught? The further he walked from the big herd, the more Oros and the other cows felt like a figment of his imagination. Fear tried to grip him but courage pushed him on. Albi walked on in the dark for one mile, two miles, three.

'You're bigger than you think, you're bigger than you think,' he said over and over to himself, over and over, remembering now that both his father and his mother and Oros too had said that to him. *You're bigger than you think,* their voices chimed in his head. But still Albi felt small and out of his depth.

And then his heart leapt. A current of air passed his nostrils. He could smell the milking-machine barn. After a copse of beech trees, he knew he'd arrived. There, quiet in the misty moonlight before him, lay the familiar sheds.

Albi made his way towards the cows' quarters. They were in the big, covered barn. Behind the fence near to him an animal moved. A familiar animal.

'Psst! Lily,' Albi whispered hoarsely. Lily looked up and jolted as she saw the glowing form of Albi.

'Who's that?'

'It's me, Albi.'

'But . . . but what's happened to you Albi? You're glowing! Are . . . are you made of snow?'

Albi stopped himself glowing. 'I'll tell you about it later, Lily. I've come to take you away from here.'

'Away? To go on the holiday, you mean?'

'In a way.' Albi was so happy to see Lily he wanted to give her a big nuzzle, but there was no time for that. 'Lily, everyone must come, but we have to be quick. I'm going to unbolt this.' Lily watched with amazement as Albi slid the bolt of the lock with his nose, then heaved the pen gate over its adjoining latch so that it swung open. 'Help me tell the others, quickly and quietly. Then we'll get Dad and then we'll go.'

'Dad died.'

Albi stopped in his tracks. 'Died? How? What of? Did the humans have anything to do with it?' Anger and sadness surged through him. He'd only met his father once but he loved him. This was a terrible shock.

'No, it wasn't the humans,' said Lily. 'He died naturally. He was in the snowdrop field.'

'Oh.' Albi didn't know what to say.

'He was happy. He was just old, Albi.'

They stood for a moment thinking about the bull.

'Lily,' Albi asked, 'maybe you are happy here. Maybe you don't want to come with me?'

'I do want to come,' Lily said. 'The others will want to as well.'

And so, Albi and Lily set to work. They woke and freed the cows and heifers, amongst them Albi's mother.

'Albi, you're safe! Oh, Albi!'

Albi nuzzled his mother's neck, drinking in her smell. But there was no time to linger and talk. All the other cows and calves bustled together to hear what Albi had to say. He spoke just loud enough to be heard over the misty rain. He spoke particularly to his mother and to Bodge's mum, the dominant cow.

'Mother, mother cows and sisters, I have come to take you away from here. I cannot explain where to now, or why, because the reasons are long and upsetting. But I assure you that where we are going is better, far, better than here. Others wait for us there. A long journey is involved. It begins with a long walk tonight, then a rest tomorrow, then—'

'You needn't finish Albi,' Bodge's mum said. 'We will all come. The bull told me everything before he died. It is good if we leave now, because tomorrow is the rest day when the farmer doesn't come to see us, so we'll have a head start.'

Albi nodded and looked at the sky. 'We must go, before the sun rises. We must hurry.'

And so, Albi led the Henge Farm cows back along the track he'd taken. Oros's force that showed the invisible way pulled him back through the night and early hours of the morning, towards the glowing auroch herd. They found them at dawn, just as the sun was rising. Albi led the cows through tunnels of bush into the heart of the snowdrop wood where Oros's herd slept and rested. It was wonderful to reunite his brothers with their sisters and mothers.

'Waking up and seeing Mum was the best thing that has ever happened to me,' Bodge said. 'I don't know how you did that. I thought I'd never see her again, or you.'

'You smell so much, Bodge, it was easy to find you.'

Bodge laughed. 'Thank you, Alb.'

'It was a hard walk, wasn't it?'

'I know,' Bodge agreed. 'Hard as a sun-dried cow pat.'

Albi chuckled. It was great to be back with Bodge again.

The herd rested all day in the coppiced wood, its central enclave so hidden by fallen branches and low trees that they felt safe. They relaxed and chewed the cud.

Albi took Lily to some milk mushrooms that were nestled under an old willow tree.

'Do these smell good to you?' he asked. 'Not the crocuses, the mushrooms.'

She nodded. 'Yes, they smell like milk!'

'I hope you can eat them. These are the mushrooms I told you about. They're good for you.'

Albi watched to see whether they tasted bitter to Lily, or sweet. He wanted another calf his age to understand things the way he was starting to understand things. He didn't need to worry. Lily took one lick of a mushroom and then began eating, eating and eating until she had eaten them all.

'They're amazing!' she gasped.

Her skin twitched and a look of surprise made her eyebrows

rise. A smile lit up her furry black face as the tickling sensation sparked its way around her body then settled where the lily mark was on her forehead, burrowing into her brain. She sneezed, then sneezed again.

'Oh, Albi! It's like night suddenly turning to day! My mind feels all bright!'

'Look at your front legs,' he said.

Lily's black fur was glowing just as Albi's had.

'I'm really glad you like them,' Albi said. 'Does the world feel different?'

'Yes, and it's strange, but I feel more curious or something.'

'Yes! I get that too. It's very good.'

Little did Albi know that his new curiosity wouldn't always be a good thing. For now, though, he couldn't have been happier.

Darkness fell and the herd set off again. They followed Oros out of the wood and up a grassy hill. The air tasted salty. Albi licked his lips and wondered why. Then they got to the crest of the hill and a strange view greeted them. Albi and his friends stood silently and looked out at it – a wide, flat expanse; a huge darkness that stretched to the left and the right and ahead to the horizon; an immense mass that moved in front of them, shivering like the back of a giant creature. Many of the herd were frightened by it.

'This is the sea!' Oros explained. 'Do not be afraid. It is simply water – salty water that divides this land from more land over there.' He nodded to the distance ahead. 'We are going to cross it. We won't have to swim.'

Albi caught sight of lights below; lights moving fast, straight towards the thing called the sea. Then the lights were swallowed up.

'That is a train,' Oros told the herd. 'Like a long truck.'

Oros led the herd down the slope and hid them behind a thicket of brambles near the mouth of a tunnel. Here, a strong, iron-railed barrier enclosed the shaft that went under the sea. When another train approached, its metal gate opened. The train shot along its tracks towards the opening and disappeared into the tunnel. After it had passed, the big entrance shut again.

However, at the edge of the enclosure was a gap in the fence where a smaller gate hadn't been closed properly. This would be their way in.

'That is a death tunnel,' a black-and-white bull declared. 'It's not natural, Mr Oros. The trains will hit us. I cannot go in there.'

Others voiced their fears too.

'I had my nose in a trough of water once, I nearly drowned. The water from the sea will surely drown us, Mr Oros, sir.'

'It may be all right for your kind, Mr Oros, but we aren't used to being in underground tunnels.'

A handful of the herd gave up there and then and turned to go back to the snowdrop wood, but the others entered the tunnel. In they walked, downhill into the darkness, with gravel crunching under their hooves and little orange lights leading the way. Albi and Lily walked at the rear but both found it difficult not to glow, even though Oros had told them all not to. They couldn't stop themselves thinking about the sea and the long tunnel that burrowed deep under it.

Inside the tunnel, the herd took a slim path beside the train track. For a while, they walked in near darkness, then what they had dreaded began. The tracks began to creak and make small screeching noises. The cows, calves and bulls pushed their bodies to the edge of the tunnel and shut their eyes.

'Don't glow,' Lily reminded Albi.

The terrifying train clapped like thunder, flashed like lightning as it passed. Then it was gone.

On they walked, hoping that the tunnel would be short. They couldn't turn back. They walked on. For hours and hours. Albi felt he was walking through the inside of a giant stone worm. Three more trains passed. Then they saw light ahead – dawn light at the end of the tunnel. They emerged, exhausted and relieved. They had walked under the sea.

The cows welcomed the rain that poured down on them. They stuck out their tongues and lapped it up. Soon they were safe and sleeping in a French forest.

Rufus Chumley was feeling exhausted but good. He'd been on a roller coaster of moods since he'd left home before dawn that morning, but now he was feeling on top of the world. It had been hard leaving home. He didn't mind abandoning his parents with their whipping tongues, especially as he knew that this way, he was avoiding the one-way Texas abattoir trip. Once he had shot the runaway calf, *then* he would contemplate America, but on his terms, because by then he would have won the Worldwide Hunting Association's prize and things would be different. But he felt sad leaving the familiar countryside that had been his comfort over the years, and he missed leaving his taxidermised friends – the animal heads on the wall in his bedroom.

He'd packed a rucksack full of essential things – a few of his clothes, some bullets, binoculars, some snacks, a solar charger for his phone and a toothbrush. His favourite small shotgun was wrapped in a jumper, hidden in a long fishing rod case. He carried a fishing net too to look the part of a keen fisherman. In his fishing tackle bag, hidden in a compartment under his fishing flies and hooks was all his loot, padded nicely with the wads of cash he'd stolen. His mother's credit card was in his top pocket with his passport, which, he thought, would come in handy if he had to con someone into thinking that he was sixteen. He didn't worry about anyone robbing him; he looked so scruffy no one would suspect that he was a walking gold mine.

The sun had been rising just as Rufus Chumley had arrived back at Stonehenge. This time he saw through the office window that the guard was asleep, so he nipped into the site and was soon at the stones. He was feeling positive and determined. Today, he thought, he wouldn't be spooked, whatever he saw.

A part of him didn't trust what his eyes had seen before, so he was very pleased when he found the calf hoofprints again – faint now, but there, still as peculiar as before, looking as though the calves had walked into the boulder.

'There must be an explanation,' Chumley told himself.

He began to look for other tracks. But instead of an explanation, he got a more confusing sight. For here, near a door-sized boulder on the hillside, were tracks showing that the calves had walked *out* of the rock. And on top of this, many of the hooves here were *giant*. Huge. Like hoofprints from monster cattle!

Chumley looked about him, wondering for a moment whether he was in some TV game show, the sort where people get fooled on camera. But all he could see was the grassy plain and the sparrows chattering in the bushes.

'Crazy. Mad,' he said out loud to try to stop himself panicking. 'Do you believe this, Rufus Chumley?'

He put his shoulder to the rock and tried to move it. He shuddered. The spooky feeling was rising inside him again. He took lots of pictures and a short video, which was difficult because his hand was shaking from nerves.

He took his gun out of the fishing bag, put it up to his shoulder and swung it left and right. He'd never heard of cattle with hooves this size. Animals this big would be dangerous, but if one of them charged him, he would just shoot it. Then a new thought occurred: monster cattle were a great thing for him. He could shoot one, put his camera on timer, pose for a photograph of himself with his kill then send the picture straight to the board of the hunting competition. They'd be so impressed!

Feeling bolder, he slung his gun over his shoulder and began to track. Every giant hoofmark made his heart sing. And so now, very excitedly, he walked eastwards. He walked and walked.

By lunchtime, he had fat blisters on each of his heels, but he didn't care. He congratulated himself on being such a fine tracker.

'Most people have no idea how to track,' he told himself. 'You're a natural-born hunter, Rufus Chumley. All that mucking about in the woods has actually taught you a thing or two.'

Occasionally, a doubting part of his mind tried to tell him he was being stupid, that surely a human was leading the herd, that it was more likely that all the cows and calves had been stolen.

But then he'd argue with himself, 'No! There aren't any *human* footprints, are there?'

After dusk, he arrived at a dense wood. He found bushy tunnels the cattle had walked through. Inside the wood, using his torch, he saw the sure signs that the animals had slept there. The grass and snowdrops had been flattened and there were fresh cow pats everywhere, often *giant* cowpats – what was more, some smelt like they'd been done only hours before.

Chumley had never been so happy to see cow poo. His tiredness vanished. He knew that this was the most exciting thing that had ever happened to him. Eagerly, he hunted round the wood for signs of where the animals had gone next. He found their tracks again. They had walked out of the wood and up a hill.

Rufus ignored his sore back and his aching muscles. He scrambled up the hill. At the top he saw the sea and, as though seeing a heaven-sent vision, he spied the herd that he had been tracking. There they were, a long line of cows and calves of all different sizes and colours, walking through a gap in a metal fence into the entrance of the tunnel that went under the sea.

He stopped stock still. Some of them were *huge*. Ginormous. Chumley blinked three times to try to adjust his sight. Surely the cows couldn't be that big? Maybe it was the dusk light playing tricks on him? Quickly, he pulled out his binoculars. Sure enough, the cows were massive but what he saw now made him even more amazed. One of the smaller calves seemed to be glowing. It was a very white calf. Was it his albino calf? He took a deep breath and reasoned with himself. He was very tired. Perhaps he was hallucinating. He lurched forward to follow, then tripped and fell. Now he came to his senses. He was famished and dehydrated. He'd collapse if he walked much further. Chumley paused.

'Eat something, Chumley.' He took off his rucksack and burrowed

into it. Soon, he had ripped the silver wrapper off a king-size bar of chocolate and was eating it. Its sweetness melted in his mouth. He chewed and swallowed, then drank from his water bottle. He felt steadier now.

'The cow pats on your shoes are real, so the cows are real,' he said. 'It makes sense that some of them are very big, too, because the hoofmarks are big. And why not? I'm big.' But then he thought about the glowing calf. 'Chumley,' he said to himself. 'Think. Was it your imagination playing tricks on you?'

He knew he'd witnessed something very strange. Why were the cows walking into the tunnel? Maybe they were being smuggled out of the country. He would get to the bottom of this. All he needed to do was follow them into that tunnel himself.

And so, even though Chumley was tired enough to drop and sleep right there on the hillside, he went forward.

Up close, he saw that the gap in the fence was only temporary. The slopes inside the barrier were being fixed and some sloppy builder had forgotten to secure the work access gate. In fact, it was wide open. Rufus stepped through, past a concrete mixer, down towards the tunnel.

He heard a noise. A train was coming. He shrank back behind a stack of iron poles as the thousand-ton weight of it thundered past. After it had gone, Chumley sat for a moment to reflect upon where he was. He looked at the pictures he'd taken of the hoofprints. He wished he'd photographed the cows entering the tunnel. No one would believe that had happened. He would have to catch up with them the other side and take loads of pictures there. He couldn't believe his luck!

'Oh, Chummers! Oh, oh, oh!'

The albino calf was even more alluring now. How had it found itself with the massive cows? Chumley felt like a scientist might, discovering a new breed of animal – for that is what the giant cows surely were. But maybe he was making two discoveries. Maybe the calf really had been glowing. A glowing calf would be an incredible discovery. And one that had escaped to be with weird giant cows was even more of an extraordinary creature.

He crunched down the gravel towards the entrance. Did the beasts know he was following them? He shivered for a moment as he considered this and as he peered into the tunnel's darkness. He saw the hoofmarks there between small orange lights that lined the edge of the train track. They showed the cows going in one direction. The wind wouldn't blow his scent in towards them. They wouldn't know he was coming. And so he began walking.

Chumley's walk was slow to start with and got even slower. The tunnel was long and in the middle of it he felt like curling up and resting. But he kept on. When trains shot past him, he shrank into dips in the wall and was hidden. It was the worst walk he'd ever made, for he'd never been so tired, but what fired him up was the intoxicating thought of shooting one of the big beasts, *and* the calf.

After eight adrenalin-driven hours, land lights appeared at the tunnel's end. Their beams were illuminating heavy rain, but he didn't mind. He was thrilled. He put on his raincoat and sang out, 'YOU MADE IT, CHUMMERS!'

His voice echoed in the tunnel. '*YOU MADE IT, CHUMMERS! YOU MADE IT CHUMMERS!*'

Elated, and with rifle to the ready, he emerged into the open air. Ahead, he saw that the tall metal railings that enclosed the French exit had been bent and opened. Chumley felt sure that the damage had been done by the humungous cows. He stepped through the opening, only to have all his thrills dashed. The torrential downpour had obliterated most of the herd's hoofprints.

Panicking now, Chumley used his torch and cast its beam over the muddy ground. For a horrid moment Chumley thought he might have lost his herd, but then he found another giant hoofmark and a small one too.

Tracking this herd wasn't going to be easy, he thought. However, the more difficult it was, the more the Hunting Association would be impressed. He took some pictures, then, buttoning his collar against the wind, set off.

And so, a journey started. A boy's and a herd's.

SPRING

Chapter Twelve

FRANCE

For Albi and the herd, the journey had been hard and wet to begin with. Later, Albi remembered this time as a blur of shivering and tiredness, of mud and sodden fur, but there were woods to shelter and hide in, and then the weather changed and it became drier.

The herd had settled into a happy rhythm, walking at night. Oros led them south through the French countryside. He told them what he knew of France – things like how the human language was different here but how the humans were still animal-eaters. They met many cows; every one they passed was locked in a field or yard or building. Most had plastic tags in their ears. Albi began to understand that no cows were actually free. They were all owned by a human of some sort. Here and there, a few French cows joined them, though most eyed Oros and the giant auroch suspiciously and didn't trust the strange, hundred-strong procession.

Sometimes they'd walk along shallow rivers. They followed the land near the coast of France. Albi and the calves especially loved it when one night, Oros took them to a remote beach and they played in the rippling waves. The wind had dropped and the sea was tranquil. A thin slice of moon hung above it. Albi thought how lovely the herd looked; a long line of cows walking on the sand under the moon.

But mostly, they walked in unvisited places out of the sight of humans. The auroch were good at sensing where humans were, where good water was, where trees and grass and leafy plants grew.

February left January behind, and soon it was March. They walked at a leisurely pace, weaving their way down through France. The auroch were pulled by a force that told Oros where to go, though no one knew their final destination. The herd didn't mind. They all were enjoying the journey and learning about the world. Animal language, from cows to horses to pigs to chickens, was the same as it had been back home. Accents were different, that was all. So, they learnt a lot from the French animals. The cows told them how French humans loved to eat. The cheese they made was often very stinky, a chicken told Bodge. Cheese was made from cow, goat or sheep's milk, an old goat told Lily. Ernie was upset by a goose who told him about the shiny axe that her farmer kept in a shed and what he did with it.

'Most humans eat animals,' Oros said. 'Before they're eaten, most of these animals live imprisoned in small places, behind bars or in cages. Humans live in cities, forgetting that they are part of nature. Most forget to look after the earth. Maybe they don't realise that they need the earth's greenness so that they can eat and breathe.'

'W-why do they need greenness to breathe?' Ernie asked.

'Because plants of all sorts – trees, bushes, even grass – make oxygen, which we need to breathe, and plants clean the world's air,' Oros said. 'They suck it in and clean it so that it is fresh and good when it comes out of them again. Humans' machines and cars and planes make a lot of gas that fogs the air, so it really needs cleaning.'

'Yes,' Bodge agreed. 'Cars are like farting machines but with cloudy gas stuff coming out of them instead of fart ponk.'

'Yes, Bodge,' Oros said, chuckling and knocking Bodge with his cheek. 'And every time we burp after chewing the cud, cows fill the air with gas too.'

The calves had competitions to see who could do the longest burp. Bodge always won. He also always came first in the rude song competition; a competition he'd invented. His favourite one was about cowpats, which he'd sing to his friends when none of the adults were listening.

'Patta-splattttttt, patta-splatttttttt!

No pain, no strain, just stand and let it drain.

This stuff smells mighty funny, it's very, very runny.

Patta-splatttttttt! Pattttttta-splattttttt!'

The cows took their time and enjoyed the spring. April saw them walking inland, into wilder, more hilly, forested parts where trees were now dense with foliage, so it was easy to hide. There were lots of milk mushrooms to eat; often they were weeks old or less potent because they had grown on a night that wasn't in the special milk moon time. But they were all good. Sometimes, if Oros thought it safe, Albi and Lily were allowed to practise their glowing, seeing who could glow the brightest.

Albi loved this game, especially when Lily called him 'The Spark'. To really glow, you had to think something special, or extra-clever. Lily was very good at it, better than Albi, but he didn't mind. Then, one night Albi found that he was glowing brighter than Lily. But it wasn't from thinking; it was from a *feeling* that he was getting through the ground.

'Can you feel that?' Albi said, glowing fiercely and pointing his nose at the rocky hillside in front of them. Lily sniffed the air and looked down.

'Yes. It's a sort of pull.' Her fur began pulsing with light too.

'It's like the tug I got the night I found the Henge stones,' Albi said.

Oros was in the distance ahead. They saw that he too was starting to glow very strongly, so strongly that it was as if he was the moon.

'He knows everything, so he must be thinking something really clever,' whispered Lily.

'Or he's feeling something like we did,' Albi said. 'He's feeling the pull too. And I bet he gets it a hundred times stronger than us.'

The rock of the hillside in front of them began to rumble and move. Stone grinding against stone; it was as if the earth was growling. Then two slabs of it parted, revealing the entrance to a cave, and two huge auroch appeared. Oros nodded to them and went in. The herd followed and the cave door shut behind them.

This cave was different to the Stonehenge cave. It had a tall wall on one side where it met the sheer rock face on the other side. High up on this part of the wall were cracks that let the light in. As a result, there were pools where rainwater gathered and patches of leafy vegetation grew. It smelt lovely – of pine and spicy herbs, of lavender and mushrooms. Milk mushrooms, but other types too – some like big spongy brown flowers and other funguses that grew like moss. The herd followed the French auroch down giant corridors, down into a vast church-sized cave. Nooks and crannies made dents in its rocks, little passages led away from it and great spikes of stone descended from its ceiling, meeting other spikes that rose up from its floors, giving the impression of columns being everywhere.

A herd of grey auroch and ordinary cows and bulls stood quietly and expectantly, as though unsurprised by their new guests. On the wall behind them were pictures of wild horses and bears, deer and big cats; of majestic animals with horns and other enormous beasts with tusks and long noses. They were all coloured with black, ochres and browns.

'Those,' Lily told Albi, 'are rhinoceroses and mammoths. I remember Oros talking about them.'

Albi and his friends looked at all the cattle in the cave. Lily knew all the breeds.

'Those golden ones are Guernseys,' she whispered. 'They make creamy milk and come from an island off the coast of France. Those beautiful white ones are Blonde d'Aquitaine, those black ones are marsh cattle called Camargue—'

Bodge interrupted her. 'Can you smell smoke?'

Albi pointed his nose to a cave a little way off. 'It's coming from over there.'

He and his friends stepped towards the smoke to get a better look. A horrifying sight met their eyes; there was a shadow cast on the distant wall. It was the shadow of a man! What was more disturbing was that Oros and some of his herd were walking with the French auroch towards it! Albi's body reacted faster than his thoughts. With a bolt, he rushed forward. Dodging other cows and bulls, he ran towards Oros and, tipping his body sideways, he threw himself at his hooves. Bodge followed close behind, Lily and Ernie too. Oros and the auroch looked dumbfounded.

'Stop!' Albi told them breathlessly. 'Don't go in there!' The massive cows towered above him. 'There's *a man*!'

The auroch glanced at each other and then they all began to chuckle.

'Really! There is!'

'There is!' Bodge insisted.

But still the auroch laughed.

Oros's laugh was deep and warm. 'We know. He lives here. He is a friend of the French herd, an extra-special man. We were just being taken to meet him. You four can watch and listen.'

The man wasn't like any human Albi had seen before. He was far more dishevelled than the people of the abattoir or on the farm. His hair was long and knotted and almost as dirty as the end of Bodge's tail. He wore tatty shorts and a torn vest. His body was covered with drawings.

'His skin looks like the cave walls,' Albi said.

'Those are tattoos,' Lily explained. 'They are a bit like our brandings, but humans do them to themselves. They make holes in their skin and fill them with paint or something.'

Albi studied the tree and leaf tattoos on the man's back and on his legs and at the other pictures and patterns on the man's body. He recognised some of the shapes there. For instance, the shapes

E, A, R, T and H were tattooed across his chest.

The man was stirring something in a pot on a fire. Albi hadn't seen flames since the ones he'd seen inside the branding machine at Henge Farm, so he was nervous. But when the man calmly smiled up at the auroch, and then rose to bow to them, Albi relaxed.

WELCOMEBIGBUDDIES, the man said in an accent that was different to the ones Albi had heard. JUSTMAKIN' MYSELFAGOOD OLD CALIFORNIAN MUSHROOMSTEW HERE WON'T Y'ALL TAKEA SEAT?

Albi didn't understand what the man had said, but when the auroch sat down, he and his friends copied them. The man got up and patted the French auroch on their cheeks.

GOTSOMEVISITORS ISEE. He bobbed his head in respect to Oros and then saluted Albi and the calves. AND SOMEYOUNG 'UNS – A FEW SEEMTOBE GLOWERSTOO BOYOHBOY THATIS COOL. The man carried on talking.

HOPE YOUALLHAD ASGOODADAY ASME. I PLANTED LIONSMANE MUSHROOMS. THEY'RE THEONES WITH FRONDS LIKE LIONS'MANES.

Oros nodded and translated what the man had said, adding, 'Lions are those big cats you might have seen painted on the wall in the big cave.'

USED TO GROWTHELIONS'MANE MUSHROOMS BACK IN SANFRANCISCO. THEY'REGOODFOR THEBRAIN. HELP METHINK.

Oros glowed intensely as his great mind translated.

WOW! The man exclaimed. AIN'T YOUA MOONY GLOWER? A BLACKAUROCH WITHPINK EYESCOOL.

Oros mooed at him and nodded. The man laughed.

CRAZY! SO, YOUUNDERSTANDME TOO JUST LIKE MY GLOWINGCAVEBUDDIES HERE! IWISH ICOULD UNDERSTANDYOU.

As he spoke, Albi and Lily attempted to decipher his words, trying to break the sentences up and understand them, but though they were glowing like small stars from their thinking, they couldn't do it.

The man stepped towards them and gently stroked their noses.

YOUAREINCREDIBLE.   NEVERSEEN   SUCHYOUNG GLOWERS! HOWTHE WORLD IS CHANGING FOR THE BETTERIFYOU KIDSARE ON THE BLOCK.

Over the next few days, Albi learnt a lot about the world by listening to the aurochs translate what the man said. He talked a lot, sometimes to himself, sometimes to the cows. The man had come from America, a scientist on a holiday to France – not the sort of holiday that the bull calves had been taken on to the abattoir, a *real* holiday. He'd come to see some other caves that were famous for their ancient paintings. He'd camped for weeks, then one day, when he'd been climbing and abseiling – dropping on ropes down the side of the auroch cave – he'd noticed some of the cracks that let the light through the rocks. Climbing in, he'd discovered the paintings, the mushrooms and the glowing herd. He'd made friends with the herd and then he'd become obsessed

with the mushrooms. Mycology, he'd told the cows, was the study of mushrooms and fungi. He now lived in the cave, in his own quarters, and farmed mushrooms – the hairy Lion's Mane mushrooms and others, like Cordyceps that looked like thin orange tongues coming out of the ground. There were ordinary brown Chaga and Turkeytail mushrooms that he grew outside in the wood and said were extraordinary because they made him healthy. He said that there were new kinds of mushrooms or fungi being found in the world every day. He talked about how all fungi – some big, some microscopic – rotted things and so helped other things grow too. He said that fungi were the oldest organisms on the planet, that they covered the earth, growing under the ground so that everywhere was connected. Albi loved the idea of this.

The man said that sometimes he dreamt that the mushrooms were speaking to him, encouraging him.

I'M LEARNINGABOUT THEM SO MUSHROOMS CAN GIVE US THEIR SECRETS FOR MEDICINE. LOOK AT MY LEGS ANDMY BACK. THESE TREEPICTURES AIN'T TATTOOS. NO SIRREE. THEY'RE JUST APPEARIN' ON ME. STARTEDWHEN I BEGANEATIN' THOSE WHITEMILKY MUSHROOMS.

Albi listened hard to the auroch translating what the man said. The human words were starting to separate out for him, though he still didn't understand them.

WHEN HUMANS POSTANDSEND STUFF TO EACH OTHER THEY WRAP EVERYTHINGINPLASTIC AND POLY STYRENE TO STOP IT BREAKING. DRIED MUSHROOMS CANDOTHAT INSTEAD. AIN'T THAT AMAZIN'?

Plastic. Albi had seen that stuff. He'd eaten some in northern France by mistake and nearly choked. The man explained post and phones and TVs and other things humans used. He told them about dark things that Albi didn't like to hear about, like destroyed forests and pollution and climate change that caused wildfires and storms and destruction.

YOUKNOW METHANE? METHANE IS A GAS. IT'S ONE OF THE BIGBAD THINGS THATMAKES CLIMATE CHANGE HAPPEN, the man told Albi and his friends. DID YOUKNOW COW BURPS ARE FULLOF METHANE? THERE ARE ONE AND A HALF *BILLION* COWS ONTHEEARTH, the man declared, MOST OF 'EM HERE FORHUMANSTO EAT OR TO GETMILK FROMOR LEATHER FROM. THAT'SA LOTTA METHANE THOSE ONE AND A HALFBILLIONCOWS BURP UP INTO THE AIR! IF HUMANS JUSTSTOPPED KEEPING COWS FOR MILK ANDMEATAND LEATHER, WHY, THE CLIMATE CHANGE THING WOULD BE ON THEWAY TO GETTING BETTER.

The man loved cuddling the calves.

I DON'T KNOW WHY ANYONEWOULD WANNA EAT AN INTELLIGENT ANIMAL LIKEYOU ANYWAYS, he told them.

Meat must taste very, very good to the humans, Albi thought – so good that it made humans forget about the life of the cow they were eating. Milk must taste great too – so delicious that humans thought it was fine to take calves away from their mothers to get it, and for all the *boy* cows, who were born who couldn't make milk, to be *eaten*. Because what would they do with the boy cows otherwise? Just let them live till they were old, while their sisters grew up and gave their milk? The meat and milk must taste so good that it made humans forget about the methane that cows made. Or perhaps the humans didn't know about this? Or maybe they didn't care about the world getting hotter and the land becoming drier and drier? But that couldn't be right, Albi reasoned. Surely if humans knew about methane they'd do everything they could to stop it gassing the air. Because they'd all want to save the green and watery world that they lived in – wouldn't they?

Albi watched the man eating his mushrooms and painting on the walls of the cave. He wished he could ask him all these questions.

After a good stay, the herd set off again, the French auroch with them. The man wasn't surprised – he said he'd dreamt of it. He was sad to see them go. Albi wondered afterwards whether his dreams had been because he'd been eating the milk mushrooms.

The herd walked through the forest and sometimes near human towns. Albi felt much more confident now, wiser from what he'd learnt from the kind man. He and Lily studied the human signs if they came to them.

LES CÉVENNES

They came to a beautiful hilly place. There was plenty to eat. Delicious grass and herbs, as well as the milk mushrooms that seemed to grow in strong moonlight as keenly as sunflowers growing in sun. Albi and Lily feasted on them, ignoring the wild horses who cantered around and teased the calves.

'Try the rosemary or the thyme!' they whinnied. 'You've been cooped up by humans so long you don't know what's what!' But it was clear the horses were also impressed. 'We've never seen your sort wild,' they told them. Then they added teasingly, 'If you want to see something special, over there where those hills are, is a cow that speaks the human tongue.' And they galloped off.

Curiosity began to stir in Albi. A cow that spoke the human language was too tempting a thing to miss.

This is where he made a very big mistake.

When the herd stopped to rest in a wood and Albi saw that dawn was still a few hours away, it struck him that he could easily investigate this talking cow. The full moon was like a great torch in the sky, lighting up the land below. He would be safely back with the herd before the sun came up.

And so, he walked to the hills. When he got there, he found one of the humans' shops. In front of it was a metal cow. Its mouth moved, so that every so often when the wind blew, the bottom part of the mouth and a noise come out.

BUY YOUR MILK HERE TODAY! the machine cow said.

Disappointed and feeling cheated, Albi looked behind to the distant wood. He was tired now. It felt much further away than it had before. He braced himself and began to walk back to the herd.

Rufus Chumley's journey had been very different. To start with, he had lost the herd completely. He'd nearly given up but, by talking to himself with a combination of scolding and encouragement, he'd persuaded himself to keep going.

An ordinary twelve year old might not have enjoyed life alone, living rough and camping – whatever the weather. But Chumley wasn't an ordinary child. He liked looking after himself. What with all his time alone at home in the woods, cooking on open fires was nothing new.

He enjoyed the nomadic life, moving from place to place. He thought about his home. There wasn't much for him there. Indeed, neither his mother nor his father seemed bothered that he'd gone. Neither had called him. Every time he used his mother's credit card to buy ham and cheese baguettes or food from a supermarket, he was reminded how little they cared about him.

He still wasn't a great shot. This annoyed him, partly because he wanted to be self-sufficient, but mostly because he knew that members of the Worldwide Hunting Association would expect him to have very good shooting skills. He practised when he could. He kept his eyes down and continued to track the herd. After a few days of losing the hoofmarks and then finding the trail again, he saw that there was a pattern to their movements. He started to be able to guess where they might be.

When he'd checked the news on his phone, or when he Googled things like 'Herd found France no owner', nothing would come up.

'Good,' he said to himself. 'I'm the only person who knows about you all.'

The idea that he'd seen a calf that glowed now seemed a bit preposterous to him. He decided that he'd been so tired he must have imagined it. He now also reckoned that the enormous cows were actually much smaller than he'd thought. After all, he'd seen them from a distance and had been cross-eyed with tiredness.

Sure, they had enormous hoofprints but chances were, they were just very big cows with extra-large hooves. Chewing it all over as he walked, the calf became more exciting to him. Its branding would prove where it had come from. It had the cute factor. Tracking that all the way from his father's abattoir would be enough to impress the Worldwide Hunting Association. He imagined his picture with it.

'They will give you a shiny medal,' he told himself. 'You'll probably be asked to go on telly, Chummers! Are you ready for that?'

Having jolly conversations with himself like this kept Chumley happy. Food was good in France, too. This was a great part of his new life that he liked a lot. He could eat whenever and whatever he wanted without anyone complaining. And with practice he did get better at hunting. He enjoyed skinning rabbits and cooking them on an open fire. It was good to know he could do this, but it was still an effort. He found it easier using his mother's credit card and buying his food. He ate salami, sausages, meat pies, kebabs, cassoulets and tarts, buying his food from takeaway cafes so that he could eat on the go and continue to look for the herd's hoofmarks.

At night, he liked to lay in his sleeping bag, under the stars, beside a burning campfire. He wiled the hours away dreaming up his ideal family. They'd adopt him. The giraffe-hunting girl would be his sister. He'd have a brother too. Sometimes they'd fight, like he imagined kids in families did, but otherwise, they'd be a team. The parents would hunt with them too. They'd hunt in all seasons. His adopted mother would be an excellent tracker; she'd admire him for the way he had tracked the herd. She'd teach him to navigate using the stars. His new father would be an excellent cook. He'd teach Rufus all the secret ingredients for his special barbecue hot sauces.

As the days went by, this conjured-up family became less and less blurred and more and more real to Chumley. He felt sure these people existed and that he was going to meet them. The idea of impressing them spurred him on to hunting down the calf. He encouraged himself by conjuring up pictures of the future – him being awarded the best hunter of the *decade* by the Worldwide Hunting Association, of being asked to sign photographs of himself or copies of his life story for fans.

He followed the tracks down through France and by late April was camping in a forest in the south of the country. Here he met a wild American man with tattoos who told him that he'd seen the animals and said they'd headed off to the north. Chumley took his tip but couldn't pick up the trail again. He had to retrace his steps. The wild man had clearly sent him in completely the wrong direction. That would be the last time Chumley listened to other people, he thought.

Then, one evening he found the tracks again; extra-fresh hoofprints. This was it! There was no way he wouldn't see the beasts tonight. He would shoot the calf. He would take pictures. He was so close that he wanted to sing. All of a sudden, he saw something in the distance that made his heart leap.

'You,' he gasped.

There on the hillside, lit up by the occasional rays of moonlight was the white calf!

Chumley paused. Was he tired? Was he imagining it? No! There it was. Not a glowing calf – Chumley laughed inside at himself for how he'd thought it could glow. What was he thinking? It wasn't magic – but it certainly was an albino bull calf. It was perfect for his collection.

He licked his finger and put it in the air. The wind was blowing away from the calf. It would never smell him coming.

Quickly and quietly, Chumley moved towards it.

Chapter Thirteen

THE HORSEBOX

Albi's legs were sore. The sandy path to the wood was a long one. It suddenly occurred to him that he wouldn't get back to the resting herd before the sun came up. So, when a short-cut of a country road offered itself, Albi found himself very tempted to take it.

The road was just becoming visible, its hedges looming on either side like dark walls. All was quiet and empty. This countryside was very remote. The cars probably only came here in the day, he thought. He eyed the tarmac. He hadn't felt tarmac below his feet since the night he'd rescued his herd. The still air smelt of spring blossom, full of hope of good things to come. With this positive feeling billowing in him, Albi stepped out on to the road. He had taken ten paces when it happened.

Albi saw the lights before he saw the machine. A truck was coming from the road behind him, its lamps beaming out like searchlights. Now he could hear its iron grinding and growling. Albi froze as fear coursed through his veins. He darted to the left, but it was too late. The vehicle careered past but then braked and, in another moment, it was reversing, backing up too quickly for Albi to run away. He hid.

The truck smelt of dogs and horses. When its front door opened, there was the unmistakeable salty smell of humans – a big man and a wiry woman. They were talking to each other, the woman *hahaha*-ing. She had a bottle with a grape-smelling liquid in it. She took a swig. Albi shut his eyes, hoping that if he couldn't see them, then they couldn't see him. But this didn't work. In the next second, he felt a thick rope around his neck.

JE L'AI! the man's rough voice announced. HA HA HA ET JE L'AI AUSSI DANS LE NOIR! He pulled at the rope.

OH! JOHN PAUL TU ES SI FORT! The woman exclaimed.

Albi wasn't sure what they were saying. The man felt fiery and aggressive. The woman smelt ill. She was. From the grape drink it seemed. She went to a bush and pink, smelly stuff came out of her mouth. Albi backed away from the sour-smelling liquid, edging himself towards the open gate to the field. If he pulled hard enough, he thought, he'd be able to tug the rope from the slurring man's hand. So, he pulled. The rope slid through the man's hand and seemed to hurt him because he gave a yelp of pain.

BRÛLURE DE CORDE! he shouted. ANIMAL STUPIDE!

Albi kept pulling. He twisted his neck left and right. The woman let out another *HA HA HA* noise.

OH JOHN PAUL, TU AS L'AIR STUPIDE.

Albi tried to think hard about what to do next, and in doing so he felt himself glowing. Immediately he stopped the glow, but not quite in time.

OOOOOOOOH, the woman said, gasping and pointing at him.

REGARDE! ÇA BRILLE! ÇA BRILLE!

In that moment, as though hit by a thunderbolt of intelligence, Albi suddenly knew that 'ÇA BRILLE' meant 'it's glowing'. He knew it as surely as he knew the ground was under his feet. It was a strange sensation to have this sudden understanding, and odd for it to happen in such a horrid situation, but the worst thing was that the brain power that made it happen caused another volt of glowing shine to come from him.

ÇA BRILLE! she shouted.

The man was concentrating so hard on controlling Albi that he didn't see. Instead, he curled his fist up and shook it at her.

TAIS-TOI! he barked.

'Shut up!' The words came to Albi but this time he stopped himself glowing.

The woman came to the man's side and took a hold of the rope too. Albi didn't know what to do. Pulling back wasn't helping. Perhaps rushing at the man would. Albi gritted his teeth and charged, butting the man with his head.

OI! he shouted.

The woman screamed. Albi realised he'd gone a bit far. Suddenly he felt a whack on his rump, then another. The woman was hitting him with a stick. The man clapped and they both started falling about making the HA HA HA noises. HAW HAW HA HA, they went. There was a thud. The back of the truck had been opened and a ramp up to its inside had been pulled out and put in place.

The moon came out from behind a cloud as though wanting to watch this show; the show where the calf gets caught. The man went up the ramp and tugged Albi in after him. The moonlight showed him the man and the woman's nasty faces. They were twisted, greedy, stupid and unkind. Albi was so scared that he pooed. ANIMAL PUANT! The man pushed past him and got out of the horsebox. He locked it shut. Albi could just see through a crack in the door. The woman threw her arms around the man's neck and put her nose near his. Then they nearly fell over. They moved out of sight. The horsebox shook as they got into the front of it and slammed its doors. Its growling noise started. Albi panicked. He had to get out. He butted his head against the horsebox door. But it was useless. He was trapped.

Rufus Chumley was running. He'd heard the commotion. Now he could see a horsebox. He sprinted towards it. This was too much! His prize was being stolen! His feet beat on the tarmac. He ran as fast as his legs would carry him.

'STOP! STOP! THAT'S MY CALF!' he shouted.

With a few extra-powerful steps, Chumley leapt on to the back of the truck, his foot landing on its bumper, his hands holding on to the bars on its back doors. The horsebox rumbled on. Chumley peered through the glassless window and gasped. There, cowering in the back was *his calf*. And it was luminescent like the moon! He hadn't been imagining it! The calf *had* been glowing both times he'd seen it before – on the hillside in the rain and by the Channel Tunnel entrance. His eyes hadn't deceived him!

Chumley paused for a second. A glowing calf . . . ? How could

that be? Was it an alien creature? No animals on earth glowed except glow worms, fireflies, and deep-sea jellyfish. It must be one of the rarest things in the world! What a trophy it would be!

Frantically, and with great difficulty, for the truck was now swinging around on the country lanes, Chumley tried to open the door, but it was locked. The calf looked up at him and their eyes met. At the same time, the calf's body seemed to surge with its cool light. Chumley gawped through the window, stunned by the incredible sight. And in that moment, more than ever, he knew that this amazing animal was his future. He beat on the door.

'YOU'RE MINE!' he shouted. 'HE'S MINE!' But the French couple didn't hear him.

After a few minutes of being thrown about, Rufus's hands and arms were running out of grip. At the next corner, when the vehicle went over a bump, he was thrown off. He landed badly. His arm cracked, and his chin skidded along the tarmac. As the horsebox shot away, he memorised its number plate.

The sun rose into a blue sky and the horsebox rolled on. Albi could feel the herd getting further and further away.

Where had the big, flame-haired boy gone? Albi wondered. And what had he been doing? For a second, Albi had thought he recognised him. But then he'd realised he was so upset that he was just imagining things. The boy was probably just a friend of the people who drove the truck.

Albi sank to his knees and buried his face between his front legs. He felt small and unworthy of Oros's great herd. The confidence he'd built had now vanished, replaced by dark disappointment in himself.

He felt a fool for letting his guard down. His mind tortured him by replaying the moments just before he'd been caught. If only he had stayed in the woods and slept with the herd. Oros had told him that there was a human expression, 'Curiosity killed the cat.' Did curiosity kill calves too? he wondered. He put his front legs on to a box and craned his neck towards a slim window on the side of the horsebox. He sniffed the air. Perhaps something good might happen, something that might reverse this horror. He waited and waited, but it didn't.

The vehicle drove on. Albi could feel the sea in the distance. It was to the left and to the right of him now. A long way off, but it was there. On they went. The air was getting warmer and dustier. He tried to stay awake in case the people stopped and an opportunity to escape arose. But on and on the horsebox rolled, its rumbling a lullaby to him, lulling him to sleep.

When he woke up, the truck was parked. He looked out. The sun was now low in the sky. He had slept all morning and for a bit of the afternoon too. He could see the couple at a roadside shed drinking from small white cups. The letters

CAFETERÍA

were printed on a board.

On the hillside behind them was an enormous black bull. Albi gasped. Then he squinted and saw that it wasn't a real bull, it was a big, flat picture of one. Underneath it were more letters:

BIENVENIDO A ESPAÑA

The place smelt new and strange. It might have been exciting, but it wasn't because Albi was alone and frightened. He was thirsty and hungry and felt desperately hopeless and ashamed.

The horsebox began to move. Albi lay down and shut his eyes. When he woke up, the truck had stopped again. He could hear hooves – or were they feet? – crunching on gravel. And running water as well. That sound made his mouth feel very dry. He got up, and peered out. Near the back of the truck was a pool of water. At one end of it was a bull, but again, not a real bull; this one was made of stone. What's more, water was gushing out of its raised front hoof. He heard voices, more *hahaha*-ing. The back of the truck opened. Rusty afternoon light filled the horsebox, turning Albi the colour of an autumn tree.

AH! a new male voice exclaimed. UN ALBINO.

Albi tried to understand what the human had said, but this time he couldn't. He backed into the truck and tried to disappear, but the rope was still around his neck. The man and woman tugged it enthusiastically and pulled him down to the dusty ground.

The new man wasn't as fierce as Albi's captors. He had a gentler way about him, as though he respected Albi, as though he had friends who were cows. Behind him was a big house. It was made of white stone and had pink flowers growing up it. Albi's knees shook in fright as the man touched his neck, then stroked him. The man led him to the water and Albi put his head down and drank. The man pointed to the decoration on his rump and shrugged. It seemed that the red moon mark obviously didn't make sense to him. Albi then saw grubby, leaf-thin things pass from the new man's hands to the woman's fingers. The two men shook hands. The couple climbed back into their truck. Its engines snarled and it rattled away.

Albi felt slightly better. He couldn't smell any cow blood and there was no fear in the air. Instead, there was a smell of cud, dung and the strong, musky scent of bulls.

Chapter Fourteen

THE SPANISH BULLS

The man led Albi along a path that was shaded by tall feathery trees. This turned a corner to a scrubby field where three bulls were grazing: a black, a brown and a tawny one. All had big horns. One pawed the ground and nudged the gate of the enclosure, making it rattle. The field had wide, low trees in it, trees that looked like great birds, their trunks like birds' legs and their branches above like wings, as though they were about to fly away. Albi wished he could fly away.

The man led Albi to a trough and opened a container with nuggets inside it. Albi ate a few.

LECHE DESPUÉS he said. His language, Albi realised, was different to the people before, and Albi couldn't understand it.

The man opened the gate to the big paddock, took off Albi's lead and pushed him in. As the gate's catch locked with a clonk, the bulls looked up.

'Mascot's arrived,' the black one said.

Albi didn't know what mascot meant. Since Mascot wasn't his name and since the bull might be mistaking him for another calf, he decided to correct him.

'Very nice to meet you, but my name isn't Mascot, it's Albert,' he said politely, deciding to use his full name as it sounded more grown up.

The bulls laughed. And came closer.

'You're our mascot, Albert,' the brown bull said.

'You don't know why you're here, do you?' the tawny bull said. He licked his lips and for a horrid moment Albi thought that maybe he was planning to eat him.

'Relax, young snow calf,' the black bull said kindly. 'All is good here.'

'How did you know I was born in the snow?' Albi asked.

'I didn't. I just called you that because you're as white as snow. We're all friends here,' the black bull went on. 'You're one of us, little albino, and we are honoured to meet you.'

'Honoured?' Albi asked incredulously.

'Yes, because you've been chosen to join us when we fight.'

'Fight?'

'He doesn't know,' the brown bull said. 'Tell him.'

The black bull nodded. 'We are fighting bulls, Albert. This is Spain. We fight for the humans. We are their protectors. We come from a long line of great bulls. Our ancestors were famous. We have their special blood. As you know, we are peace-loving creatures but there are monsters out there and so we must fight for the safety of all. The humans wear warrior skins and we help them fight the monsters, often to the death. We are heroes, for without our bravery the monsters would win.'

Albi's eyes were wide as he listened. 'Where do you and the humans fight the monsters?' he asked, amazed by the idea that cows and humans could be so courageous together.

'In a big sandy place,' the tawny bull said.

'It sounds very frightening.'

'Bravery is in our blood. We sacrifice ourselves for the peace of the world. We fight for calves like you.'

'Thank you,' Albi said humbly. 'I don't think many cows know about this brave thing you do. Have you fought the monsters before?'

'No, but years ago, a bull from our farm was told all about it by a small white pony who had been to the fighting place. The pony told of the courage of a bull that slayed one of the monsters. The pony was the mascot, as you will be, Albert. He had to walk ahead to proclaim the beginnings of the fight. As you will when the time comes. You are our mascot, the harbinger of good luck.'

'Are you sure you've got the right bull calf?' Albi asked, uncertainly. 'My friends and family call me Albi, you see – Albi's not as proper-sounding as Albert and . . .'

'Yes, you are the one,' the brown bull said, and all the bulls mooed and chuckled at the same time, something that reminded Albi of Bodge, who called this noise 'moockling'. Albi felt braver, thinking of Bodge. Buoyed up, he told the bulls about his herd and his journey. They listened but he knew they didn't believe him.

'Good stories,' they said.

Albi settled into life in Spain. In May, the orange trees blossomed, filling the air with an intoxicating, sweet smell. On quiet evenings, when the cicadas were chirping in the bushes, he could be silent and focus his mind on feeling where his friends were. Even though he couldn't see Oros, he could sense the herd somewhere in the direction of the hills but far, far, far away. He imagined the mushrooms and fungi under the ground connecting him to them all. He chided himself again for his foolishness. He had to admit that he might never see them again. For one thing, he noticed that the gates of the field were always firmly locked with a heavy, fixed bolt. For another, his confidence had been knocked. Since his big mistake, he didn't think himself clever enough to be able to escape.

Life wasn't bad. He liked his new home. The bulls were kind to him and they were all treated with great affection by the humans of the place, as though they were special. Albi knew he wasn't as important as the bulls who were going to have to fight to save the world, but he felt very privileged to be amongst them.

Sometimes, the man would come into the field on a horse. The horse was strong and acted loftily, as though he was better than the bulls, but Albi could sense that he was nervous of them. Perhaps he'd had trouble with one or two bulls in the past, Albi thought.

The man walked and trotted his horse between the oak trees, as he inspected the place and checked that the bulls were happy.

The days rolled past, getting hotter as spring ended and summer began to descend. The shade from the winged oaks became more and more welcome and Albi and the bulls would stand under their green branches, half asleep, as the warmer midday hours passed.

'Talk about sweltering!' Albi said. 'So, this is summer!'

'Ha!' the bulls laughed. 'We don't call this summer! There are still damp places in the field. Summer gets much, much hotter than this.'

When the full moon came in early June, the milk mushrooms grew in its light. Albi found them to be just as milky as the mushrooms he'd had before. The bulls thought them disgusting and spat them out.

'They're toadstools,' the black bull said. 'You will turn into a toad!' He impersonated a toad jumping about, which made Albi laugh a lot because a jumping bull is a funny thing to see.

The bulls loved it when Albi mooed tunes and glowed in the dark. 'You are our mascot moon calf. You're *Albi, the Glowing Moon Calf*,' they declared.

Albi thought about the names he'd had, from 'Albert', the name his mother had given him, which had shortened to 'Albi', to Bodge's 'Glow Worm', to Lily's, 'The Spark'. One French boy with very white hair and pink eyes, who'd visited the Spanish farm had stroked Albi's nose, and whispered to him, 'Cow boy. You're just like me, aren't you? A boy, but in a cow's body.'

Albi had thought about this a lot since. In France, Oros had told him that his thinking power was as good as any human boy's might be.

'It's *Albi, the Glowing Cow Boy*,' he told the bulls. They laughed at this.

'But you're not a boy. You're not human!'

'I think I feel like a boy,' Albi explained.

The black bull knocked the side of Albi's head fondly. 'You're whatever you want to be,' he said. '*Albi, the Glowing Cow Boy* it is.'

And so they wiled the time away, but then, one very hot day, everything changed. A hustle and bustle and a buzz of excitement descended upon their idyll. Something was happening near the man's house.

'The monsters have come again,' the brown bull said knowingly. 'It always happens when the hot weeks arrive.'

They heard the coming and going of machines. The man came to the field. He put a halter around Albi's head and, making encouraging, clicking noises with his tongue, led him out of the field.

'Don't worry,' the tawny bull assured him. 'He's taking you to the special place where they get you ready for the fight.'

'But I don't want to go.'

'We will miss you too,' the bull said, licking Albi's forehead fondly. 'But you have been chosen and must play your part. Look at you, Cow Boy. You're growing faster than a fat orange on a tree. Next year, you'll be too big to be the mascot. Make the most of it.'

Albi followed the man. The truth was, he had no choice. The human led Albi up the dusty avenue of cypress trees. They walked past the stone bull that spouted water. All the while, Albi thought of the monsters. What were they? What did they look like? They went through a gate to a barn where the man tied Albi's leading rein to a post. A long, coiled-up worm-like thing hung on the wall. Albi wondered what this was. The man took hold of it, then fiddled with a metal object on the wall. Water came out of the end of the worm. Albi jumped in surprise. The man made clicking noises with his tongue, as though trying to assure Albi that everything was fine. He squirted some slime that smelt of flowers on to Albi's back and, adding water from the worm thing he began to rub his fur.

Soon, a froth was lathering up, from the back of Albi's ears down his neck to his chest, from his sides to his stomach and his legs. The man made sure that he washed every part of him.

Whatever the gooey stuff was that was making the bubbles, he used a lot of it. He scrubbed Albi's hooves, cleaning the bottom of them too. He washed Albi's face with a wet rag. And then he rinsed Albi down. Albi watched as dirty, bubbly water swilled down a hole in the ground.

The day sun shone down and he could feel himself drying by the second as the water evaporated from his coat. It was a still a soft calf coat, with only a few coarse hairs in it. And now, free from dust and dry mud it sprung up extra-white and extra-fluffy.

OH, DIOS MÍO! ERES UN ANIMAL HERMOSO. UN ÁNGEL ALBINO. HARÁS EL TRABAJO.

Albi tried very hard to understand what the man was saying. He began to glow before he remembered to control it. It was too late; the man had caught a glimpse.

ERES BRILLANDO!

A flash filled Albi's head again, the same as the one that he'd had when he'd first eaten the milk mushrooms, the same as the light that had filled his head when he'd understood the horrible woman's French words, though this flash had more sparks in it. At once, Albi knew what 'eres brillando' meant. It meant, 'you're glowing'.

Albi was amazed. Spanish! He was understanding it! And the meaning of its words had come as easily as air to his nostrils. But more was happening. This time, the language understanding was bigger, as though the flash in his head had turned a key and unlocked a massive door in his mind; a door that now swung wide open. He knew that human language was going to become as easy to decipher as animal language now, knew it with the same certainty as he knew that water was wet. His mind had taken an extraordinary leap, one as miraculous as a cow jumping over the moon would be. Were the Spanish mushrooms different to the others? Or was it because he had eaten so many milk mushrooms before now? Or was it because his brain had grown bigger? Whatever the reason, Albi wasn't sure it was a good idea to let the man see him glow, so he quickly stopped.

The man rubbed his eyes then shook his head. He laughed. He led Albi to a trailer. Albi hardly noticed; he was so stunned by what had just happened.

BUEN BUEY, the man said. The words were clear as spring water. 'Good bullock.'

Albi mooed at the man to make him speak again.

'It's all right, you are going to have a good journey.' The man said and chuckled.

'I can understand what yoOOOOu're saying!' Albi mooed. But the man only heard a bullock complaining.

'In you go, boy,' he said.

Albi did as he was asked.

SUMMER

Chapter Fifteen

PAMPLONA

Chumley had broken his arm. His left arm. A French doctor had put it in a plaster cast. Rufus didn't have any friends to write on it, so it was plain white, though very grubby because two whole months had passed since the accident.

It had been tricky visiting the doctor as the nurse had asked nosy questions about him, so he didn't want to make a trip back to a surgery to have the cast taken off. It was too much of a risk – his true age might be found out and then he'd be sent back to England. He was sure that leaving the cast on for a few extra weeks wouldn't hurt. In any case, he wanted to spend as much of each day as possible tracking. He had completely lost the herd, and now he regularly wondered whether he'd made everything up. In these moments, he'd look at the pictures he'd taken of the giant hoofprints. These would reassure him and he'd believe in the herd again and the glowing calf too.

With clever searching on the internet, he'd found out that the horsebox that had carried away his calf was registered in southern France, so he made his way down there. He bought a better sleeping bag and a bigger tent, as well as a lightweight frying pan, a plate, a fork and a spoon. He cooked on fires and washed up in rivers, where he bathed too. He stole from people's vegetable gardens or ate by shopping for groceries in the villages that he walked through. He avoided speaking to people – in any case, his French was almost non-existent – and then he'd retreat to the woods where he camped.

One evening in late June, when his arm was getting unbelievably itchy in its cast, he walked past a cottage garden and spotted a pair of sharp secateurs on the ground near a wheelbarrow. He slipped his hand through the fence and took them. Then, that evening, he carefully clipped away at the plaster fabric of the cast. His arm felt wonderful out of the dirty shell.

'You're a hatched chick!' Chumley told it. It was white and very withered compared to his strong, tanned right arm.

Soon he was making good use of his gun again by hunting rabbits, sometimes to eat but at other times just for fun.

He'd noticed that whenever there was a big moon, large white mushrooms sprouted under trees. When they did, he liked to use them for target practice. He'd bought a quality hunting knife and liked to hurl this from a distance away. He'd pretend he was competing with his imaginary sister and brother. They'd have a go and miss, then he'd show them how to throw a knife like a pro.

'Shot!' he'd congratulate himself when he hit one. Being a sharp shot with a knife was a useful skill to have under his belt, which is precisely where he kept his knife; in a leather sheath under his actual belt.

Every day, he would nervously check the news pages on his

phone to see whether anyone had reported a glowing albino bull calf or a wandering herd of big-hooved cows. He hated the idea of someone else getting the credit for his discoveries. He comforted himself with the thought that he still had the rest of the summer, autumn, and winter to catch up with the calf. The hunting competition's last entry date was right at the end of the year.

Today, Chumley sat in a café eating breakfast. He was getting accustomed to his life of waiting. There was lots of cash in his wallet, since he'd been living in his tent and not spending much. He still had all of his mother's jewellery to sell, and her credit card.

He stirred his hot chocolate and dipped a fresh croissant into it, then stuffed the croissant into his mouth. As he munched, he thought about his parents. It would be nice, he thought, if they cared about him enough to send out a search party for him. The more time that passed with them not bothering to telephone him, the happier he was that he had stolen their stuff. He'd become more and more convinced that he wasn't their real child.

Whenever he sat alone eating garlic snails and boeuf bourguignon or horse-meat steak, or as he gorged on gateaux and chocolate soufflés, he would picture his imaginary hunter parents sitting with him. Even though he was always alone, amongst other tables full of jolly people having fun, he didn't care. He didn't need the sort of cosy family life that he saw around him. One day, he would be with his hunting family. All he needed was his prize albino calf and then they would know that he existed and they'd come for him.

This morning, as he sat in this café, he smiled and thought of the calf's stuffed head on a wall and him beside it, having his portrait painted. Maybe, once he had caught his calf, he should learn to do taxidermy and start a business? He'd be so famous people would queue up to meet him. Business would be fantastic. He would be paid to be in gun adverts! He would become a young celebrity and be a social media hit!

'Yes,' he said out loud to himself, practising for his future fame as he stirred the last dregs of his hot chocolate. 'I did indeed hunt it down myself. Yes, I taxidermised the whole body but in separate parts. The head, as you see, hangs here. The body is in my living room. I'm an artist as well as a taxidermist and a hunter.'

'Excusez-moi, monsieur. Plus de chocolat chaud?'

Chumley realised the waiter had been standing beside him for a while.

'Oui,' he said, not embarrassed at all.

Chumley liked to sit in cafés with hot chocolate and croissants and then scour the internet for clues as to where his calf was. He would search under all sorts of hashtags: #albinobullock, #glowingcalf, #glowingcow, #albinocow. He'd seen pictures of albino calves and cows from every part of the world. Albino *whale* calves too, glowing toy cows, cows with light behind them so that they looked as though they were glowing. 'That's not a real glowing cow,' Chumley would grumble to his phone. 'Not like *my* glowing calf.' Like a treasure-seeker, he hunted and hunted.

After the waiter had poured his hot chocolate, Chumley mechanically tapped #albinocalf into his phone. This time, something different happened. A host of pictures began crowding the screen. Today, #albinocalf brought up scores of pictures of a small albino bull calf. Chumley sat up. He scrolled through them. They were all from a town in northern Spain called Pamplona. First, there were pictures of the calf at dawn, in a pen. The calf was definitely very shiny, almost glowing. His pink eyes were like gems. Chumley's hands began to sweat from excitement. With a quivering finger he tapped #pamplonacalf into his phone. This led him to #pamplonamascot. More photographs filled his phone's screen. Pictures of the calf being promenaded up the old streets of Pamplona with crowds cheering from behind barriers. The people were dressed in red and white, with red sashes around them. The calf had a red sash about its neck too. Chumley even found some film – videos of the calf being led up cobbled streets to an arena with people throwing petals down from their balconies on to him; petals that landed and spotted his white fur with red.

'Happy Saint Fermín Day!' the people shouted.

Chumley saw that the footage had been taken that morning. He looked at his watch. It was still early. Pamplona wasn't that far away. He couldn't believe his luck! If he moved fast enough, he could be there by the end of the day.

He hauled his rucksack on to his shoulders. Quickly as he could, he picked up his bags, and put some money on the table to pay for his breakfast. Then, grabbing the two last croissants from the dish, he stepped onto the street and flagged down a taxi.

'Happy Saint Fermín Day!'

Albi was nervous. The crowds were heaving behind the barriers. 'Crowds', 'barriers', 'flags'. The human words for things were now coming as naturally to Albi as leaves to a tree. They were sprouting in his mind even without humans saying them. As Albi listened, his coat sometimes pulsed but he stopped the glow because he didn't want to draw that sort of attention to himself.

The people were very excited; Albi could feel the fizziness of it in the air. As Albi approached, they waved red flags at him.

'Hooray!'

'Hurrah!'

'Happy Saint Fermín Day!' a sweet young boy called to him. The boy had kind eyes and a sunny face. Albi decided he ought to make an effort. After all, he was the mascot. He mooed at him in reply.

'Ha ha ha!' The boy's laugh was light and sweet and thrill-filled.

Albi lifted his head high. It was a special day and the humans had chosen him, Albi, to be mascot of the beast-fighting bulls! He mooed up to the morning sun as though to tell it that everything was wonderful. And around him, the mass of humans ha-ed and hee-ed and laughed and clapped their hands. Albi thought to himself how marvellous these humans were, and how wrong his dad had been to think of all humans as harsh and cruel. He felt enormously proud as they cheered, and he sprung off his feet in the way that he knew would please them.

The man led him up the street and under an arch to a big sand-filled arena with many, many seats around it where people sat. He paraded Albi around the ring. The crowd applauded. Then the man led him up a slope at the edge of the ring, up to a higher place under shade. It was a pen decorated with red flowers.

'You're a very good snow calf,' the man said to Albi, patting his nose. 'They love you.'

Albi liked this enclosure – it was quieter and away from the crowds, and its lofty views meant that from it, he could see the last part of the street that he'd just walked up, and the arena too.

The man shut the pen's gate and went away. Albi looked down at his red sash and felt very satisfied. His heart began to quieten. He realised now that it had been racing. He lay down for a rest to think about what had just happened and to wonder what this all meant. Was he going to be a mascot of some sort for the rest of his life?

The crowds began making a noise. A loud *CRACK BANG* hit the distant air. All the humans hushed.

'They're coming!' somebody called from the street.

The bulls who were protecting the humans here weren't his friends from the farm, but Albi was very fearful for them. He wondered what the beasts that they were going to have to fight would look like. He shivered, sensing that some dark force was coming his way.

Chapter Sixteen

THE MONSTERS

Hundreds of voices rose up from the street and rolled towards the arena where Albi was waiting in his pen. Something big was coming. With a colossal whoop, the street nearest to him burst into animated applause. And then he saw the oddest sight.

Men came running around the corner below him. They were dressed in red and white with red ribbons around their heads. Three, four, then five . . . no – *nine* men, all with looks of alarm on their faces . . . Or was it excitement? Albi couldn't tell.

Bulls were running behind them; more men ran beside these bulls. They all were running as though they were being chased. Albi craned his neck to see what the monsters looked like.

One man had run ahead of the others. He now twisted round. He seemed to be waving his red scarf mockingly at something beyond the distant bulls who were all still charging up the street towards him. The bulls got closer and closer. The man turned to run again. Albi still couldn't see the monsters.

Then something deeply shocking happened. One of the bulls

dipped his head. The man who had waved the red scarf tripped. And when he did, the bull's horns scooped under him, and he tossed him high into the air, as easily as a dog tossing a bone. The crowd cried out in dismay. The other men in the street kept up the sprint, dodging the other bulls that ran beside them and behind them. In the chaos, the man who'd landed on the street was trampled by hooves. It was a horrible sight.

The remaining men ran ahead and into the arena. The eight bulls followed, thundering through the gateway, shocked to find themselves in the arena's wide open space. The audience bellowed. The men jumped over the arena barriers to safety and the bulls ran around the centre of the ring, snorting and cooling down.

Albi watched the street, where people dealt with the hurt man. Albi was very confused. First of all, he didn't understand where the monsters had been. But mainly, he couldn't understand why the bull had tossed the man. He, Albi, had been treated so well by these people and the men in the street had been running with the bulls in a friendly way. The bull who'd tossed the man had behaved very badly. Albi was suddenly very ashamed of his kind. He watched as the bulls were led to shady resting places at the sides of the arena. Then he lay down. The combination of heat and tiredness lulled him into sleep.

The day went by with the audience in the arena ebbing and then building again. A woman came to Albi's enclosure with a metal spade and shovelled his cowpats into a bucket. Albi thought of Bodge, and wondered where he was now. Bodge would have said something funny about the woman and what she needed a bucket of cowpats for. Albi suddenly felt an overwhelming sadness. He could appreciate that he was a lucky calf to be with all these good humans, but he would rather be with his herd. He tried to sense where they were. He shut his eyes and quietened his thoughts. And in his mind's eye, he suddenly saw them. They were in a wood, asleep. The cracks in the foliage around them showed that they were near a lake. Albi knew they were hundreds of miles away. Suddenly Oros's voice came into his head.

'*We are in a country called Romania. We are walking towards where the sun rises. Escape, Albi. Join us.*'

Albi felt himself glowing strongly. He opened his eyes, expecting to see Oros. The voice had sounded so clear and real. For a moment, he thought that he must have fallen asleep again and dreamt him. He hadn't been asleep. The vision had been real. He shut his eyes again. '*I want to be with you,*' he thought, as hard as he could. '*But I'm so little, I don't know how.*'

The sun was fairly low in the sky now. It was cooler. The seats of the auditorium had filled up. Young humans sat beside their parents. Albi had never seen humans so beautifully dressed. A girl near him wore bright-red clothes. They flounced around her like the petals of a crimson rose. Her dark hair was plaited in the way Albi had seen horses' tails twisted and tied. The boy next to her wore tight red trousers and a shiny silver top. Lots of children were dressed in this colourful way. They punctuated the crowd like flowers growing amongst plain leaves in a flower bed.

A high-pitched honking sound cut through the hubbub. Albi looked to where it was coming from. Two humans held shiny tube-like objects to their lips and were blowing through them. Trumpets. The word popped into Albi's mind. Their noise announced the arrival of three horses that walked into the arena, each with a man on their back. The men were dressed in black and white, and wore black head coverings too. They reminded Albi of the black-and-white magpies he'd seen in the fields. The horses were clad in shiny red cloaks, their eyes blinkered by red masks.

Albi rested his nose on the bar of his pen and watched with interest as six humans, all in coloured clothes, walked into the arena. They each carried large pieces of floppy red cloth that they flapped about behind them in the same way as Albi had seen birds display their tail feathers.

So, the monsters must be coming now, he thought. How did the humans know when they would arrive? Albi looked up at the sky. Could the monsters fly? Would they swoop down? Were they snakes that would slide under the gates of the arena? Or were they snarling, fanged beasts that came out of holes in the ground? He peered over the edge of his pen and waited. The horses and humans left the arena, leaving just one man in the sand.

A door at the edge of the arena opened. One of the bulls came bursting out. He ran around the sand, then stopped abruptly. He seemed perplexed. He looked at the man who was waving his large red cloth thing at him.

'AY! AY!' the man called. Why was he doing this? Was it because the monster was near and the man was trying to get the bull to help?

Bulls, Albi knew, were gentle creatures, but if they thought they were being attacked, would charge. The strangely dressed, noisy man in front of the bull was shouting rudely. He waved his red cloth so that it looked like the cloth itself was about to fly up and attack. The bull looked muddled and upset.

Again, Albi looked up for the arrival of the monster. He saw something distant in the sky, but then it flew over and he realised it was just a plane. When he looked back, he saw to his horror that the bull was pawing at the dusty ground with his hoof. Had Albi misunderstood? Was *the red cloth* a monster? The audience cheered. The bull charged, his head down, his horns set to pierce the sheet of red. They nearly did. As they touched it, the man whipped the cloth away. He made a move as though in some sort of dance, jumping away from the bull. And as the bull ran past, the man did something vicious; he stuck a long striped spike into the bull's neck. A spear. Albi glowed as the word came to him. The audience clapped and cheered more. Albi glowed from his tail to his ears as his mind scrambled to work out what was happening. The audience had cheered. Did this mean that they were on the man's side? The audience went silent. They gasped as the bull charged again; they whistled as the cloth was whisked through the air. They whooped as another spear was brandished.

Albi saw the truth. The man was the monster and the arena was full of monsters too. Albi couldn't bear to watch. He bowed his head. The noise of the braying crowd told him what was happening; their quietness told him that the bull was pawing the ground, their cooing told him that he was charging, their cheering that the matador was flapping his red cape. Matador. Cape. The words came to Albi. When the audience shouted, 'OLÉ!', the matador's spear flashed.

Albi re-ran what he'd seen on the cobbled streets. The man had been waving his red scarf at the bull, goading him to attack. All the men in the street had been teasing the bulls for fun. There was no noble fighting of monsters. How wrong the bulls from the farm had been!

Albi screwed his eyes tight and strained to hear Oros again.

'*We are here, Albi. You can join us. You are bigger than you think.*'

Rufus Chumley was nearly in Pamplona. He looked at his phone to see where the bull fight had got to. He saw that the animal would soon be dead.

'Now the good old matador will finish you off,' he said. He watched with satisfaction as the matador flourished a sword. 'That will sort the furry brute out,' Chumley said, laughing at the footage.

Then, out of the blue, two men holding a banner ran on to the sand.

'ASESINOS!' they shouted. 'MURDERERS!'

'Don't be stupid!' Chumley scoffed. 'It's good sport, you idiots.'

A thought hit him. Perhaps the organisers in Pamplona were planning to slaughter his albino calf and barbecue it tonight!

'DRIVE FASTER!' he shouted to the taxi woman. 'VITE! VITE!'

Albi watched the men who had run into the sandy arena. One carried a banner with more human shapes on it.

BULLFIGHTING IS BARBARIC

'BULLFIGHTING IS BARBARIC!' the man shouted passionately.

And in a swift and strange way, Albi suddenly knew that the words he had shouted were the same as those on his banner. Just as his mind had leapt when he understood human language, now his mind finally understood their written words too. Albi could see how the word BARBARIC in the banner was mouthed by the man, 'BARBARIC!' Albi knew at once what each one of the letters sounded like – the B, the A, the R. He thought of the signs, HENGE FARM and CHUMLEY'S ABATTOIR. The B and A and R were in those signs. He was reading! And his understanding was happening as easily as a bird takes off and flies.

Albi's fur stood on end, glowing the brightest he had ever felt it glow. But though Albi knew that reading was truly marvellous, he didn't feel happiness about it at all because the cruel sights he was seeing made him so scared and sad.

In the arena, the crowd jeered and booed the protestors. Other men grabbed them, broke their banners and dragged them off.

Albi heard a child's voice crying, 'Mama, I want to go home, this is so cruel!'

The mother replied, 'Yes, Tomas, I will take you home, this is horrible. I'm sorry I brought you here.'

Albi wanted to go wherever they were going, too. He knelt down. He was shaking. He tried to separate himself from what he was hearing. But he couldn't. As the sky grew darker and night fell, he heard the bullfighting go on and on and on.

Chumley sprinted through the streets of Pamplona, cursing his heavy backpack. The ground beneath him was strewn with red petals and litter. He could hear the applause in the arena ahead. He ran under the arena's entrance arch. Panting, he bought a ticket. He spotted the place where his calf had been put and saw that he could easily make his way to it under the audience seats. As the crowd cheered the matador, Chumley felt like they were cheering him.

'I'm bigger than I think!'

Albi's eyes suddenly opened very wide. Seven bulls had died. There was only one more alive. And he, Albi, was full of life and as *worthy* of life as any of the humans in the arena. He must stop these feelings of smallness in him. He must believe himself and escape. Why had he doubted himself? He *was amazing!* He could understand humans, he could *read* their writing! He might not understand the world, but no one did, and he was trying, and that was amazing in itself. He'd made a terrible mistake the night he'd left the herd, but it was out of curiosity, which was an admirable thing. He *must* stop feeling small. Right now, he had to feel as big as he could and muster every cell of his brain power and get out of this bad place.

It was night now. Lights lit up the arena and the passageways near where the people were standing and sitting, but around Albi's pen it was dark. He looked at the pen's gate – it had a bolt that he knew he couldn't unlock. Albi's mind raced. There must be another way of getting out. His eyes fell on a bale of hay in the corner of the pen. Quickly, he shoved his forehead behind it and knocked it across the pen so that it was near the gate, making a step. With a little run and a bold leap, Albi jumped on to the bale and, springing high enough off it, he cleared the pen fence.

The thump of Albi's landing was drowned by the audience's applause and horrible cheering. No one was in the wings of the arena; everyone was watching the fight. He nipped along the passage and trotted down to ground level, then ducked into the shadows under the scaffolding of the seats where the clapping audience sat. He hid here as a person passed – a sweaty boy with red hair who had been running. For a moment, Albi thought he recognised him, but he suspected it was just his nervous mind playing tricks on him. When he'd gone, Albi made for a big exit door and stepped out into the open air.

The night was his friend. He was in an unlit court at the back of the arena. Albi saw an entrance to a garage or something. Taking a chance, he reached it and slipped inside. He found a truck and next to it a small, parked car that was covered by a large piece of blue plastic. Cleverly, Albi burrowed beneath this plastic and then edged his way to the back of the truck, so shielding himself from the world. And here he stayed, trembling. He heard music, he heard crowds leaving the stadium, he heard people looking for him.

'Thieves are everywhere,' he heard the man from the bull farm say. 'He will have been stolen by now.' He sounded disappointed and upset.

'You should have kept an eye on him,' a younger voice chided. Albi thought he recognised that voice. It sounded like someone he'd heard in the abattoir months before. Was that possible? Then he realised that this younger voice had spoken in English. *That* was why it had sounded familiar.

Albi saw the light of torches. None of them would have thought a bull calf clever enough to hide.

But Chumley *was* thinking that a clever calf might hide. His calf was special; intelligent enough to leap out of its pen and escape. Chumley had seen the signs on the ground. Skidding hoofmarks showed where the animal had landed after his jump and a few further hoofprints showed that it had set off down the ramp. Chumley had been devastated to find the calf gone but he'd also been impressed. And now he felt calm because he was so hot on the calf's trail he just knew he was going to catch it. If he was the calf, he thought, what would he do?

There was an open garage in the alley, where a car was wrapped in blue plastic. There was a truck there too. Chumley investigated. He poked at the blue plastic but nothing moved. The calf wasn't there. Not wanting the other searchers to find his calf first, he left. He followed them out into the main street, then he broke away from them.

'He will have run to the countryside, Chummers,' he muttered to himself. He turned his torch on and studied the ground.

Albi heard the humans go. He stood perfectly still, though inside he was shivering. It had been very difficult not to tremble when one of the searchers had come close to his hiding place. The person had poked the plastic near his head. Albi's heart had thumped so violently he had thought the human might hear it.

Albi stayed quiet, though his thoughts were loud and painful. Visions of the bull in the arena haunted him, dark feelings pulled him down – fear about what would happen to him if the humans caught him, then a deep, deep dislike that he supposed must be hate for the people who'd killed the bulls. But this was all overwhelmed by sadness. He'd believed that humans were good. In the turn of that afternoon, everything had been broken. Heavy longing washed through him. He longed to be with his herd. He thought of them and cried.

Time went past. Albi slept in bursts. The town's bell struck four times. Most people had gone home now. The streets were quiet, the humans were in their beds. This was his chance to get away. He remembered his father's, his mother's and Oros's words – that he was bigger than he thought. Perhaps, if he just believed this, everything would be all right? He decided this was a good way to think – he'd have faith in himself. Beyond this, all he had to do was stay free and keep walking towards the herd. He thanked the garage, the small car and the blue plastic that had hidden him. And, taking a determined breath he poked his head into the empty alley, then made his way to its entrance. Crossing the road to the gutter, where it was dark, Albi trotted out of town.

Chumley, on the other hand, was feeling less and less sure of himself. He was on the other side of the town, in a field. He stumbled about, searching, pointing his torch this way and that.

'You idiot!' he scolded himself. 'They were right. You're a complete waste of time. No wonder no one likes you. Who wants to know a *useless* person? You couldn't even find the calf when he was right under your nose!' He dropped his torch and fell to the ground. 'You're conning yourself, Rufus Chumley, if you think the Worldwide Hunting Association's going to want a pathetic turd like you. You can put that dream of being someone who matters right out of your stupid head.'

Rufus was exhausted, he felt beaten and now very, very hopeless and sad.

He began to sob. Tears rolled down his cheeks, for it occurred to him now that if the Hunting Association weren't going to enrol him, then his dream family certainly wouldn't want him. No one had ever liked him. They'd be the same. Limping towards a dumped tractor trailer and feeling utterly dejected, he crawled onto it and went to sleep.

Chapter Seventeen

CAMILLE

Albi didn't like being on the main road. The verge at the side of it wasn't shadowy enough because there were streetlights. He kept going, though, hoping for an opportunity to get into the fields where he would be safer.

His chance came in the form of a quiet lane that seemed to lead to scrubland and low trees. Beyond these, lit up by moonlight, was a very, very large tent. Albi had never seen a tent this big, but it was quiet and he reckoned this was the way to the open countryside, so he took the turning. However, at the end of the lane, when he rounded the low trees, he found himself in a clearing with lots of caravans on it. As the word 'caravan' came to him, Albi felt a tingle of electricity rush over his back and out through his tail. He stopped himself glowing and paused as the meaning of what these caravans were sunk in. And he considered his position. Going back to the road wasn't a good choice, he thought, and the people in the caravans were probably asleep. He could make it past them and would soon be in the woods and the hills beyond.

But suddenly, a window in one of the caravans lit up. Albi saw the shape of a man. The door of the caravan opened and the man came out, climbing down its silver steps until he stood on the dirt ground. He yawned and stretched like a cat, though his hands were stretched into the air.

Albi was struck by how like other animals humans were. Humans *are* animals, he realised, even though they wore clothes.

The man began talking into his phone. He hadn't seen Albi, but Albi knew that at any moment he might. So, quietly and slowly he backed away.

His back hoof bumped something. It was a ramp. The man looked up inquisitively. Albi glanced behind him. The ramp led up to a small horsebox. The man was now bending down and straightening his trousers, his phone tucked under his chin, still talking into it. Albi kept an eye on him and walked backwards up the ramp and into the safe box. He'd hide here, he thought, in this horse-smelling, straw-lined refuge, until the man went.

Unfortunately for Albi, the night wasn't as young as he had thought. Dawn was breaking. And with it came human voices. People shouting orders to each other, humans laughing. Through the crack in the horsebox wall Albi could see lots of humans now coming out of other caravans. They were starting to dismantle the giant tent, taking it down as easily as a cow might reach for a branch with tasty leaves and tug it down. And then, amidst the hustle and bustle he saw four black ponies being led by a young girl towards the horsebox that he was in. Albi shrunk to the back of the box, shutting his eyes, wishing he could camouflage himself. Hooves clopped dully up the ramp and in the next moment, the four ponies were in the box with him. They were as shocked as he was. One of them whinnied.

'Oh, don't make a fuss, Beatrice, get in,' the girl outside said. She spoke French. Albi's head tingled as his mind twisted to understand her words. When the girl was satisfied that the ponies were in, she slammed the horsebox door shut.

It took a second or two for everyone's eyes to get accustomed to the light. The ponies were jittery, and rightly so, for as far as they could see a bull-calf imposter was in their box. They kept their distance, which could only be a few steps away because of the small space. But when they'd seen Albi's wide eyes and felt his nervousness, the smallest, fattest and oldest of the mares stepped forward aggressively and stamped her hoof.

'What on earth do you think you're doing in here, young bull?'

Albi could feel himself blushing. 'I'm very sorry,' he began. 'I didn't mean to intrude. It was an accident.'

'An accident indeed. Expect you're after our hay,' the mare said. 'You're probably a bad 'un.'

'N–no I'm n–not!' Albi stumbled over his words.

'Why should we believe a word you say?' she neighed back accusingly. Her whinny was like an alarm bell. If she carried on, a human would be alerted and open the horsebox. 'Come on, speak up!'

Albi didn't know what to say. He'd seen such frightening things the day before that he didn't know what to think of the world – of humans or of other creatures, even. Perhaps the old mare had met bad cows. *He* knew he was good but he couldn't blame her if she was suspicious of him. The pony bared her teeth.

'I'm sorry,' was all he managed to say. Then, 'Please don't tell them I'm here.' He shut his eyes. Visions of the horrific bullfight and the laughing crowds swam in front of them. Great big tears began rolling down his cheeks. The engine of the horsebox gave a mechanical cough and it began to move. One of the younger ponies nudged past the old mare and stepped sideways in front of her, so that Albi was shielded.

'Look what you've done, Maman,' she said. 'Honestly, he's only a kid.'

'I'm a c–calf,' Albi said, correcting her with a sniff. 'Kids are young goats.'

The pony nodded. 'I know that, sweetheart.' Then, 'Don't worry,' she whispered. 'Our maman's whinny is worse than her whip. My name's Isla and this is Isabella.'

'Hello,' said the other black pony. 'And our mother's name is Beatrice.'

The old mare grunted.

The young mare nudged Albi gently with her nose. 'What's your name, little bull calf?'

'Albi,' Albi said quietly.

'Do you want to tell us why you're hiding? It's not often that we find a young calf in our box. Something out of the ordinary must have happened to you.'

And so, Albi told them what had happened in Pamplona. The ponies had seen pictures of bullfighting on posters pasted on billboards in towns that they'd visited in Spain. But they had never seen what actually happened in a bullfight. Then Albi told them about the abattoir. It all came tumbling out of his mouth, painting a horrible picture.

'We're sorry you've seen all these things,' the young mare said. 'We feel for your kind. We are lucky that humans don't eat horse.

Over the years we've helped them, taking them on our backs, pulling their carts, their carriages, so they would never eat us.'

'I heard they do,' Isabella corrected her. 'The donkey on that farm told me. They make donkey-meat salami. And they eat horse steak. In some countries they even eat dog.'

'Oh, rubbish!' said Isla. 'They don't. You believe everything, Isabella. Humans love horses and donkeys. They would never eat dog. They love dogs too.'

'I don't,' the older mare grumbled. 'Kicked one once because it was nipping at my heels.'

'There are good dogs, mother. Remember we saw that kind dog leading a blind woman once.'

Albi shut his eyes tight and shook his head. Isla stroked him with her nose.

'Do not give up. There are humans who don't eat meat. Our miss – Miss Camille, the girl you saw, we never see her eat animal meat. We never smell it on her.'

'Mind you, there are a few humans in the circus who *do* eat animal meat,' Beatrice warned him. 'You can smell it on them. They smell like dogs do, or like the lions who used to be in the circus.'

'Mother, don't alarm him.'

'They are carnivores,' Albi said.

'Aren't you a fancy one? Knowing long words like that,' the old mare said.

Albi nodded sadly. 'My mother taught me. Humans who don't eat meat are called vegetarians.' The ponies were quiet. A thought suddenly hit Albi. 'Do they eat each other?'

'I'm not sure,' said Isla worriedly.

The old mare frowned. 'What a silly question. Of course, they don't. You're letting your imagination run away with you, young bullock.' Then, kindly, she added, 'It's because you've seen some dreadful things. Try not to think of them. Try to rest now.'

The ponies settled Albi in, giving him a corner of the horsebox to lie down in. The journey would take a good few hours, they said. So, Albi slept for a while. When he woke, he felt better and had an appetite to hear about the circus.

'Stay quiet there and we'll tell you,' Isla said. And so they did. They told him about how it went from town to town, forever on the move; about the circus tent, the 'big top'.

'The big top goes up and down as easily as a butterfly's wings opening,' Isabella said.

'Not as easily as that,' the old mare piped up. 'Don't talk claptrap.' She was still grumpy but Albi could sense that she was a little softer than before. They told Albi about the humans who lived in the caravans, from the many circus workers to its performers – the flying-trapeze artist, the strong man who could carry five people on his shoulders, the daredevil tightrope-walkers and the buffoon clowns who ran around in the ring, chasing each other with buckets of water.

'It's the Greatest Show on Earth,' said Isla. 'And we do tricks to make it even better.'

Albi had never heard of tricks.

'We walk on our hind legs, we dance to music, and when we canter around the ring, Miss Camille hops from my back to Maman's back to Isla's. She is an acrobat. She is amazing.'

'We wear feathered plumes on our heads and she wears sparkling clothes like a bird of paradise. The audience loves Miss Camille and us. They clap and clap!'

The thought of a clapping audience made Albi shudder. It reminded him of the bullfighting arena. 'What will Miss Camille do when she finds me in here?'

The ponies went quiet.

'Not sure,' Isla eventually said.

The horsebox drove on. Albi and the ponies looked out through the spy holes in its side and watched the world roll by. Dry brown, undulating hills became flat plains with villages and fields with sheep. There were lots of cars and trucks on the road. Every so often, they'd pass fields of purple lavender.

After a few hours, the horsebox came on to smaller roads again. Albi could smell the sea. And then, he could see it, shimmering and blue. It reminded him of his mother, and his friends and Oros; of walking in the moonlight with them beside the sea. He shut his eyes and, as though he had invisible antennae, he could feel their presence far, far away.

'We always head to the empty land outside the human warrens,' Isla said.

The trailer was driven through a town and then stopped on a barren piece of open ground where scruffy trees and bushes grew. The driver got out and walked away. Then they heard lighter footsteps and the metal sounds of the horsebox door being unbolted. Albi knew his time was up. He started to imagine his future unfolding – one that ended badly. He shivered as the door opened and the ramp was pulled down.

'Come on, my beauties,' he heard the girl say.

'Good luck,' Isabella said to Albi. She and the other ponies clopped down the slope. Past them, Albi saw the girl, their Miss Camille. She was wearing a red top and brown jodhpurs – the word 'jodhpurs' filled Albi's mind. She was a handsome, brown-haired child, her skin very dark. She looked athletic and confident. She patted the old mare on the rump and was just about to shut the horsebox door when she saw Albi.

She squinted, as though the sight of a young white bull calf in the back of the horsebox was just a trick of the light, then her face lit up with surprise.

'You've got to be joking. Where did *you* come from? You're so white. Almost glowing.' Albi realised he'd been so scared that he'd forgotten to suppress his 'jodhpur'-induced glow. He stopped it at once.

She stepped up the slope of the ramp. Albi backed further into the horsebox. She smelt of rosemary and wheat, hay and horses. Her eyes were green and it seemed to him that they had sparkling bits in them. There was a gentleness about her.

'Don't worry, little fellow. I won't hurt you,' she said.

Albi knew that first impressions were very important. He also knew that humans could find big animals scary and he didn't want to do anything that would suddenly alarm the girl. He stepped very slowly towards her, nodding his head as he did. He decided to be bold. He dipped his head and pushed his forehead into her hand.

The girl felt good, and very kind, and it was a funny thing, but Albi felt that she loved him at once. It was unlike any human love he'd felt before. He realised that all the other gestures of affection from humans, even the bull-farm man, had been shallow. The feeling that he got from this girl was deep and caring and safe. It felt like the love he had felt from other cows.

He stepped out of the box. The black ponies were standing in the shade of a low, wide tree. They watched as Camille patted Albi, then as she walked slowly around him. She ran her hand along his back, as though measuring the distance between his shoulders and his rump. She checked his tail, inspected his legs and hooves and stroked his furry cheeks. She peered in his ears.

'No bugs in there,' she said. Then she wiped his eyes. 'Haven't you got long lashes?'

She brought him a bucket of water. Albi nodded gratefully and drank. The girl sat on a wall and watched him. It was almost as though she was expecting something.

Albi saw quite clearly that the only way to stay safe now, until he could get away again, was by impressing the girl, Camille. He'd promised himself he'd be bolder and more confident from now on, and so, trusting his instincts, he summoned all his wits and mooed, 'What abooOOOout this?'

The bucket was nearly empty. He took its handle in his mouth and with a flip, he swung the bucket up so that it landed on his head like a hat. Then, since he wanted to really entertain her, he rose up on his back legs and walked backwards. He stopped, flipped the bucket back on its base and he gave another little moo.

The girl sat stock still. The ponies stared at him, all rigid too.

'Do you think she liked that?' Albi asked them.

Chumley was woken up by a chittering noise. He opened his eyes. It was still the very early hours of the morning and it was still dark. Two rats were perched on the side of the trailer, chatting

with each other. Chumley didn't know rats chatted like this. He wondered what they were talking about. They seemed very happy. He wasn't. He was very unhappy. He felt very alone. An outcast. No one wanted to know him. No one cared about him. He didn't even like himself.

He thought of his calf. Yet again, it had slipped through his fingers. Was he tracking the calf or was the calf leading him on a wild-goose chase? Was it a trap? He felt stupid and useless again. He sat up and the rats fled.

He was feeling something else, too. He was hungry. Very hungry. The town's shops wouldn't be open for hours. He looked desperately inside his rucksack for a snack. He started to moan. He was so hungry it was painful.

'You shouldn't be so big, then you wouldn't be so hungry,' he told himself. 'Useless, overgrown lump.'

He pulled out his frying pan and found a small bottle of oil and some salt and pepper, but other than that there was nothing to eat. He eyed the rats, who were now over by a tree. Barbecued rat. What would that taste like? As he thought about this, and about how he probably wouldn't be able to shoot the rats anyway, he noticed some big white mushrooms glinting in the moonlight at the base of the tree. He didn't usually eat mushrooms, because of the brown ones that had poisoned the girl in Henge. Maybe these were poisonous too? Chumley was too hungry and miserable to care.

'If you get poisoned,' he said morosely to himself, 'no one will miss you.' He imagined a farmer finding his skeleton. The farmer would find his mother's credit card in his rucksack and his parents would be informed.

'*We don't have a son*,' he imagined his mother saying.

Chumley clambered down from the trailer. Greedily, he picked all the mushrooms. They smelt milky. 'That'll make up for no butter in the pan,' he told himself, cheered by the thought of breakfast. He lit a fire and soon had his pan on and the mushrooms sizzling. He added salt and pepper and when they were done, tipped them on to his plate.

He leant back against the trailer wheel to eat. Another meal alone. He took a spoonful. This was when he got a surprise. The mushrooms melted in his mouth. They were delicious! They were the best thing he'd eaten on the whole of his trip! Famished, he ate the whole plateful. He was so hungry, he realised, that his body was a bit shocked by the food, for it began to tingle. A sparkling feeling filled him. It shot up from his feet, all the way to his neck and head, where the fizzy feeling exploded into a pulsing, throbbing lightness.

'Don't leave it so long between meals next time, Chumley,' he told himself. He lay back and shut his eyes. The fizzy sensation died down, but his head felt clearer than before. On top of his comfortably full feeling, another good thing happened – the nasty thoughts Chumley had about himself receded from his mind.

'Goodbye empty hole, hello, energy ball!' He gave a little whistle. 'That's the power of food, Chummers!'

And now, good thoughts began springing into his head. He was actually quite an impressive person, he thought. He was only twelve, but here he was, surviving on his own, often in the wild. He'd tracked the big-hooved cows and then the calf. He *was* a real hunter. He didn't need a prize to know that. 'You're very talented, and brave,' he told himself. 'And self-reliant and tough.'

Normally, when Rufus tried to celebrate himself a big horrid, doubting part of him would block these thoughts, reminding him what his parents and the children at school thought of him. But today, Rufus's mind took a leap, karate-chopped this doubting wall and blew it away. Today, he suddenly saw himself anew. He was all right. More than this, he was extraordinary!

'You, Rufus Chumley,' he said, pointing to himself, 'are *incredible*!' And for the first time ever, he knew that he truly was! He felt hugely relieved, as though dark clouds had left his head. He let out a massive sigh. Then he kicked his legs and punched at the sky. 'You are amazing, Rufus Chumley!' he shouted. 'Wooooooohooooooo!'

The rats sat on the ground a way off, watching him, enjoying the show. They watched as the boy in the field lay on the grass, his eyes shut, laughing and throwing his arms around in the air.

'Why haven't you thought this before, Rufus?' the boy exclaimed.

Rufus made a promise. He vowed that from now on, he was going to only think good things about himself. He shut his eyes. He felt wonderful. A horrible monster had left him. He imagined what it had looked like – a many-headed ogre, he thought, the biggest of its heads being his mother's and his father's. The other heads belonged to his teachers, his mean nannies, the unkind children at his school. The heads all shared one big, malicious mouth. In Rufus's mind, he threw a flaming spear at the monster. It fled.

'Shot!' he congratulated himself. 'Good shot, Rufus Chumley.'

The rats watched the boy. They'd never seen a human do what he was doing now.

He was glowing.

Chapter Eighteen

THE CIRCUS

The girl jumped down from the wall. 'Again!' she demanded. Albi did his trick again.

After that, things picked up speed. The girl ran across the clearing where other trucks were parked. She returned, pulling a man by the hand, who, by the similar earthy smell he had, Albi guessed must be her father.

'Watch!' she told him.

'Again, please!' she said to Albi, putting the bucket down in front of him to show what she wanted.

Albi repeated his trick. He did it once more when the girl's mother, a beautiful, dark woman with short hair had been fetched, and again, when a group of other circus people – clowns without their make-up or red noses, a tall, scrawny juggler, a dwarf and three muscly acrobats – had assembled to watch.

It struck Albi that this might not be enough. If he didn't impress these circus people they might sell him. Then he'd be back in the abattoir in no time. So he decided to really shock them. Thinking of the peculiar dancing cows he'd seen on the television in the Henge Farm house, he attempted copying them. He jigged his body to the left and the right. He swung his head and tapped his hoof. The audience of circus people laughed and clapped. Albi paused. They liked him. But he needed to astound them. The Spanish bulls had loved it when he mooed tunes. If he showed these people how he could sing, surely then they'd think him worthy of joining their troupe?

Oros had taught Albi one of the human songs that he'd heard through the cracks in the rock at Stonehenge, a song sung by a shepherd who used to watch his sheep near there. The words to it went, 'Twinkle, twinkle, little star . . .' Albi mooed it now.

His audience were more than astounded. Flabbergasted, gobsmacked and thrilled, they hooted and whistled. Some simply sat with their mouths open.

'He is a magic calf!' The girl rushed towards Albi and threw her arms around his neck.

'Show off,' the old mare grumbled from behind him.

'Oh, I love him! Mama, Papa, can I keep him? Please, please, please! He can be my second act. Please!'

Her parents looked at the picture in front of them – their bold, wild daughter, with all her naughtiness and zest for life, and the angelic albino bull calf with his pink eyes and intelligent face and his cleverness. How could they say no?

'If we say yes, Camille, will you promise to keep his stable clean?'

Albi's first performance with Camille and her trio of ponies didn't happen for a few days. The circus lorries and animal wagons drove from Spain to France, stopping at towns where the circus was booked. In the evenings Camille let Albi stand at the side of the stage to watch her pony show, and then in the empty days, when she could, she'd work on a new show with Albi in it.

Camille did not have a lot of spare time as she was often being taught by her mother; something that involved her reading from books and making marks on paper.

Books, paper, writing. These words came to Albi. It was amazing to him that humans could talk to each other through writing and reading. A human could write anything and another could read it, and the reader could be thousands of miles away or even be reading the words years after the writer had died. Albi liked to come up behind Camille and peer over her shoulder to look at her books. He loved reading. He concentrated hard, making sure that he didn't glow, since he wasn't sure it was a good idea to let humans know about this.

A clever white calf has joined us, Camille wrote, one afternoon. *Snowy. His nose is on my shoulder now, almost as though he is reading this. He is wonderful. We all love him.*

When Camille was free from her work again, she, Albi and the ponies spent hours rehearsing their new act. Finally, the night came to show it to the world.

Albi stood behind the big black curtain that shielded backstage from the circus ring. It was nearly the time for his debut performance. He peeped around the velvet. Camille was in the spotlight, dressed in silver and blue, riding around the sawdusty ring, first on Beatrice, then on Isla and Isabella. The ponies galloped faster and faster but still Camille moved from one horse to the other. She called to them to go slower. There was a drum roll. Camille stood tall on the cantering Isabella, jumped on to the moving Isla and from there, somersaulted on to Beatrice. The audience, full of holidaying families and gangs of children, clapped enthusiastically.

Albi turned his head to look at his beautifully brushed body, as washed and shiny as it could be. He knew how to turn on his glow just enough for it to seem that he was simply extraordinarily white. He had silver bows around his neck and all his ankles. He looked wonderful but he felt sick. They'd rehearsed the show scores of times, but he was queasy with nerves. What if the bright lights out there stunned him, or if the audience scared him so much that he forgot his part? He tried not to think about it. One of the circus helpers stood by his side, stroking his ear, making sure he didn't move until he was supposed to.

All at once, the moment of truth was upon him. The ponies, encouraged by Camille, rose up on their hind legs and walked backwards out of the ring. This was Albi's cue.

'Good luck, Albi,' each pony neighed as they walked backwards past him.

Albi shut his eyes and reached for his courage.

Oros's face smiled at him. '*You'll be brilliant,*' he said, his voice as clear to Albi as though he was in Albi's head.

'They're going to love you,' Isla insisted. And Albi was on. Up he got on his hind legs, with his front legs in front of him in the air like a begging dog. This, for starters, was a sight for the crowds.

Albi tottered over to Camille, who beamed at him and winked. Then bowed. And their act commenced. First was the bucket act.

This had become more elaborate. There were now six buckets, each sparkling orange and shiny yellow. Albi took a deep breath and went towards one. His mouth felt dry from nerves as he put it about the bucket handle and lifted it. But then he heard some children laugh and clap and his stage fright disappeared. He liked the idea of making them happy. And so, he carried on, stacking the buckets, carrying them to the other side of the room, unstacking them, then fetching apples from Camille and plopping each in a bucket.

Next was the comedy part. The ponies came back on. Albi led each of them to a bucket and stamped his hoof to tell them when they could eat an apple. Beatrice's job was to steal a whole bucket of apples from Albi when his back was turned and to trot off with them. Albi acted confused and the audience roared with laughter. The ponies left the ring.

'Oh, Snowy!' Camille said, a microphone in her hand. 'Those cheeky ponies are so naughty. You were only trying to teach them table manners. What shall we do? Shall we sing a song to make you feel better?' Albi nodded. The audience laughed. 'What shall we sing? "Frère Jacques"?' Albi nodded again. Camille began the song.

'Are you sleeping? Are you sleeping?
Brother John, Brother John?
Morning bells are ringing, morning bells are ringing!'

And then Albi came in, leaning towards the microphone. 'MOO, MOO, MOO,' he went. This was the part that was normally sung as 'ding dang dong'. He mooed in tune and in time. And the audience went berserk. They laughed and applauded rapturously.

Camille gave Albi a huge hug. 'You're a hit,' she whispered in his ear. 'They adore you.' Then, 'Would you like to sing another song?' she asked him, this time with her voice amplified so that the audience of six hundred-or-so people could hear easily.

Albi nodded. The audience laughed. Then he put his mouth near the microphone and mooed a whole song. He'd made up the tune himself. The audience didn't clap when he'd finished. They were too astonished to.

Then, a small boy shouted, 'YOU ARE AMAZING!' and the waves of applause rolled in.

Albi became a phenomenon, a star attraction. His picture was plastered on billboards that he'd see when the horsebox was driving into a new town. He drew large crowds, and because of him, the circus's shows were always sold out. The circus moved from town to town, giving the holiday-makers and townsfolk something spectacular to go and see in the evenings. Now it was an even greater show on earth.

Albi decided to keep his glowing a secret because he wasn't quite sure how it would change things if the humans knew about it. He felt safe with Camille and the audience was happily entertained. Everything was going well, so there was no reason for the humans to know about how he could light up.

At night, Albi slept well. Sometimes he dreamt of a boy who was longing to stroke him. It was slightly odd, as the feeling of the dream was very strong, and the boy was always the same red-haired boy. Albi couldn't exactly place him, though supposed he must have seen him somewhere – many children watched the show every night. And so, he shook off the dream every time he woke up and, lightened, he'd get on with his day.

But Albi's dreams had some truth in them. For, like the holiday-makers and townsfolk, Chumley had one day seen Albi's face on a giant billboard. He'd recognised him. He'd bought circus tickets and sat in the crowded audience and watched the show. Rufus started to come every night. He took lots of pictures. He filmed his bull calf pirouetting on the spot to violin music that the circus girl played. Sometimes, the girl stood on the calf's back as he trotted round the ring. The calf did tricks and made the audience laugh.

'Génie! Fantastique! Superbe!' the audience cried.

He's mine! Chumley felt like shouting at them. *Not yours, not hers. He's mine!*

After the show, people would queue to gawp at the calf in its pen. Chumley watched the girl as she groomed it, fed it, checked its hooves and teeth and tail and ears for bites or sores; as she lay in the hay singing to it. He'd never seen a calf with such polished hooves. The creature was very special and the circus people knew it. But it never glowed in their shows, so it seemed to Chumley that they didn't know about the calf's glowing power. This secret knowledge made him feel very superior and even more proprietorial.

His calf was guarded and penned in by high fences. Chumley was pleased because this meant it was safe. Sooner or later, an opportunity would arise when the circus's guard would be down and then Chumley would let the animal out. He'd let it escape and he'd count to ten thousand. That would be fair sport. After that, he'd hunt it down.

There was a chance though, that someone else might try to steal the calf before Chumley was ready. He decided to take precautions. He couldn't have his calf being stolen or escaping without him knowing.

There was a high-tech spy shop in the local town. Chumley had researched what he needed from it. He pushed its glass door open and went in.

'Bonjour?' the tidily dressed shopkeeper said, eyeing the scruffy customer that had just entered.

Chumley pointed to the device he needed. It was in a box on the shelf behind the assistant.

The shopkeeper wrinkled his nose and sniffed at the air. Then he placed the box on the counter. Chumley pulled out his card. The man looked surprised. He studied Chumley's card, then eyed Chumley suspiciously.

'Votre identification, s'il vous plait,' he demanded.

Chumley took off his grubby rucksack and dug around for his passport which he then handed to the man.

'Hmmmmph.' The shopkeeper grunted as he inspected it. The name on the card, R. Chumley, matched the passport. Little did he know that the R on the card stood for Rebecca and not Rufus.

Rufus tapped the credit card's code into the authorisation machine. The receipt was printed out. Holding his nose aloft the shopkeeper passed Chumley his purchase.

'Merci, Monsieur.'

Chumley left the shop, seeing himself in its mirrored door as it closed behind him. He looked very dirty and unkempt. No doubt he smelt too. Perhaps, he thought, he ought to do something about this? After all, he did have a new respect for himself, so he ought to be looking after himself better too. His new hunting family would like him more if he was presentable, he thought. The time had come to clean up.

Rufus stepped into a men's clothes shop. Inside were rows and rows of hanging trousers and jackets, and shelves piled with smart shirts and nice T-shirts. New socks hung on a revolving display, and underpants were neatly packed in a glass-doored cabinet. He definitely needed new underpants. He'd been wearing the same ones since the beginning of his trip and, he had to admit, he hadn't washed them that often. He chose two pairs of trousers, a jacket, six pairs of striped underpants, four pairs of socks – one pair with rabbits on them, three shirts, three T-shirts, a jumper, a belt with a deer on its buckle – his new family would like that – and even a suit. He got a new pair of shoes and a pair of trainers and finally, he bought a shoulder bag and a case with wheels.

'A new me,' he explained to the shop assistant.

The woman smiled broadly, thrilled to have made such a good sale.

'Formidable!' she said.

'Oui, oui, oui. No more smell of wee on me!' Chumley said back to her.

He took his new things and went back to the field on the outskirts of town where he'd been camping. He retrieved his gun from a ditch where he'd hidden it. Then he left the tent and his smelly sleeping bag for anyone who wanted them. Soon, he was in a comfortable hotel room, having his first shower in months. Grimy water swilled down the drain as he rinsed the dirty suds of shampoo out of his hair. He put a handful of conditioner in it to help him tease out its knots. Then he wrapped a towel around his waist and switched on the hairdryer. The red in his hair would look good with the blue suit. He put it on and looked in the mirror.

'Not bad, Chummers,' he told himself. He thought of the girl in the dead-giraffe picture and of the boy who still could be his brother; of the hunting man and his hunting wife who he was sure would adopt him if he met them. He imagined them all standing beside him, looking out of the mirror. Perhaps they were already a famous hunting family. They'd be so happy when he joined their crew. He wasn't going to give up on that dream.

He put his old rucksack in the bin, then packed his new piece of high-tech equipment into his new shoulder bag. He made his way back to the circus.

The show was over. As usual, a gaggle of children were petting his calf. He got in line to do the same. He took more pictures of it. As the children fed it some nuggets, Chumley stepped up to the fence. He liked being so close to the animal. He studied the red, moon-like branding on its rump. He'd have to look that up on the internet, he thought, to see exactly what farm his calf came from, so that when he shot it, he could prove how far he'd tracked it. Then, turning his mind back to the task in hand, he leant towards it and gave it a pat.

Albi let himself be patted. The little hands stroked his nose and his ears. For a moment, the feeling from his dream about the

red-haired boy stroking him flashed in his mind. No wonder, he thought – children were crowding around his pen. He felt a sharp pain on his rump where an insect stung him. He swished his tail to get it away then turned back to a child who wanted to take his picture.

Chumley walked away from the circus and sat down on a nearby park bench. He turned on his phone and switched on the tracking app. There on the map on his phone was a bright yellow light, blinking at him, showing him that the tiny metal device that he'd implanted in the skin of his calf's rump was working.

'Just you try to escape me now,' he said.

MAGICAL SINGING BULL CALF

MELODY MOOOER

First in France, then in countries beyond, newspapers and internet sites punched out their headlines, telling the world about the small French circus's phenomenally intelligent performing calf.

Television companies from Sweden to South Africa, from China to America, from Kuwait to Australia sent reporters to film Albi for their news shows. The miracle of what he could do was all to do with the milk mushrooms, Albi knew, so whenever he found them growing under a tree or near a hosepipe tap, or somewhere damp, he'd eat them again and his mind would grow brighter and brighter and brighter.

He was enjoying life at the circus. He liked to use his inventiveness to think up ways to make Camille's show even better. He loved her and the ponies and the great times they were having. Now the idea of running away felt like a mad thing to try to do, for he was happy, and even though he could still sense the herd, far, far away, the risks of being caught on the mighty journey he would have to take to get to them was too high. What was more, he sometimes felt that Oros was watching and was proud of him. Proud of what Albi had achieved and the new family he'd found. Because the circus was like family. Albi adored Camille and was content to stay with her. Life was good. But, one night, things started to change.

It was the beginning of August. They were in a fancy seaside town. The show had been a success and Camille had brought the ponies and Albi out of the big top tent to their small paddock. Albi and the ponies noticed a musky, pungent scent in the air. They heard voices locked in intimate conversation. The first belonged to Camille's father.

'Take a look at him, he's over here,' he was saying.

Camille's father smelt of the grape drink. Wine – Albi knew its name now. His guest peered into the paddock. Beatrice's nose twitched.

'That new man smells of passion flowers and racehorses,' she said. 'Very grand indeed.'

Albi could smell horse on him now too. He was dressed immaculately in a crisp dark-purple suit.

'How much will you take for him?' the new man asked, in a deep voice that reminded Albi of the low bells that he'd heard ringing in some of the towns they'd been to. Albi didn't know what 'take for him' meant but he knew it was something serious because Camille's hand tightened around his ear.

'Oh!' Her father laughed. 'He's not for sale.'

'Everything has a price,' the man said.

'*He* doesn't,' Camille piped up. 'Papa, make him go away.'

The man did go away, but the next morning, when Camille had taken the old mare to the blacksmiths, he returned. A gleaming silver horsebox was driven near to Albi's paddock. The driver got out of one side of it, and the man who smelt of racehorses got out of the other side.

Camille's father appeared. He came into the paddock, walked past Isla and Isabella and stopped at Albi. He put a halter around Albi's head and led him out through the gate. Albi didn't like it. When the horsebox's back door opened and a ramp came down from it, Albi started to feel very nervous indeed.

Camille's father clicked his tongue, 'Come on, lad, up you go,' he coaxed.

Albi dug his hooves into the gravely ground beneath him. 'NO!' he mooed.

Where was Camille? Had she come back yet? Could she hear

him? Camille's father pushed Albi up the ramp. Albi could have kicked him but he didn't want to hurt him. Instead, he just mooed a plea to not be shoved into the horsebox.

'Where are they taking you?' Isla whinnied from the paddock.

'I don't know!' Albi mooed desperately back.

The lower part of the horsebox door shut so that Albi could just see over it. He saw the man give Albi's father a big case and then saw the men shake hands. It reminded Albi of the French man shaking hands with the Spanish bull-farm man months before. Albi knew the word for the grubby stuff that he'd seen so often in human's hands. Money. He imagined that a lot of it was in the brown case.

The horsebox shook and made chugging noises and began to move. It noisily wheeled its way over the stony circus ground, away from the big tent towards the road. And then Albi saw her. Camille was in the distance coming round the side of a caravan, leading Beatrice. She took one look at the silver horsebox, at the case in her father's hand, at the enclosure where Albi had been and she guessed what was happening. She dropped the ponies' leads and began to run towards the moving horsebox.

'No! NOOOOOOO! You can't take him! NOOOOOO!'

Her father caught her but she broke free and she began sprinting towards Albi. He mooed back at her.

The last Albi saw of his dearly beloved friend was her frightened and scared, with begging eyes and tears streaking down her face; with her arm outstretched and her mouth open as a terrible scream came out of it. Albi mooed to her. Of course, to a passer-by it just sounded like the loud moo of a cow, but to the tuned ear it was an anguished cry of a calf being ripped away from a human that he deeply and truly loved.

As the vehicle drove on, Camille's cries rang in Albi's head. If he'd been with her, he would have enjoyed the perfect, chamomile-smelling box he was in. But instead, he hated where he was, because the shiny horsebox was tearing him away from the friendship and love that he'd found, stealing him from Camille, Isla, Isabella, Beatrice and his circus family.

Yet again, he'd found happiness and it had been taken from him. He ignored the clear mineral water in the silver trough on the side of the box; he didn't care about the views outside. He lay listlessly on the floor. He wasn't scared; he was shocked and sad. So sad that he couldn't care what happened to him next.

The vehicle slowed down. Albi got up and looked out of the window, a small part of him hoping that Camille would be standing there, that everything had been a terrible mistake.

There was no Camille. They had arrived at a wide, open expanse of fenced-off ground. The air smelt of the liquid that the circus fire-eaters used to make flames. Huge machines with wings stood on the tarmac, glinting in the sun.

Aeroplanes.

Chapter Nineteen

AEROPLANES AND LABORATORIES

Chumley had been keeping track of his albino calf. He had to admit, this made a part of him feel sad. For, he saw how easy it was to keep track of something and this brought home the truth – that the people he called his parents did not care enough to keep track of *him*. But, when he forgot about this and remembered what a talented young adventurer he was, it put him back in a good mood.

He'd been staying in small hotels in all the towns that the circus stopped at, and he liked his new life. Today, he was sitting on the balcony of his room. It had views of a pretty garden square. He sat down in the sunlight and delved into his phone to check on the location of his little bull calf. The yellow star on his phone blinked.

ST TROPEZ AIRPORT

Chumley frowned. That couldn't be right. Sometimes the app

had a glitch. He switched the phone off and on again. To his horror, the star blinked again from the airport. He stood up. What could this mean? Was the circus leaving town by aeroplane? Impossible. Had the calf been killed and was someone taking its skin, with the electronic tag still in it, to another country? Or had the calf escaped and accidentally walked to the airport?

Soon, Chumley was standing beside the wire fence of the airport. He watched as a small, sleek plane took off. As it did, Rufus had the oddest sensation. It was as though he could feel the calf's presence pulling away from him. Then the yellow star disappeared from his phone.

NO LOCATION FOUND

the app told him.

'NO!' Chumley shouted at his phone. 'This isn't true!' He hailed a taxi and made his way back to town.

The circus big top was still up. Chumley rushed to the enclosure where the animals were kept. He found the circus girl sitting on an overturned bucket, her three black ponies leaning over her. She was crying. Chumley knew how she felt. He was tempted to go and talk to her, to commiserate with her. His French was almost good enough to, as, recently, for some reason he'd suddenly got very good at it. But he didn't know what to say. He watched the girl with her ponies and wished he had some animal friends to comfort him.

The plane vibrated and hummed as it shot through the sky. Albi didn't care where he was going. He never wanted to care about anything ever again.

He thought of Camille. How he wished he was with her. Why had her father given him, Albi, away? He'd taken him away from Camille and the ponies as if he were a toy that they had all been given to play with. Camille's father wasn't a bad man, Albi thought. But he had done a very, very bad thing.

Albi felt like he'd been locked in a prison of sadness. A deep, dark place under a mountain of unhappiness, far away from fresh air and light – Camille was like oxygen and the sun to him. He needed her. His heart was breaking. And he was full of regret too, that he'd never even showed her how he could glow. He knew that she loved him. That was the only comfort that he had. He wanted to snuffle his nose under her chin and hear her laugh, and knowing this would never happen again was horrible. She was gone from his life now.

He shut his eyes and Oros came to him now. 'Breathe in, then moo out for as long you can. You will come to a quiet place inside you that is your true self, Albi, not the Albi that is pulled down with dark, sad feelings. Lift yourself up. Stay with your breathing. Don't think of anything except for your breath. In and out. This is a calm place. You can be at peace here.'

Albi took the advice. He began to breathe in and then moo out for as long as he could, and he kept breathing like that. Albi stopped letting himself think about the things that made him sad. He just thought about his long moos. He lifted himself up and away from the feelings of missing Camille and the ponies and Bodge, Lily, Ernie, his mother, and Oros; he lifted himself up from the feelings of anger he'd felt towards Camille's father and towards the matadors and the people in the arena in Spain. All the horrible things he'd felt dropped away. It was just him and his moos inside an aeroplane that flew he knew not where.

It was a long ride and Albi slept, sleep healing his broken heart just a bit, filling its cracks with courage. As he slept, the plane bumped along, rocking him. Then, after what felt like a day, he woke up. His eyes were dry and his head foggy. With a thud and a rumble of its wheels the plane landed. And as it did, Albi's heart lifted. For, although a very bad thing had happened to him and Camille now felt very far away, something good had come out of it – the herd felt *closer*. The pulling feeling told him that they were still a long, long way off but they were definitely much nearer than before. Suddenly, a hope that he hadn't entertained for a long time came to him; hope that he might actually see his herd again!

Albi took a few swigs of water from the dispenser and had a think. He was here, he knew, because of his impressive performance at the circus. The humans admired his intelligence. Albi's mind whirred. If there was still a chance that he could catch up with the herd, he had to do everything in his power to make sure he survived to find them. To survive, he knew he must be as bright and entertaining as possible. And so, he made a positive decision: he decided to put all his sadness behind him. He decided to focus his mind on what he had control over at that moment, and to again use his cleverness to survive.

'I'm bigger than I think,' he told himself, as the back door of the plane half-opened.

Dense heat flooded in. A dry, spicy smell filled the air. Albi squinted to see what was outside. The place was even hotter than where the bull farm had been. There was no smell of green vegetation. All around was sand. There wasn't a plant or a tree in sight. He smelt manure but it was unlike any manure he'd smelt before. In the distance, he saw a large animal – a swan-necked, long-legged animal with a rubbery muzzle, big eyes and, very oddly, a huge *hump* on its back. Then, another one of the same creatures stepped out from behind a sloped wall of sand. This one had a man sitting on its back. In his hands were reins decorated with coloured ribbons and small bells that jingled when the man tugged at them.

A man in a uniform stood at the back of the plane as the ramp was brought out. He held a rope with a metal connecting clasp on it. Albi realised this was for his halter. Starting as he meant to go on, he took the opportunity to impress the human. He stepped down the slope towards him, bent his head, and politely took the rope from his hand with his teeth. Other men nearby laughed and made exclamations of delight and amazement. One point up, Albi thought. His nose caught the scent of passion flowers. It was the smell of the man who had come to the circus.

The man looked different today. He was dressed in a long white robe with a red and white chequered scarf on his head, held in place by a black cord. The other men were dressed in these clothes too.

Albi decided not to feel hatred for the man. There were very few humans like Camille, who appreciated that animals had feelings. This human was simply like most humans. He had plucked Albi from his life as easily as a bird might peck a berry from a tree. He didn't know any better. Albi also knew that most animals didn't have as good a memory as he, Albi, did. Beatrice, for instance, couldn't remember the farm she'd lived on as a foal. Perhaps this human thought Albi would forget Camille as easily as a squirrel might forget where he'd hidden a nut.

Albi walked over to the man and tapped the ground in front of him three times. He mooed. The man turned to his friend and smiled broadly,

'A'taqid innahu yuhib hadha al-makan,' he said.

Without being asked, Albi walked to a horsebox that he could see was for him, went up its ramp and trotted inside it.

'Hayawan dhaki,' one of the men said. Albi felt his skin shiver and tingle. He stopped himself glowing but he let his mind open and receive what it needed to grow and understand. And 'Hayawan dhaki', though said in this very different, new tongue, made sense to Albi. 'Clever animal,' the man had said.

Clever animal indeed, Albi thought to himself. If they only knew how much he understood.

The horsebox drove along desert roads, past dry dunes that rolled away for miles all around, then it turned off and crossed a cattle grid into a lush, grassy park. Fans of water swooped left and right over its green meadows, their wet arches catching the bright sun so that rainbows hung in the misty air.

Albi smelt horses. And then he saw them. Huge, beautiful horses; black, brown and white horses standing in fields under trees with fronded tops. They looked up then they returned to their grazing. Their backs shone. Albi had never seen animals more beautiful or more handsome, with such muscles and gloss.

The horsebox rumbled under a stone arch, into an enclosure. The back door to the horsebox opened, and a see-through tunnel was attached to it. People came near and peered through it. Albi could feel they meant no harm. Without coaxing, he walked along the tunnel to an open door at its end. Albi walked past a bearded human and into the room beyond.

Albi's eyes took a while to adjust to the bright light of the room. The bearded man wore a smart white coat-like layer over his clothes. An overall. The word came to Albi. Another man, one with a moustache, who smelt of hay and horse sweat gently led Albi over to a wall. Here, he took some broad straps from the ceiling and belted them under and around Albi's chest and tummy, buckling them tight so that Albi had the sensation that he could, if he wanted, lift his legs off the ground and his body would be held up by the straps. Albi knew the body harness was to hold him in case he suddenly decided to charge around their little room. There was a lot in the place that could be damaged – delicate-looking metal and glass objects and things with screens on them. Computers. Scientific instruments. This was a laboratory. The words flooded in.

The door opened and the man who'd come to the circus entered with a woman; she was the first woman Albi had seen here. She was wearing a scarf around her head. The humans spoke quietly about him. Albi, now fluent with their warm-tongued language, knew what they were saying.

'Isn't he well-behaved?'

'He's certainly highly intelligent.'

The man who'd visited the circus asked, 'What do you think, Miss Safar?'

'He's extremely calm,' the woman – Miss Safar – answered. 'It's as though he understands we will not hurt him. To fly from the South of France to Kuwait and be so cool and calm is extraordinary.'

'I told you he was no ordinary cow. Perhaps you can start now?'

Miss Safar came over to Albi and gently stroked his head.

'Hello,' she said. Albi mooed at her which made her laugh. 'Aren't you adorable?'

She patted Albi's neck and at the same time pressed a button on a disc she was holding. Slowly, lots of wires descended from the ceiling above his head. He blinked up at them.

'I am going to do some tests on you,' she said.

Albi wasn't sure what tests were, but he mooed in reply, saying he didn't mind.

'The sheikh wants to know why you are so clever.' She nodded at the man who had come to the circus, the sheikh. 'Then maybe we can help the sheikh's horses be clever too.'

'And then they'll be the smartest horses in the world and win every race!' the sheikh said and chuckled.

The woman stroked Albi's nose. 'Doesn't he look like he understands what we're saying?'

'Steady on,' the sheikh said. 'Remember, Miss Safar, he's only a cow.'

And so, the tests began. The moustached horse handler put a covering around Albi's head. His ears stuck out of holes in it. As the humans busied themselves with devices that they clipped to his ears, Albi thought about how he knew the language they spoke was Arabic. He didn't know how he knew that – he just did. Just as he knew that day was day or that night was night.

He knew that this sheikh man was important. He knew that he had mountains of the money stuff that humans loved so much. Albi wondered whether these people would be able to work out why he was so clever. Would they find out about the milk mushrooms? Were there going to be any mushrooms here?

Miss Safar poked a sharp, thin metal spike into his foreleg. It didn't hurt much. Albi watched as red liquid came out of him, through the spike and into a small, clear container. It was amazing that this red stuff was inside him under his white fur. He'd seen the red stuff before, of course. Blood. The word for it came to him again. Blood could come out of a creature and it didn't have to mean death.

Miss Safar patted him on the shoulder. 'I don't eat meat,' she whispered.

Albi saw that she was very kind person, for she was saying reassuring things to him even though she thought he couldn't understand. He could smell that the man in the white overall and the Sheikh both did eat meat.

There were so many names for the different meats that humans ate. Albi knew many of them now: spare ribs, steak, veal. Leg of lamb, sausages, liver, kidneys. Heart, bacon, salami, trotters. He looked down at his hooves. Did they eat hooves?

Miss Safar took the container with his blood and slotted it into one of the silver machines on the wall. Lights flashed on the machine's dials.

'Good, that's done,' she said. Then she came back and checked the wires attached to the gear on Albi's head. 'We're ready,' she announced to the bearded man who was now sitting in front of a computer screen with lines and shapes on it.

The sheikh sipped at a lemon tea and settled into a chair to watch. 'What are you going to call him, Miss Safar? I can see you already adore him. You can choose.'

Miss Safar smiled. 'Thank you. I think his name is Snowy.'

'Snowy it is!' the sheikh said, laughing and raising his glass of tea. 'Let the experiments begin!'

'I will familiarise him with the animal cards first,' Miss Safar said. Frowning, she began to show Albi cards with pictures of horses on them. 'Horse, horses,' she said, very seriously. Then she showed him a picture of a cow. 'Cow,' she declared. She showed Albi more pictures of horses. 'Horses, horses,' she said again. She got to another cow card. 'Cow!'

Albi smiled to himself. When a card came around with a calf on it, he gave a big moo. The sheikh spluttered on his drink. The bearded man gasped. Miss Safar clapped her hands delightedly.

'Do you think he really recognised it was a cow?' the Sheikh asked.

Miss Safar placed all the picture cards on the ground: sheep, pigs, chickens, horses and lots of cows. Albi tilted his head to make it look as though he was thinking hard, then he lifted his hoof and began to point out the many cow cards by touching them with the tip of it. He looked at the humans. They all had their mouths open like frogs about to swallow bugs.

'What's the matter? Thought animals were all completely stupid, did you?' Albi said, though of course, all that the humans heard was a moo.

Albi didn't want to impress the people so much that they moved him somewhere else. He felt safe with Miss Safar and thought this a good place to stay for now. So he slowed the pace down. In the next card tests, he acted as though he didn't understand. He pretended he didn't know how to walk on the treadmill. Eventually, the sheikh got bored.

'He's certainly a very bright animal,' he told Miss Safar. 'Please find out why.' And he left.

Miss Safar looked quizzically into Albi's eyes. She nodded. 'What's going on in that head of yours?'

Albi was right. The sheikh's stud was a safe place to stay. A stud was, he found out, the word for a big home for lots of horses. Albi's quarters were a luxurious stable where he slept and his own personal paddock that he could enjoy in the evenings when it got cooler. From it he could see a few of the sleek racehorses in other fields.

The days were very hot. Albi stayed inside doing Miss Safar's tests. He tried to learn as much as he could from her. He listened to conversations she had on the phone or with the moustached man and so found out that the stud was in the countryside but near a train station. Sometimes the sheikh's camels were transported by train to other places. This was useful information.

Miss Safar gave him free rein to walk about the laboratory. It was obvious to her that Albi was not going to be like a bull in a china shop. He was calm and well-behaved. She was so relaxed about it that sometimes she listened to music with her headphones on, not noticing what Albi was up to behind her. She liked it when he put his head on her shoulder while she was working.

Albi discovered that, though she didn't have tattoos, she was very like the man in the cave. She loved nature and wanted to do something to stop climate change. Climate change was something Albi knew a lot about now. Miss Safar liked to record herself talking about desertification, which was when green places get so dry that plants stop growing. She knew about a place in China where a desert as big as Belgium had been turned to greenness again. Her ambition was to go there and learn what they'd done and then help turn other deserts into places with lush plants. Like Albi, she wanted to leave the stud.

Sometimes he watched the computer screen with her, which was very interesting. He saw more in a few minutes about the world than he'd seen in a day of walking with the herd. Sometimes she watched funny TV shows where humans wore silly outfits and talked in a jokey way. Albi would moo, laughing with Miss Safar. There were serious things he saw on the computer screen too. News stories that showed humans fighting. And others that showed some of the disasters happening in the beautiful world. Fires, floods. Sometimes the things on the computer made Miss Safar cry.

'If only humans put more energy into fixing the world, instead of destroying it and fighting,' she said as she wept. 'You know, Snowy, there is a way. It just needs humans to care enough that they give up things. Do you know, if humans stopped farming animals, there'd be much, much less methane and global warming gases in the air. Methane. So much of it comes from cows burping. Humans eating meat makes twice as much greenhouse gas as humans eating plants and vegetables!'

'I know,' Albi mooed to her, thinking of what he'd learnt from the American man in the cave.

Miss Safar went on, telling him, 'So much land and forest that should be cleaning the air is cleared to grow food to feed cows that humans eat. It's wrong. You'd think humans could just give up meat and milk and cheese and butter just to sort things out. But no, they won't. Why, Snowy? Why?'

Albi would snuffle into her neck when she cried to try to cheer her up. That usually tickled her and made her laugh.

'What about the burps of humans too?' he asked. But of course Miss Safar didn't understand what he was saying.

Albi loved Miss Safar's writing, with its curls and swooping lines. He liked it when she wrote with a pen that she dipped in ink. This was usually to put her signature on documents that she signed.

The writing was very different to the writing near Henge Farm or in France or Spain and Albi found it difficult to fathom. Then one afternoon, it all fell into place. It made him glow, but Miss Safar didn't see. And with the understanding of the Arabic writing came a brilliant idea. One that involved Miss Safar's cards that had *writing* on them. Albi trusted Miss Safar enough to try it out.

Albi knocked the testing cards on the floor. They scattered. Some landed picture-side up. A dog, a cow, a horse, a boy, a baby human, a car, a bed, a kennel, a stable, a garage, a cot, a barn. Others landed word-side up. One had the word, سيارة on it. سيارة sounded like *sayaara* when spoken. It was the Arabic word for *car*. Near to Albi was a card with a picture of car on it. Albi saw his opportunity. He gave a little moo to get Miss Safar's attention, he reached his hoof out, tapped the word سيارة, and then, very deliberately, he tapped the car picture.

Miss Safar's body went rigid. She swung round in her chair. Then, slowly, she stood up.

'Did you . . . ? No.' She shook her head. 'No. It isn't possible.'

Albi nodded, he mooed. She looked around her to check there was no one else in the laboratory.

Miss Safar bent her head and shut her eyes. 'Ya Allah!' she whispered.

Albi knew this word – he'd heard a circus man praying to Allah. He'd seen an acrobat sitting cross-legged praying in another way too and Camille's mother on her knees whispering prayers to God. So, he knew Miss Safar was probably praying now. He let her do it for a bit then he mooed.

Miss Safar opened her eyes and she nodded. Fumbling, she sorted out the picture cards so that they were equally distanced on the floor; cards with different animals on them, and pictures of other objects and things. Then she shuffled the word cards and finally placed one down. It was upside down so Albi couldn't read it. He twisted his head round to see.

'Aauuuuurghhhh . . . !' Miss Safar let out an almost pained sound. Albi hoped she was all right. 'Oh my goodness, you *knew* it was the wrong way around! I think you are, are . . . *reading*!'

Her hand shaking, she placed another card on the ground.

بقرة

بقرة meant 'cow'. Albi tapped his hoof on the word بقرة and then on the picture of the cow. Miss Safar sat back on her heels. Then she leant forward and looked into Albi's eyes. 'You understand me, don't you?'

Albi nodded and mooed.

That same afternoon, Rufus Chumley sat under a shaded awning in a palm tree garden café in Kuwait. A man-made mist dropped from sprayers in the ceiling at the edges of the café. Like a cold curtain, it kept the place cool, which was good because Rufus felt very ruffled and overheated. He'd had an extremely nerve-wracking morning. A ghastly morning. His mother's credit card had stopped working. This meant he'd had to quickly find a jewellery shop and sell her rings and necklaces to get some cash. He spoke Arabic surprisingly well, but he'd never sold anything in his life before. He wasn't sure whether he'd got good money for the diamonds and gold. Chumley took a few gulps of his lemonade.

He opened his phone and looked again at the flashing yellow dot that showed him where his calf was being kept. It drove him crazy that it was being kept by this sheikh, this imposter who knew absolutely nothing about his calf's real past. If only he could steal his calf back, he thought. But it was impossible. How was he going to get into the billionaire's guarded stud? What was the sheikh keeping his albino calf for, he wondered? A pet for his child? Or had he noticed that it glowed sometimes? Or had the sheikh had the calf killed and stuffed it, just as Chumley planned to?

Ever since the night in Pamplona, Chumley had mixed feelings about the calf. He dreamt about him a lot. Dreamt of stroking him. Half of him wanted to keep the calf alive, as he admired it so much, but the other half still really wanted to kill it. Because he so wanted to have the the Worldwide Hunting Association see what a brilliant hunter he was and then be part of their big family.

It was August. There was the rest of the year to go before the hunting competition deadline was up. Chumley looked online to see pictures of other competitors' entries so far. A man from Oregon in America had shot a bear; a young girl in Russia had got herself an enormous elk. His glowing bull calf would be far superior to their kills, he thought. Mind you, it might not glow when it was dead. This was a bit of a problem. He would have to get pictures and film of his calf glowing when it was alive to show what a rare animal he'd hunted down. The other amazing thing about this creature of course, was how far it had travelled. He knew it had come from near Stonehenge and would prove that from its branding. He had evidence from the internet of both the time the calf had been a mascot in Pamplona and of its time in the circus. He had taken his own pictures too. People would be flabbergasted to learn that he, twelve-year old Rufus Chumley, had tracked this creature from England to Kuwait! The creature would be a remarkable kill. Chumley would be crowned a legendary hunter.

Chumley sat at his café table and watched people come and go, in pairs and in families. Chattering away, like those rats had on the trailer in France. It would be nice to have a companion, he thought. Even if only at the end of a telephone. The other day he had phoned his mother and his father, but neither answered nor called him back. Suddenly, he felt very sad.

He shut his eyes and thought about friends he might have. The face of the calf came into his head. He imagined stroking him again. Then stopped himself.

'No, Chumley, he's not your friend. He's your prey.' He thought instead of other animals he'd enjoyed the company of. The songbirds in the forest had been nice. He imagined one now, a blackbird. When he opened his eyes, a small blackbird was standing on the table looking at him. It tilted its head as though trying to read Chumley's mind.

'Will you be my friend?' he found himself saying to the bird. Slowly, he put a piece of his bread on the table. The bird ate it. 'Is that a 'yes'?' Chumley asked shyly.

Chapter Twenty

COMMUNICATION

'So, you can read. You can understand what I am saying.' Miss Safar shook her head in disbelief, then she gazed at Albi and sighed. 'You're a miracle.'

Albi shook his head.

'You're not?'

Albi went to her desk and, being as careful as possible, nudged the ink pot there with his nose. It tipped over. Ink spilled all over the floor. He felt bad about that, but needn't have worried – Miss Safar was thrilled.

'Yes, yes. Of course!' She rushed out of the room and was soon back with a big bag. In it was a large pad of what the humans called paper and a tin that read

طلاء أسود

She eased the lid off to reveal the black paint inside, and pushed the tin towards Albi. She put a big piece of white paper beneath his nose.

'Can you?' she coaxed.

Albi thought for a moment. The word car, or سيارة in Arabic, came to mind. He dipped his hoof in the paint. Miss Safar held her breath. Albi didn't blame her; it was a very exciting moment. When his hoof was treacly with paint, he lifted it out. A few splodges dropped on the paper. Taking care not to glow, because he didn't want Miss Safar knowing about that yet, he started. But writing was not easy. Hard as he tried, he could not coordinate his hoof with his mind's intention. His hoof could hold his weight, it could tread the ground for him, but it could not do this fiddly thing of manipulating paint on to paper. He tried again on another sheet, but this time made an even worse mess. He gave a moo of annoyance.

'Don't worry,' Miss Safar said, though Albi could see that she was a little disappointed too. 'Hoof to eye coordination is hard. Writing is hard for humans too, when we learn as children. Your leg has never had to use its muscles to control a paintbrush-hoof before.'

Albi stamped his hoof on the ground in irritation. He'd never felt so clumsy.

Miss Safar's eyes lit up. 'Oh my goodness!' she exclaimed.

She rushed over to the table and her fingers played on the computer keyboard. She pressed a button, and another machine on the other side of the room began spewing out pieces of paper. Twenty-six pieces of paper; Albi counted them as it spat them out. Excitedly, she brought them over. She began pinning them to the wall.

'This is a very long shot,' she said. 'But you are so bright, my little Snowy, that I think you will understand this.'

Albi looked at the wall as she put the paper up. Every letter was one that he knew. And beside each letter were a series of dots or lines or both. The letter A had one dot and one line beside it. B had one line and three dots beside it. Each letter had a different set of dots and lines.

Albi looked at the pieces of paper and tilted his head as he thought. He couldn't help glowing a little as he did, but the lab lights were so bright, and Miss Safar was so interested in what his hoof was doing that she didn't notice.

A . –	B – . . .	C – . – .
D – . .	E .	F . . – .
G – – .	H	I . .
J . – – –	K – . –	L . – . .
M – –	N – .	O – – –
P . – – .	Q – – . –	R . – .
S . . .	T –	U . . –

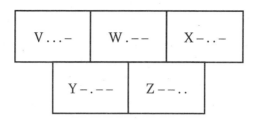

'This is called Morse code,' Miss Safar explained. 'It was invented by a man called Mr Morse. Before telephones were invented, messages were sent by breaking up messages into noisy dots and dashes and sending these bleeping signals through wires.' She picked up her phone. 'You know what telephones are, don't you?' Albi nodded. She sighed and smiled. 'Ohhh.'

For a moment she paused. She touched Albi's fur. Albi knew she was wondering about it and whether it was glowing or not. She seemed to decide that it was a trick of the light, because she shook her head and continued. 'Dots and dashes. A dot sounds like this . . . *BEEP*. A dash like this . . . *BEEEEEEEEEP*. So . . .' She paused again and put her hand on his head. 'It's as if there's a human boy inside you.' She shut her eyes and opened them again, as though she hardly believed what was happening to her, then went on. 'So, my dear Snowy. Look here. The letter A is a dot and a dash. I was thinking that perhaps you can stamp or tap your foot for a dot, and you could wipe your hoof on the floor for a dash.' She took a deep breath. 'So!' she said, her eyes wide with anticipation. 'Shall we start?'

Albi nodded.

'How do you do an "E" in Morse code?'

Albi looked at the chart. E was just one dot. He lifted his hoof and tapped it once on the floor as precisely as he could. Miss Safar lifted her fingers to her mouth, amazed.

'Can you show me a Morse code "A"?' she asked. Albi tapped his foot once, then wiped it across the floor. 'Yes! A dot and a dash – yes, that is correct!' She rubbed her eyes, as though she thought she might be dreaming. 'Um . . . Um. Goodness! I'm so thrilled that I'm not sure what to ask you to do next!'

Albi helped her. He dragged his hoof along the ground twice.

'M?' she asked.

Albi nodded. He studied the Morse code on the wall.

'Go on!'

Albi continued. Drag, drag. Pause. Drag, stamp, drag, drag. Pause. Miss Safar wrote down the letters.

$--- . --$

'M . . . Y?' she asked.

Albi nodded and went on. Drag, stamp. Pause. Stamp, drag. Pause. Drag, drag. Pause. Stamp.

$- .. --- .$

She drew what she was hearing.

'MY NAME?' she said, incredulously.

Again, Albi nodded and went on and wrote down the letters he was giving her.

$. . . . .$

'IS?'

Albi nodded once more.

$. - . - .. - ...$

'A . . . L . . . B?'

$. .$

'ALBI?'

Albi nodded.

'Albi? My name is Albi!' she practically cried out. Albi nodded. Miss Safar gasped. 'And to think, I've been calling you Snowy! I'm so sorry! I'm so, so, sorry, Albi. My name is Miss Safar.'

. .

'Dot, dot,' Miss Safar read, as the letters came. 'I.'

−.−−.−−−.−−

'K . . . N . . . O . . . W. I know? You know! Oh my goodness!' She looked embarrassed and spluttered. 'Oh, but of course you know! You've been listening to our conversations and heard my name a hundred times.'

Albi mooed a laugh and Miss Safar laughed too.

'But Albi, my first name is Maryam. So, call me Maryam!' She smiled. 'Oh! It's so nice to meet you properly at last!'

Maryam flung her arms around Albi's neck and hugged him. And that was when Albi let all his pent-up glow shine. Maryam stepped back in awe.

'Oh my goodness! You *were* glowing . . . You *are* glowing!'

This was how Maryam and Albi became real friends. Their secret conversations were very long-winded to start with but in a couple of days they both got very good at it. Albi told Maryam about the milk mushrooms and his glowing. He told her about his life and his travels, about Oros, his mum, about Lily, Bodge and Ernie. He told her he could feel that they were somewhere, hundreds of miles away to the north, and about how he wanted to get back to them. He asked Maryam about a camel train that went north that he'd heard the moustached man talk about. Maryam said she would try to think of a way to help Albi get on to it.

A person looking into the room would have seen a young bull

calf knocking the ground with his hoof as though he had a nervous tick. And they would have seen a woman in a white laboratory coat sitting in front of him, listening and talking to the cow in the same way that humans talk to other humans.

When August's full moon came, Albi predicted that the milk mushrooms would sprout near the water trough or the tree, and, sure enough, they did. Maryam, who had stayed late to see the mushrooms and collect some to test, crouched down in the grass to look at them. But when she reached down to pick them, she couldn't. They felt too special, she said.

Albi touched the ground with his nose. He felt very clear-headed, charged by the special milk-moon mushrooms. When he shut his eyes, it was as though Oros was beside him, talking right into his ear.

'*You are strong now, Albi. You must leave this place.*'

Albi picked up one of the milk mushrooms in his mouth. Maryam followed him inside. He placed the mushroom on her desk and, tapping out what he wanted to say, told her, 'These mushrooms are for you to do great things with. The milk mushrooms will help you with your work.'

'Thank you,' Maryam said. She sighed. 'I have thought about the train, Albi. It is safe . . . to a degree. It will get you to the north, closer to your herd. The sheikh puts his racing camels on it. He has a special camel carriage. You can hide in that.' Her eyes filled with tears. 'I don't want you to go, Albi, but I don't want to control you and keep you here if you want to leave.' She wiped her nose and gave him a hug. 'Your courage inspires me. I will be brave now and pursue my dreams too. After you've gone, I will go to China to meet the scientists who are turning the deserts there green.'

Maryam reached into her pocket and pulled out a beautiful moonstone, set in macramé on a long loop of strong string. She put it over Albi's head, squashing it into his fur so that it couldn't be seen, and she gave him a kiss.

'This is for you to remember me by. It comes with all my love for you. I hope my love will help to keep you safe. Stay away from humans, Albi. Most will want to . . .' Her voice trailed away.

'Eat me.' Albi finished her sentence.

Albi understood what Maryam's fears were for him. محل in Arabic, viande in French, carne in Spanish, meat in English. The whole world over, humans ate animals. Humans were lucky that they didn't get eaten, he thought.

To cheer Maryam up, he mooed her a tune that he'd made up for her, but this made her properly cry.

'I'm sorry. I didn't mean to upset you,' Albi said.

'Oh Albi, don't worry. I'm just crying because I love you so much. I will miss you so badly when you're gone.'

The little birds on the café table tweeted up at Chumley as he fed them.

'Oh, so the bread is too fresh? I'm so sorry, I will make a complaint to the management.'

Chumley had a few bird friends now and today had been lovely because they'd all been pleased to see him. The café cat had also been friendly and Chumley had spent a good ten minutes stroking

it. He looked at the supper menu again. It had been difficult to choose between the beef steak or the pork chop or the skewered chicken. He had gone for the steak.

His favourite bird, the blackbird that he'd named Mr McFeathers, hopped near his water glass and then on to his finger. Chumley smiled and Mr McFeathers flew up on to his shoulder. Chumley felt good, contented. In another life, he might have been like that French girl – a circus boy with tamed animals, he thought.

The bird flew off and landed on the ground. Lots of Chumley's other feathered friends hopped near it. He threw more crumbs for them. And then, it happened. The cat pounced. All the birds scattered, flying away. Except for one that the cat had caught. With one sharp bite, the cat had killed Mr McFeathers.

'NO!' Rufus cried.

The cat looked up angrily. Who was this man, interfering with his sport? He picked the dead bird up in his teeth and with a few deft leaps, was up on the wall in a place where no one would find him.

'Everything all right, sir?' the waiter asked, seeing his regular customer was distressed. He placed the man's plated steak in front of him. 'Mustard?'

Chumley looked at the meat on his plate. In his mind he saw Mr McFeathers' flesh in the cat's mouth.

'Please take this away. I'm sorry, but I have lost my appetite.'

He shut his eyes. If he hadn't, he would have seen that the skin on his hand was glowing.

Chapter Twenty-One

THE CAMEL TRAIN

Three days later, Albi was on the road again, on the way to the train station. He was hidden in one of the sheikh's animal trucks and sharing the space with one of his camels.

'You'll be fine,' the camel said. 'Good luck.'

Albi nodded gratefully. 'Thank you.'

When the truck arrived at the station, Albi did what he had practised with Maryam. He squeezed his head out through an open gap at the rear of the truck and, using his teeth, slid open the bolt there. Pushing the door open, he quickly leapt out. Then he hid behind some dustbins. The stable man got out of the vehicle. Discovering his truck's door ajar he looked panicked but, finding the sheikh's camel still inside, he relaxed.

A long train pulled up, its brakes screeching. Albi spotted the carriage with the sheikh's emblem on it. Sticking to the plan Maryam had devised, he stayed hidden in the shadows. People walked past. The station became a hubbub of whinnying and bleating as horses, goats and sheep were loaded into carriages. The door of the sheikh's carriage would be opened soon, the sheikh's camel would board and minutes after the train would roll away. Albi's heart pounded. He knew he had to move soon.

A man in a brown uniform laughed as he shared a joke with the train driver. He sang along to the music he was playing, then he switched on his torch. He stepped to the sheikh's carriage, behind the driver's cabin. Albi watched as he pressed a simple code into a box on the side of it: 101010. The numbers stood like a line of sticks and balls in Albi's mind. The carriage door opened and a ramp began sliding out, meeting the concrete platform with a *THUNK*.

Albi eyed the ramp longingly. The plan was, he'd run up it and get on board, but he didn't know how he was going to do this without being seen. Maryam had said that the platform would only be dimly lit by station lights. This was true, but she and Albi had forgotten about the moon. Tonight it was low and very bright and it shone down through a cloudless sky.

The driver opened his window, stuck a pipe in his mouth and put a flame to its tobacco. He began to suck and puff out smoke. Puff, puff, puff. The man puffed along to the music on the radio. When the driver blew out a big puff of smoke it was as if he had disappeared. For a moment too, the platform was hidden from the driver. Albi saw his opportunity. The next time a cloud of smoke came, he shot out from his hiding place and, with the sound of his hoofsteps drowned in the music he trotted up the ramp. Once inside the carriage, he dived behind a pile of hay, getting down on his knees and rump and backing himself into the corner so that he was buried.

The sheikh's racing camel was led to the carriage. He lumbered up the ramp, then with a nod to Albi he turned to his handler and snorted and spat at him. A big blob of spittle landed in the stable hand's eye.

'Ah!' he cried. 'That's filthy! Get in, you stupid animal.' When the camel spat again, the man ran out of patience. He shut the door and locked it. 'Settle your own self in.'

The camel gave Albi a wink.

'Thank you,' Albi mooed quietly.

'My pleasure,' the camel replied. He yawned. 'Get ready for a long journey.'

Albi's heart quietened and he breathed in the sweet smell of the carriage. It smelt of hay and farmyard and for some reason, of human children.

As the train started moving the air filled with a new, pungent smell.

'Terribly sorry about that,' the camel apologised. 'Sometimes my posterior has very bad manners.'

Then a small voice to the left of them both piped up. 'Thank you very much, stinker. Just so you know, you're not the only one in this wagon.'

Albi leapt to his feet.

'Sorry,' the young voice said. 'Didn't mean to shock you, fella.' A hand, a child's hand patted Albi on the neck.

Fear coursed through Albi and he dodged sideways, making sure that whoever this person was he didn't get a hold of him. Light from the outskirts of the town illuminated the back of the carriage and Albi, quivering with fright, saw a small, dirty boy with a friendly face standing in front of him.

'Don't worry,' he said. 'I won't hurt you. Lucky you can't talk,' he added, 'because I'm a stowaway.' He said this proudly. 'So how do you do? My name's Tishk.'

Albi could tell that the boy had spent time with animals, firstly because he was entirely comfortable to be in such tight quarters with Albi and the camel, and secondly, on closer examination, the boy smelt of them – dogs, cats, horses, mice and camels.

'Don't worry about him,' the camel grunted, his eyes still closed. 'I saw him at a race in Abu Dhabi. He's a jockey.'

'A jockey?' Albi mooed. 'I thought only adult humans were jockeys.'

'In the horse-racing world, yes,' the camel said, 'but in the world of camel racing, adult humans are so greedy to win that some of them use children as jockeys. They don't weigh much, you see, so the camels can run faster. The sheikh doesn't use kid jockeys, but others do – even though it's not allowed.'

The train left the station and rumbled away from the town, making its way along heavy metal tracks out into the desert and the cold night air.

Chumley stepped out from a cinema into the cold night air. He had an odd, pulling feeling in him, as though he was losing something. The movie had been set in British countryside which reminded him of his old life. He had certainly lost that. But when he switched on his phone, he saw that he had lost something else.

The yellow star that usually showed him where his albino bull calf was, now read:

NO LOCATION AVAILABLE

He began to sweat. Why had the star disappeared? Had some meddling person removed the chip he'd put in the calf's skin? Or had it been flown somewhere again? He tried to calm himself.

'Don't worry,' he said to his phone. 'This is probably good. I bet you'll pop up again somewhere soon. The sheikh won't have you guarded all the time. Soon, very soon, I'm going to get you.'

He went to his hotel room to pack his bag.

The train journey was indeed a long one, just as the camel had said. During the week that followed, Albi, the camel, whose name was Sarie, and the boy, Tishk, passed through sparsely shrubbed desert where the sand stretched for miles around. Tishk talked to his animal companions a lot.

'It's been two years since they took me away. I was so small when that nasty man and his wicked wife stole me. They stole me and sold me. Sold me! I never should have gone with them. Puppies and sweets. They tricked me. There were no puppies. I wonder how much they sold me for?'

Then, another time, 'Mother always said I was a champion. When I was five, I rode the winner in the town's race. Sand King was his name. I loved that camel. He and me were like that.' He crossed his arms together over his chest. 'I wish we'd never entered that race. Sand King and me, we wanted to win that one so badly. That was when we were spotted. That greedy old man and his cunning wife with her popcorn. I always had a sweet tooth. I will get back to Lahore . . .'

He'd say 'Lahore' over and over, as though saying it would make him get there. 'I am lucky. I will get to Lahore . . . Lahore . . . Lahore . . .' Sometimes, he'd get out a whistle and play tunes on it. Some jolly, some sad.

The boy ate nuts and stale bread that he had in his knapsack, and he drank the same water as Albi and Sarie. He would often sit on the hump of the camel's back, from where he could see out of the high stable-carriage windows. He'd talk about the sandy world that stretched into the distance. Albi thought of Maryam and her ambitions to turn the deserts into forests and grassy plains. He missed her. He missed Camille and the circus ponies too. But he could feel his herd getting closer and this made him feel better.

'You're a beauty,' Tishk said, stroking Sarie's nose. 'I bet you run like hot fire.' He ruffled the hair on Albi's forehead too. 'And you, what a wonderful creature you are.'

Albi didn't glow or moo in tune with Tishk's whistle because he didn't want the boy to keep him. Albi needed to stay free.

As the journey progressed, Albi, Sarie and Tishk felt more and more cooped up. They took it in turns to pace the length of the carriage. Once a day, the train would stop at a station and someone would board it to check the water and the food. Sarie would kick hay over Albi and the boy and hide them. He would stand rooted in front of them like a camel shield.

'So, you're hiding too,' Tishk said, the first time it happened. 'Afraid of being caught, just like I am?'

Albi tried not to think of nets and nooses and ropes. It made him shiver. If he was found, he'd be sausages or steak or roast beef in no time. It was horrific to think of, but it was true – everywhere, most humans would eat him. The thought of kind Camille and Maryam gave him hope. As did animal-loving Tishk.

The boy longed to see his parents again. He knew the stations that had to be passed to get to Lahore. They crossed the giant country of Iran and entered the next country, Pakistan. Tishk celebrated this border by singing its national anthem, for Lahore was in Pakistan.

The train's metal wheels beat on and on in a rhythmic roll, over and over and on and on, clunking iron castanets, steel fingers tapping. It sped eastwards, then north. One evening, after lots of track changes, the train pulled into a very large station and backed itself up into a sleeper track.

Albi read a sign:

لا محور

This was a new written language to Albi; it was Urdu. So, it took a few seconds for his brilliant mind to understand. They had reached Lahore.

'Lahore?'

Chumley had much less money now. He'd sold all his mother's jewellery and his father's watches. And the piles of expensive Kuwait hotel and restaurant bills had eaten through his savings. He hoped he had enough to pay for a plane ticket to Lahore.

Chapter Twenty-Two

PAKISTAN AND KASHMIR

Sarie said goodbye to Albi and wished him more luck, then disembarked, clomping noisily down the ramp.

Albi and Tishk huddled together, hidden in the hay. The station's hubbub filtered through the carriage walls – camels grunting, humans calling, dogs barking. Albi could smell Tishk's salty fear. Then the wagon door shut, its ramp rumbling back into its holding place. Whistles blew and the carriage was shunted to an even quieter place.

Dusk was falling but Albi knew that sooner or later, a human would open the carriage and step in with buckets and brushes and a hose. He and Tishk couldn't wait for this. Tishk obviously had the same thought, for, as soon as the station was quiet, and the rats were out, squeaking on the tracks, he climbed on to Albi's back and peered out through the window.

'They've all gone home.' He jumped down and beamed at Albi,

patting him on his neck. 'Bet you never knew you'd get this far away from Kuwait, little bullock!'

Tishk put his ear to the door, nodded, then then reached for the door's handle. He tried to turn it. His smile faltered. He tried again. A look of dread dropped through his face.

'It's locked! Why would they lock it tonight? There's only hay in here! They think it's empty, so why would you lock a thing that has nothing to steal inside! Why?' His eyes moved to the code box at the side of the door. 'Oh, no!'

Tishk fell on his knees and began to sob. 'It's numbers, and I don't know the numbers. It could be any numbers in the universe!' He crumpled into a weeping heap on the floor, his head in his hands. 'What am I to do?'

He looked like he was praying. Albi wondered if he was praying to Allah, like Maryam had, or God, like Camille's mother used to.

Albi gave a quiet moo, but Tishk was a shaking wreck and paid no attention to him. Albi gently butted the boy's shoulder with his forehead. He mooed again. Tishk opened his eyes.

'Not now. Can't you see? We're stuck!' he cried.

Having him look up was all Albi wanted. With a swift dive, he pinched the boy's whistle from his pocket. Gripping the whistle between his teeth, Albi pulled himself up on his hind legs so that his forelegs were on the wall, and he punched the numbers into the pad. Sticks and balls. 101010. The locking mechanism inside the door gave a clunk and the floor of the carriage shook as the ramp started moving out. Now Tishk's eyes opened wide.

'You . . . you *are* a miracle!' he spluttered. He dropped to his knees and stretched his hands up above him. 'Thank you!' He flung his arms around Albi's neck, squeezed him and kissed him.

'Oh, thank *you*!' He took the whistle out of Albi's mouth. 'Is this a magic whistle?' He shook his head and put it back in his pocket. Then, taking a deep breath he stepped towards the open door. He paused. 'The way out of here is for you to look like you belong to me,' he decided. 'Do you understand, young bullock?'

Albi nodded.

'Is that you just shaking the flies off?'

Albi shook his head.

Tishk laughed.

'Heel,' he said. 'Follow me.'

Tishk walked slowly down the ramp without looking behind him, then, as though testing Albi, he suddenly turned. Albi was right there.

'Good!'

The platform was deserted. It was getting darker by the second.

'OK,' Tishk said. 'When we find some rope, I'm going to put it around your neck so that you look like you're mine, then hopefully no one will bother us.' Albi nodded his head. Tishk laughed, then frowned at Albi. 'I think you are a bit too white. We don't want you attracting attention.'

He led Albi to a muddy place at the end of a track near the platform. He didn't need to tell Albi what to do. Albi just lay down on his side and rolled.

'You are the best!' Tishk exclaimed. 'You've been sent as a present to help me! Come on, little bullock, walk with me. Let us get to my village! If we take the road north to a big town called Jammu, we will get there. You can't miss my village. It's on the way to Jammu, you see. There's a tall water tower outside it with a blue flower on it. Are you ready for a long, long walk?'

Albi felt very fortunate to have found the boy too, for with Tishk by his side, he was protected. So, with both of them feeling happy and optimistic, they set off to the place called Jammu.

The light was fading in the big city, Lahore. Its dusty pavements were sparsely lit by street lamps and the cars on the roads began to turn their lights on. There were mopeds and scooters and tuk tuks, people busy with their own business. Very few noticed the bull calf and the boy heading purposefully out of town.

After hours of walking, when the city was well behind them, they found a disused barn to shelter in. They slept here for a few hours, then got back on to the road. Albi walked keenly, for though the herd was still far off, every step brought them closer.

The edge of the road wasn't always easy to walk on; it had stones and overgrown parts and there was a lot of traffic. First of all, night lorries, then morning trucks and buses, vans, cars, motorbikes, tractors. Sometimes, they passed carts pulled by horses or camels, or oxen pulling wagons.

By mid-morning, they came to a crossroads with seven possible turnings. Tishk looked worriedly up at the sign with its list of directions to go in. He was tired and hungry and, on top of this, now anxious too.

'I can't read,' he admitted to Albi. 'I don't know which way Jammu is. Maybe if we wait here, I can ask someone.'

He tried to flag down cars, but no one stopped. Tishk slumped into a heap on a hump of grass and for the second time, he began to cry. Of course, there was no need for his despair. Albi had already read the sign.

ج م و ں

'Jammu!' He mooed, tapping his hoof in the direction that they should go.

Tishk's face twisted. 'You don't know either! Don't pretend.'

But Albi nodded and tapped again and again, until he felt like a mechanical toy whose settings had been stuck. To sway Tishk completely, he got up on his hind legs, as he had done in the circus and walked like that a little way in the direction that he knew to be right. This made Tishk sit up. He stared at Albi in amazement. Then, to help Tishk really believe, Albi decided to shock him. Remembering the tune that the boy had so often played on his whistle, Albi mooed it to him now.

Tishk sat bolt upright.

'You are a gift from the heavens,' he said incredulously. 'How could I have forgotten what you did in the train with that lock? I trust you, my friend.'

They began walking along the road that Albi suggested. Half an hour later, an old man came hobbling along the road, leading a donkey.

'Excuse me sir, is this the way to Jammu?' Tishk asked.

'Yes, young man. You should cross into Kashmir tomorrow and get to Jammu tomorrow night. What a handsome bullock you have!' he added.

On they walked, stopping at streams to drink and for Albi to eat some camel nuggets the boy had taken from the train. Tishk was so hungry that he ate a few of the nuggets too. They walked through the rest of the day. The sun sank in the cloudy sky. They sheltered and slept and walked for a second day but slower now, much slower. A second evening approached. Night fell again.

'You are my magic bullock!' Tishk sighed, stroking Albi. Albi could feel the child was deliriously tired. They were walking across fields now, away from other people, so to give Tishk strength, he made himself glow.

'I'm dreaming!' Tishk laughed. 'Let me ride you. I am too tired to walk. Yawning, he took the rope off Albi's neck and climbed on to his back. He was a light load. It was a warm night and soon, he was asleep.

It was a sleeping boy that Albi carried into Kashmir and to the small village on the outskirts of Jammu. He lay him down on a slope of grass there, near to the water tower with a blue flower on it. Tishk rolled over, snug and snoring. Albi gave him a goodbye lick on his ears, then quickly left.

The village was twinkling with night lights. Albi could smell wood smoke from the chimneys of people's houses. From down the hill, he heard the warm voices of two adults and some children.

'It's bedtime now,' a woman was saying.

'But I don't want to go to bed,' a small, cross voice replied.

'Mum, LOOK!' a young girl's voice suddenly exclaimed. 'It's a boy!'

Albi walked on into the woods. He imagined Tishk waking and looking for him, then his happiness at seeing his village and the friendly people. Albi smiled as he thought of Tishk being reunited with his family.

He remembered Bodge's mum's words. *The more you care about others, the stronger you get.* It was true. Albi felt extra-strong because he had helped himself *and* someone else as well. He thought of the days when he'd been a young calf, when he'd felt small and wide-eyed, when he'd thought that the most knowing calves were better than him. Now, he was as clever as a bull calf could be and he knew that cleverness wasn't the best thing. No, kindness was. Kindness was a superpower. He thought of the kindness others had shown to him, from his mother to his friends, to Oros, the Spanish bulls. Camille and the ponies, Maryam. Their kindness had been a power that had helped him. And as a calf, he may have been young, but he had always been kind. All his life, he'd had that power.

Chuffed by this realisation, Albi walked on.

Rufus Chumley had spent the last of his money on a plane ticket from Kuwait City to Lahore. And with very few possessions stuffed into a ruck sack – a toothbrush, passport, a blanket, a sleeping bag, a thin tent, a few coins, a spoon, a plate and a solar-powered phone charger – he'd left the airport.

His phone had picked up intermittent signals from his albino bull calf, so, buoyed up by a renewed optimism, Chumley had started walking along the main road. He tried to hitch lifts, but no one picked him up. He must look dodgy, he thought. He'd hidden his knife in its sheath on his belt under a cloth so it couldn't be that. Undeterred and fuelled by the prospect of catching his calf, Rufus kept on.

One day, he found a stray dog walking beside him. It was thin and very scruffy with a scar on its face and it was missing the end of one of its ears. It seemed to like Rufus a lot, which was a spectacular feeling because he had never felt anyone like him this much before. He called the dog Snoot. Snoot was a better companion

than Mr McFeathers had been. He liked to play fetch. He'd lick Rufus fondly and tilt his head when he was trying to understand what Rufus was saying. When Rufus slept, Snoot curled up at his feet. He woke him with a gentle bark every morning and made Rufus happy.

Snoot seemed to be able to find things to eat in the scrubland and bushes. But food came less easily to Rufus, and he was always hungry. Ever since Mr McFeathers had died, Rufus had lost his taste for meat. The milky mushrooms he'd eaten in the field outside Pamplona stood out as being one of his best meals, and so, when, one full-mooned night he found some more under a tree, he ate them raw. They were creamy and sweet. They made his stomach warm and sent him to sleep. He had very good dreams that night. He dreamt that he was glowing and then that a huge bull was talking to him. The bull said, '*Trust the feeling. You will find the glowing calf.*'

When Rufus woke up, he was sure that he could feel where the glowing calf was even more than before. It was strange; it was like a tug, as though a big invisible rope connected him through the ground to the calf and was pulling him towards it. An odd new part of him wanted to meet the calf and get to know it, but the old hunter part of him scolded him.

'Make friends with the calf? Are you going mad? Chumley, you're going to hunt that animal down.'

The day after his milk-mushroom meal, Rufus was hungry again and took to begging. An old widow was very kind and shared her lentil soup with him. She also gave him a woollen coat that had belonged to her husband when he'd been alive. 'You will be needing this,' she said.

'No one has ever been so nice to me,' Rufus told her. 'You're very kind. Thoughtful. Generous. Thank you.'

The old lady smiled broadly, impressed by the scruffy young person who spoke in her tongue. If Rufus hadn't been so tired, he might have noticed that he was speaking a language he'd never spoken before. He might have seen that under the blanket that he wore like a cloak, the skin of his legs was glowing.

Soon, Chumley was reduced to rifling for food in bins. One afternoon he found a packet of biscuits. He popped them open and shared them with Snoot.

'We're the same, you and me,' he told him. 'Both animals.'

Rufus said this with pride. He felt close to animals now. The idea of killing them wasn't attractive any more. 'We're both alone, Snoot. You know what?' he confided in the dog, 'I had an imaginary family once. A hunting family. I was so lonely that I imagined they existed. But now, I'm not interested in hunting.

'*Really?*' the hunter part of him asked.

Chumley paused, picked up a stick and broke it. 'Except for one animal.' He frowned darkly. He was filled with a deep dislike for the calf. 'I think that I hate that calf, Snoot. Because, and this may sound crazy to you, but it's not really an animal, you see. It's more of a *beast from another planet*. It glows. And that's not right, is it? It's dangerous, Snoot. So I've got to kill it. This is a very different sort of killing. It's very important that I track it down. I think maybe that calf is a danger to the world! And guess what? This is going to sound weird. But sometimes I think I can feel where it is, through the *ground*. It feels like the mushrooms are whispering to each other about where it is and then telling me. Like they've chosen me and are helping.'

The tracking device led him to the foothills of some mountains. It was wetter and the slopes were greener. Rufus was grateful for the fruit trees here. Like fruit shops, he could stop at them and get what he wanted. Sometimes the trees were in orchards, and it was clear that they belonged to local farmers. Rufus didn't like stealing any more so when he could, he only took the fallen fruit; apricots and plums on the ground that were often infested with flies and wasps.

He found an old sack and filled it with whatever he could forage. Figs, pears, potatoes. He ate the potatoes raw, biting into them like apples. And he laughed to himself, amazed by how he was living. On a few occasions he found wild almond trees. He eagerly picked the nuts from the low-hanging branches. The almonds were rich and oily and made his mind feel sharper. Nuts had lots of protein, he remembered. That was probably why.

'Brain food,' he told Snoot, as he filled his sack. 'Those milk mushrooms are brain food too. Certainly are. I'm sure they're how I learnt French and Arabic so fast. Let's keep a look out for them, Snoot!'

Walking with the heavy sack was difficult, but worth it because the land was becoming more rugged, with less food about. Rufus was getting much thinner and very muscly. The fat that had built up around his stomach from all the French café cakes had gone.

The hills grew steeper and lonelier and colder. There were less and less signs of other humans, less houses and then less mountain huts. Rufus made fires to keep him and Snoot warm, using the ancient method of rubbing two flints together to start flames. When there were no more nut and fruit trees, he began to dig for root vegetables and wild tubers.

Chumley became extremely hungry. Snoot was so famished he ate the turnips Rufus gave him. Rufus remembered seeing jungle people in a documentary eating insects and so he began looking under rocks for bugs and worms and grasshoppers; anything that was edible. He ate the insects raw. He felt bad about eating them.

When the turnips and bugs and insects weren't enough for him and Snoot, Chumley decided he would have to hunt something to eat. His old knife skills came in handy and he easily killed a rabbit. But it wasn't the same as before. Before, he'd enjoyed killing and paid no attention to the life he was taking. This time he said a prayer to the dead rabbit. He thanked it for giving its flesh so that he and Snoot could survive the mountain.

Rufus was no longer interested in The Worldwide Hunting Association. He didn't want to be like those people who killed for fun. He watched the mountain animals – the wild pigs, the bears, the deer, the foxes – and had huge respect for them. He admired the great birds that flew above him – eagles, hawks and kites. He felt clear-headed and good.

But as the days passed, he became thinner and more tired and at night his sleep started to teem with strange dreams. Rufus's thoughts became confused with mad ideas.

'I've been thinking,' he told Snoot as they walked. 'That calf probably isn't even from this dimension. It hangs out with weird huge beasts. You should have seen their giant hoofprints near Stonehenge! They were walking into the rock there! You've got to be from a different dimension to do that stuff.' He shivered. Then he started to laugh. 'Maybe when I find the calf it'll make us some milkshakes!' Rufus thought this was the funniest thing he'd ever heard. He laughed for a good ten minutes, rolling around on the ground. 'Of course it can't! It's a bull calf!' His smile suddenly dropped. 'When I kill the calf, Snoot, its glowing will go into me. But I have to kill it. If I don't, who knows what dreadful things will happen to the world?

'TELL THAT CALF I'M COMING TO GET HIM!' he shouted to a golden eagle who flew over him often. 'TELL HIM THAT HIS TIME IS UP!' His voice echoed through the rocky outcrops. 'His time is up! His time is up!'

One night, he was sure he saw a tiny glow in the distance. When he shut his eyes, the tugging feeling came from that direction too. It was soon after this that his tracking device stopped working but Rufus didn't mind. He could feel the bull calf very strongly now. Soon, he picked up its hoofprints too.

'I'm coming to get you,' he whispered.

AUTUMN

Chapter Twenty-Three

ALONE IN THE MOUNTAINS

Steep, misty slopes rose ahead of Albi like steps to a grander world. He began to climb. The paths were rubbly, and he had to be careful not to twist his leg or trip.

The weather was getting colder. A new moon grew in the sky as his fur grew thicker. He kept his coat dirty and mud-matted. He wanted to be as disguised as possible, even though there were very few humans living here in this wild, rough place. Albi still had to be very careful. The people here were hungry, and they might lick their lips when they saw him. Lots of steaks, scores of sausages and a nice big stew could be made out of him. He might not have a chance to moo them songs or make them laugh or impress them with his glowing. They might prefer him as a feast on plate.

The mountain pastures were empty now, the once-rich grass of the summer thin. Albi was always hungry. Snow-capped mountaintops were ahead and a frost bit the night.

Albi grew very tired. His energy dropped. Weak and exhausted, he began to lose the feeling of where the herd was. And then it disappeared entirely. All at once he felt utterly alone. A suspicion dawned on him that maybe his knowing where the others were was just a figment of his imagination, just like a mirage of an oasis would be to a thirsty, confused camel.

And so, the next part of his journey was a very difficult one. Albi told himself that the knowing feeling would come back. He kept walking towards the mountains, to where he'd felt the herd before, expecting it to rise up in him again. But the feeling didn't come back. Albi had to face his loneliness.

It was very rugged and remote now. He copied other animals and ate bitter thistles and twiggy leaves. As the place became wilder, he grew bolder, and he began to walk in the daytime. He brushed the dirt and dried mud off his fur by walking through bushes and, after rains, it became bright and white again. He met wild goats and forest boar. Once, near a mountain pool, a woolly ram with huge horns charged at him. Before he knew what he was doing, Albi dipped his head and his own new horns tipped forward. That was enough to scare the ram off. When Albi looked in the water, he saw a reflection that was very different to the one he'd seen in the farm trough months and months before. His face was much furrier, his cheeks had more muscles, and his horns were now more than stumps.

'You certainly are bigger than you thought,' Albi said to himself.

He learnt to like it in the mountains, with its crowned stags, handsome and beautiful, royal and antlered. He admired the majestic eagles who ruled the skies. One golden eagle flew above him often. Albi mooed in greeting whenever he saw him.

He loved the company of rabbits and hares, foxes, hawks and songbirds. And he came to be happy with his life, whatever was going to happen now he'd lost his herd. Perhaps he would stay in the mountains forever, he thought. Perhaps he would live out his days contentedly, like the other animals here. He could make new friends. But still he was hopeful the pull would come back, and so, he walked on towards the mountaintops.

When the October full moon came, the milk mushrooms came too. Albi spotted their silver spores falling from the sky, and the next day the mushrooms grew, and he feasted on them. They restored him. That night, he slept soundly and woke up with the wonderful feeling of knowing where the others were again. They were much nearer. But with this feeling came another. Albi could feel something, somebody behind him. And whoever it was was getting closer and closer.

Morning was almost breaking. The golden eagle had landed on a rock near to him. It flapped its wings and looked out over the valleyed hills below.

'Good morning,' Albi said, not expecting a reply, because he'd found eagles to be very solitary and usually silent.

This one surprised him. He turned his brown and orange head and replied, 'Good morning, young bullock. I have been watching you. I have seen your fur light up, as though you had the moon inside you.'

'Yes.' Albi smiled. 'My fur does glow sometimes.'

'I have seen other cows like you,' the eagle declared. 'Their herd walks the other side of that mountain.' He nodded his beak to indicate the direction he meant.

'H–how far away?' Albi stuttered.

'For me, if I fly on the high winds, a morning. For you, two weeks, if you take that path.' He pecked at the air to show the direction he meant. 'Down and up. There is a thick forest that will be difficult to pass through. There are humans there. And hungry wolves.' Albi shook his head as he absorbed this horrible truth.

'Or you could brave the ridge.' The eagle indicated the flat, rocky mountaintop to their right. 'It is very treacherous and dangerous. The rocks are bare and dry. It can be windy and its sides are steep. If you slip, you may slip to your death. But if you don't slip, you would get there in three or four days.' He rustled his feathers as he prepared to leave. 'There is one more thing. A young man follows you. Take care, young bull.'

He spread his wings. A powerful beat of them lifted him, and in a few seconds, he had flown up and away into the cold air.

'Thank you!' Albi mooed loudly after the eagle.

He glanced about. Who was following him? Where was this person? Were they good or were they bad?

As if in answer to his questions, a boy suddenly came rushing out of the bushes.

'AAAAAAHHHH!' he shouted, his voice full of fury.

His long red hair was dishevelled and dirty, his expression was wild, his eyes were greedily wide. Albi recognised him at once.

In the boy's hand was a sharp knife.

Rufus Chumley charged forward. He would be on top of the bullock in just a few seconds. And then he was. The animal's legs gave a little as he landed on him. Chumley braced himself for it to buck. But it didn't. Chumley snarled and clutching a handful of the bright white fur, he raised his other hand with the knife in it to the skies.

'YOU'RE MINE!' he shouted. And, using the last of his energy, he brought the knife down.

But, in that moment, the most peculiar thing happened.

It was as though a force sucked the strength out of his arm. His hand went limp. He dropped the knife. It clattered to the ground. Rufus gasped, froze, then collapsed. His head fell into the bullock's white fur.

And now, like a child with a long-lost pet, one that he loved as much as he loved himself, Rufus Chumley held his arms around its soft, furry neck. And he knew, knew for sure, that the last thing he wanted to do was kill the bullock. He felt more love for this animal than any other living being. This strong, magical bullock that stood quietly under him, gentle and soft; a creature that smelt of grass and salt and life. How had he thought that it was bad? It was just like the other animals Rufus loved, though even more special. It was warm and comforting and good. All Rufus's confused thoughts melted away.

Albi stood still. What was the boy doing? Had he fallen asleep? Albi felt wetness on his skin where the boy's face was. Tears. The boy was crying. He was desperate, sad and lonely and needed to

be carried. Albi could sense that. So, without shaking him off, he began walking. A dog joined them. Albi supposed it was the boy's friend. The boy didn't speak. He just lay still. And Albi walked.

Albi walked all day. And as he did, the truth of who the boy was came to him. He'd seen the boy before. In the abattoir, on the back of the horsebox, at the bullfight. He was the boy from Albi's dreams.

Albi didn't feel that this boy was a threat though. Quite the opposite. The boy obviously wanted to be with Albi, and Albi felt good being able to help.

When night came, the winds became harsher, so Albi found the biggest boulder to sleep beside. He and the boy and the dog slept together.

Revived a little, the next day, the boy chose to walk, though he held on to Albi's tail. Albi set his back and shoulders determinedly and trudged on, along the craggy ridge. The dog walked faithfully behind. From high in the sky the eagle watched them. They looked like small insects walking along the back of a grey cow.

On the third day, Albi found some small, shrivelled milk mushrooms nestled near some low bushes. He took some for himself and with his nose, nudged the others towards Rufus and Snoot. Snoot preferred the mountain moss but Rufus ate them gratefully, then climbed back onto Albi's back.

Rufus Chumley shut his eyes and held his arms around the bullock's neck. The four hooves beneath him clopped over the stony ground; the furry bed under him swayed and rippled as the animal's muscles carried him; the rhythm as gentle as lapping water under a boat. The ground was gravelly and easy to slip on, but the young bullock kept walking, step after steady step, as though he knew exactly the path to take, as though guided by something. Rufus didn't care where they were going. He felt like he had come home, so wherever the bullock took him was the right place.

Rufus thought of all the killing he'd seen – of his father's abattoir, where dead calves hung like picked ripe fruit; of the animals he'd shot and gutted and stuffed. And he saw how blind he'd been to those animals' lives. He had never thought of their feelings. But now he saw that their lives were as important to them as his was to him.

He thought of the people he'd grown up with – of his cold mother and his cruel father, of how they didn't love him. But that wasn't his fault and it didn't make him feel bad. It made him feel strong. He felt sorry for them that they were so rotten. He felt lucky because he wasn't them. He felt wise because he could now imagine how horrible it must be, living such mean lives. He forgave them, which felt good, but he also felt sad for them, because they didn't know how to think about other people's feelings. They were shallow. They could only think about themselves.

'I'm sorry,' he mumbled in his sleep, over and over again. 'I'm sorry. Please forgive me, forgive me.' And his body and his hair glowed.

Albi wondered what the big boy felt so sorry about.

'Thank you,' the boy kept saying. Then, 'Thank you, glowing boy cow.'

'That's all right,' Albi mooed.

Albi could feel the herd getting closer and closer now. The ridge started to slope downwards. Albi's vision was bleary from fatigue, his ears were numb from the wind. Then his leg buckled. He tumbled a good distance down. The boy fell too. Albi clambered to his hooves and now walked with his eyes shut. The boy was no longer on his back. The songs Albi had learnt ran around his delirious mind. The words jumbled in his head.

Twinkle, twinkle, little star,

میرے دل کی

The cow jumped over the moon,

خواہش ایک دعا کے

Frere Jacques, Frere Jacques,

Sonnez les matines!

The dish ran away with the spoon.

His mind grew forgetful. All that he knew was that he wanted to get back home. But home wasn't a place that he could remember. Home was a feeling. A safe feeling. All he wanted was to be there.

He heard the cries of birds roosting. They roused him from

his sleepwalking. But this awakening made him fall again. The ground smelt of grass. He opened his eyes. The snow had gone. He saw trees.

He was at the bottom of a mountain – or was he imagining it? The boy had gone. Albi wasn't sure whether he'd ever been there at all. A glowing ball was coming through the dim dusk light towards him, getting bigger and bigger.

Was he dreaming that too?

Chapter Twenty-Four

THE HAPPY HILL

Albi woke up a few hours later, with the warm smell of his mother nearby. His eyes flickered but stayed shut. He smelt and felt her wet nose on his.

'Albi. You found us.' It was Oros's voice.

'You fainted, Albi,' Bodge's voice was deeper than Albi remembered.

He felt something being nudged towards his nose. Wet grass and milk mushrooms.

'Eat these,' Lily said.

Albi was too weak to reply to any of them.

'Where have you been?' they asked. 'How did you find us? How did you get here?'

'I don't know.' Albi's life since leaving the herd felt unreal to him; his past a story that he'd heard once but nearly forgotten.

'I missed you all the time,' he said. 'I was always missing you. I don't want to ever leave you again.'

Over the next few days, Albi recovered. One afternoon, feeling stronger, he got up from the leaf-lined, makeshift stall that his mother and Oros had made for him. The herd gathered and a hush fell as everyone eagerly waited to hear what had happened to him.

'I've never seen them so well-behaved,' said Bodge, breaking the silence. 'It's quiet enough to hear a caterpillar fart!'

The herd laughed and so did Albi, which felt good because he hadn't laughed like that for weeks. And he began. The herd settled and listened as he told them how his life had turned. It was a long telling.

'That's what happened to me,' he said, when he'd finished. 'That's the short version.'

'Interesting,' said Oros. 'That matches some of the dreams Lily here had about you. Lily has visions about the future and sees things in far-away lands. So we had an idea where you were. Lily is rather brilliant.' Lily bowed her head modestly.

'What happened to you?' Albi asked.

'It was a tough journey,' Oros began. 'Wasn't it?' The cows around him mooed in agreement. Albi noticed some very young moos – there were two fluffy black-and-white calves who looked only a few weeks old. 'It was often wonderful but sometimes sad. You may have noticed there are no more auroch, Albi. I am the last. Others of our herd died along the way too – cows, calves, bulls, bullocks, heifers; to old age, sickness, hunger, thirst. It is a miracle that we are here. And that you are here, excellent Albi.' Again, the herd mooed. Albi felt warmed to his soul.

'We felt your presence often,' Oros said. 'As you felt ours. And what did we do? Well, we walked, and walked.'

'I trotted!' one of the calves exclaimed.

'Yes, you did,' Oros agreed. 'Some of us walked and some of us trotted. We found refuge in other caves along the way, under other ancient stones like those of Henge. First in the mountains north of Italy, under the holy rocks there, then under the ground in Slovenia and Croatia. We journeyed on through Europe, at one point on a big barge that carried us down a long river called the Danube. That was a wonder. Lily dreamt about the barge and how we should get on to it.'

Lily nodded. 'After that,' she said, 'we got to a port in a country called Romania, and we smuggled ourselves on to a ship that I'd dreamt about too. We travelled across the Black Sea, to another country called Georgia. The way was easier there.'

'Until we got to the next s-sea!' Ernie said. 'So many s-seas. The mushrooms told us w-where to go and showed us a t-tunnel, a n-n-natural one, unknown to the humans.'

Oros nodded. 'And so, we walked under this sea and under the next countries too. Turkmenistan, Iran, Afghanistan. When we emerged, the land was dry, with only thistles and cacti to eat. It was summer and very hot. But finally, we got to the foothills of the mountains in Pakistan and the rains came, and with them, more fertile places.'

'The grass was juicy again,' Bodge said. 'It was amazing. We slipped by the humans like ... like snakes through the garden.'

'Every full moon the milk mushrooms came. And we all ate them,' Albi's mother said. 'Our time has had its sad moments and its frightening situations, but we made it here, and, beloved Albi, it is a heavenly thing to be reunited with you.' She rubbed her nose on Albi's back.

'You'll never guess what the others called me,' Bodge said.

Albi smiled. He always loved listening to Bodge.

'They called me Poo Hunter.'

'Oh dear,' Albi said. 'Why?'

'Because I got so interested in other animals' poos. It wasn't fair. But oh, how foolish they were!'

'We were,' one of the bulls said and laughed.

'You see,' Bodge explained. 'One night, my smelling talent made them realise I am very, very useful. We were in one of the wilder countries. We got to a wood. I saw this pile of dung on the floor and renocised . . . I mean, recognised the smell of it. It was wolf poo! Wolf poo has a certain grim stench. Rotten. Like dog dung but twenty times worse. Dog poo mixed with sour milk and slimy rotten leaves, I think. Bad. So, I warned the herd. And sure as pats is pats, a couple of wolves *did* come that night. And because of my poo skills we were ready for them. Saw them off. They stopped calling me Poo Hunter after that. Now they call me The Nose.'

Albi admired his friend's big black nose and laughed. 'Bodge the Nose. I like that.'

'Just goes to show, good things come from poo,' Bodge concluded.

That evening, Albi joined Lily and Oros on a grass-cushioned outcrop of land that overlooked a lake below. Autumn boasted in red, orange and ochre in the leaves of trees that grew there, and the blushing sunset above, with its pink clouds, was reflected in the water.

'The lake is like a mirror,' Lily said. 'Do you think the sky admires itself in it?'

'I love the idea that the sky has a mind,' Oros replied.

'Did the sky send the mushrooms to us, to set us free?' Albi asked.

'I don't know,' Oros said. 'What is for sure is that the silver milk-mushroom spores fell from the sky, and the milk mushrooms opened our minds.'

'I wonder whether humans will eat them and become more intelligent and better and kinder, and save this beautiful world,' Albi said.

Oros nodded. 'However they do it, I hope they start to properly care about each other and this planet and the animals they share it with, and soon.'

'So many do care,' Lily said. 'I dream about them. They grow things and are careful about what they take from the earth. And more and more humans are becoming like this. I dream of many that are just children, but they are powerful and brave and determined. They will stop the bad humans destroying this place.'

'That's good to hear,' said Albi. He looked up at the sky and thanked his lucky stars that he was back home.

To start with, Albi felt a little distant from the other cows, because they'd shared in a journey that he hadn't been part of. But by talking to them, he relived their journey with them, and they learnt about his. And then he felt part of the herd once more. He was pleased that all the cows had come to love the milk mushrooms, and so had a high understanding of the way the world was. Oros explained that Lily had been touched by one of the silver spores, which was why her dreaming skills were so good.

It had become a habit now for Albi, Lily and Oros to sit on the hillside talking as the sun went down.

'I couldn't have got the herd all the way from Stonehenge without Lily,' Oros said, smiling at her. 'She has a sense of knowing things. She has finely tuned those talents of hers. You have both overtaken me.'

'I never could overtake you, Oros,' Lily declared.

'I've learnt things you haven't, that is all,' Albi said to the old bull. 'You are much wiser than me.'

Oros chuckled.

'I felt like that about my father. I was sure I would never have my thoughts as cool and balanced as his. Felt like a sapling beside a great oak. When he told me that I would step into his hooves, take on his position as head of the herd, I remember shivering from the apprehension of it.'

A fresh gust had whipped up in the valley. Albi looked at three trees that stood on the mountain side – a great, deep-rooted tree with strong branches and heavy bark that hardly moved, and beside it, two small trees whose trunks were swaying and shaking in the strong breeze.

'And so,' Oros said. 'I know what you are both going to feel when I tell you what I'm about to tell you.' His big pink eyes looked at Lily then at Albi. 'You are both ready. And I am getting old, so I have to tell you this. I've been on this planet for many years. This journey has wearied me. Just as you two have grown up, I have grown tired. I won't be here forever. When I go, you two are my obvious successors.'

Albi knew what losing friends was like. He didn't want to lose Oros.

'You'll be around for a long time yet, Oros,' he said.

'I'm not so sure.'

Albi looked into the old bull's eyes. 'But I've only just found you again. And the herd will be empty without you.'

'Albi . . .' Oros sighed. 'Do you remember when you were a calf? You felt very small. The truth is, you have always been big, because even when you were small you were good and brave and kind. And intelligent.'

'But we're too young to lead the herd.'

'I can't be here forever. One day you too will be old. Before then, you must both show the herd the way. Teach them. There will come a time when you have to speak to young ones and tell them that *you* are going. The river of time rolls on and no one can escape being caught up in its stream. This is the way of Nature and Life and Death. You must be grateful for our meeting, for our time together. When I go, you will feel the pain of it but you will learn to be happy without me. You will be happy to be alive. You will help your children understand the good way. Show them that kindness is the greatest power. And then you will have grown even stronger than you are now. Trust me. It is true.'

Oros took Albi and Lily down to the sunset lake. It was warm because hot springs heated its water. They stepped in and then swam, and it was lovely.

The herd moved on, walking further down from the craggy mountain to creased foothills where the earth sprouted with more and more green vegetation. The hills seemed to tumble down like great, green stairs to the valley's bottom.

One morning, they came through a cedar forest that opened on to a view of a plain. Beyond it, the morning sun rose up over the horizon. Oros walked out of the forest and stepped into its light. Up and up the October sun rose, now illuminating the land below; its cultivated fields with neat lines of crops of wheat, corn and barley, its orchards of fruit trees and its stone cottages. And Oros stood like a silvery-black mountain god on the hillside, in full view of the humans below. Albi watched as the old bull walked towards some tall stones and lay down beside them.

Albi and Lily approached him.

'Are you all right?' Albi asked. 'You should come back to the cedar wood. Humans might see you here.'

The old bull smiled, his pink eyes twinkling with the kindness that Albi loved so much.

'This is my final resting place,' he told them. 'And that village there? That is your destination. It is where you and the herd will be safe.'

Albi looked down at the cottages with smoke coming out of their chimneys.

'But Oros, why should these humans be any different from any other humans?'

'Because' – Oros smiled – 'this is India. And in this part of India, cows are holy.'

'Holy?'

'Yes.' Oros chuckled. Albi wondered whether Oros was so exhausted that he had lost his senses. 'There are many human religions,' Oros said. 'The one here is Hinduism, and it very good for us. It all came to me in a dream last night. Let me explain. Hindus have always believed cows to be generous and nurturing, like Mother Earth.' Albi thought of the paintings on the cave walls under Stonehenge, of the ancient people bowing to the cows there.

Oros looked up at the sky. 'Hindus believe in a great God who they call Brahman, but they think there are many other gods and goddesses too.'

'Like his helpers?' Lily asked.

'A little like that, I think. In the holy pictures of Hindu gods and goddesses, there is often a white cow, painted with garlands around its neck. One of the goddesses has the head of a human woman, the body of a cow, and wings. The people in this part of India believe that all bulls, ox, cows, bullocks, heifers, calves are the children of this goddess.'

'But my mother is my mother, not a cow goddess with wings,' Albi said, frowning.

'Yes, Albi, but they think that right at the root, before the earliest of cows, this winged half-cow , half-human goddess was the original mother of all cows. They think that if they are kind to cows, the goddess will be good to them. So, cows are free to wander where they wish. Strangers feed them. Yes, cows are sacred here.' He chuckled again. 'There is even a holiday when all the cows are washed and decorated with flowers. How about that, Albi and Lily?'

Albi thought about the dangerous humans he'd come across. He was doubtful that a whole villageful of them could think cows were sacred.

'It is true, Albi. It is what they believe.' Oros lay his head on the ground and smiled. 'Here, humans won't hurt you at all. Here, you are all safe.' He shut his great, black-lashed eyes. Albi and Lily watched him breathe slowly. Then Oros gave a long, satisfied sigh and was gone.

Albi got down on his knees, Lily on hers too. They willed the old bull's big chest to rise again. They waited and waited, but it didn't.

Oros was still. Still as the rocks beside him.

Albi and Lily stayed on their knees, both bowing their heads as the long mountain grass bent in the morning breeze. Soon, Bodge and Ernie were by their side and then the rest of the herd. Every cow stood quietly, almost as still as Oros, all bearing witness to the moment when the great bull's spirit lifted and drifted up and away. And then they went back to the forest and fetched branches in their mouths. They laid them in a wreath around Oros so that it seemed he was in a wild green boat, its sail the rocks above him. They put leaves and flowers over him like a wild blanket.

'Where shall we go now?' Bodge asked Albi and Lily.

'We are going down to the village,' they replied in unison.

'Cows are sacred here,' Lily explained. 'We will be free.'

By now, the sun was a burning orange sphere in the blue sky. People were starting to come out of their homes. The herd waited for Albi and Lily to lead the way.

'You go first,' Lily said.

Albi felt humble with the honour as he led the magnificent procession down the hillside into the Indian village. What a sight it was! Cows, bullocks, bulls, and so many breeds. All shades of black, white, cream, brown, grey. Cattle of all shapes and sizes with all types of fur and horn. The cows came down slowly and carefully, timidly, because they were walking towards humans.

The villagers looked up in amazement. They dropped their buckets and bags, their spades and baskets and they stood, gaping. Never before had they seen or heard of such a sight. The herd coming towards them was led by a beautiful, young albino bullock whose shaggy fur seemed to glow in the fresh morning light.

A girl was the first person to move. She didn't find these animals frightening, for she sensed that they were unsure. She walked towards them until she and Albi met. The young bullock looked at her with his shining ruby eyes. She took a purple flower from her hair and ever so gently put it into the fur of his fringe. She looked into his eyes. The bullock looked back at her with so much intelligence and feeling that she felt that if she spoke to him, he would actually understand what she was saying.

'Welcome, and thank you for coming,' she said.

Twenty-Five

PEACE

Later in the day, Albi, Lily, Bodge and Ernie went back to visit Oros's body. He was gone. The branches, leaves and flowers that the herd had piled on top of him were exactly where they had been put, not a petal disturbed. And yet, the great body of Oros had vanished into the thin mountain air.

Then they noticed that the semi-circle of stones that Oros had laid down beside were not ordinary stones scattered there in a haphazard way.

'They're like the r-rocks at Stonehenge,' said Ernie. 'But smaller.'

'Without the top bits,' Bodge agreed. 'They're laid out in a crescent-moon shape.' He walked around them.

'Why didn't we notice this before?' Albi wondered.

'We were all a bit pepculiar . . . I mean, peculiar in the head, paying our respects to him and all that,' said Bodge.

Albi nudged one of the rocks. 'Do you think this stone moves? Maybe he's under here, in another cave?'

Bodge mooed. 'Don't start that again. I like it here.'

Lily and Albi gave the rock a push, but it was far too heavy to be budged.

'Did O-Oros really exist?' Ernie asked.

'Of course he did!' Bodge said.

Albi thought about it. Oros was so magical that it felt like perhaps they'd dreamed him. Albi found that the time behind him, the whole of his life so far, all felt like a dream now.

'The time we had with Oros was real,' Lily reassured him, as though reading his mind.

They looked out over the hillside. The village children played, rolling down its slopes, their bodies like human wheels. A small bird landed on a stone and began to sing, its iridescent blue feathers flashing in the morning light.

'Everything glows and flashes in a wonderful way if you look at it right, doesn't it?' Albi said.

'Yes, because life is a miracle, a magical thing,' Lily agreed. She smiled. 'I am sad Oros has gone. But I am so happy we are all here. I feel safe.'

Albi nodded. 'Safe at last.'

He mooed at the children.

And the children looked up, waved at him, and laughed.

Chapter Twenty-Six

THE GLOWERS

Rufus opened his eyes. He'd been sitting cross-legged for he wasn't sure how long. He was in a small wooden hut, in front of its big open window. He liked this place. The people here were friendly and kind. He enjoyed helping them and they seemed pleased to have him there.

A soft evening breeze ruffled the cotton curtains. Snoot lay curled up, asleep in a basket. Around them, carved wooden animal heads on the walls smiled. Some children in the village had made them. A carved dog head, a black cat head, a green crocodile head, a goat, a small mouse head, a black horse head, a brown cow.

Rufus got up and put a shawl about himself. He lit a match and set the fire in the grate going until the wood in it was crackling with flames the colour of his hair. It was growing dark, so he lit some candles too. The flickering light from them made the wooden carvings around him seem alive.

There was a knock at the front door. He opened it. His two young friends had come to see him again.

'Hello, Rufus Chumnow' they said together, giggling at the nickname they had given him.

Rufus smiled. He liked his new name. The Indian boy pulled a cloth-wrapped parcel from behind his back and offered it up to Rufus.

'For you!' the girl said. 'Because you teach us so nicely. We carved it for you.'

Rufus opened the package. Inside was another wooden head for his collection. A bull's head. It was white and its eyes were painted pink. He smiled. It reminded him of someone.

'Thank you!' he said, admiringly. 'It is I who should thank you. You teach me so much too. And helping you makes me stronger.'

The children laughed.

'That is very funny, Rufus Chumnow,' the girl said. 'Our mother's food make you stronger, I think.' She passed Rufus a basket with lidded bowls inside. 'She made some more for you.'

'Please say thank you to your parents,' Rufus said. 'They have been so kind to me.'

'They like you,' said the boy. 'They like to help you. They say that it makes them feel good.'

'And,' the girl added brightly, 'we like you too!' Then she asked, 'Has your tree grown any more?'

'Good question.' Rufus rolled up his right trouser leg and the three children bent to look at his calf. A strange picture had started to grow there, its trunk starting at his ankle and its green branches spreading out across his calf muscle. It wasn't a tattoo, though it looked like one.

'Yes, it has!' the girl exclaimed. 'Look, those leaves weren't there yesterday.'

'You're right,' Rufus said. 'Maybe soon I'll look just like a tree! I like the idea of that.'

Just then, there was a mooing outside. The children gasped and ran out to the hut's stone steps. Rufus let a spider scuttle over the stone flags and out of the way before he stepped out too.

In front of them on a bank of grass were their regular evening visitors, a beautiful black heifer, and her friend the albino bullock. A little distance away was a hefty grey bullock with a smaller tawny-red. All of them had garlands that people from the village had hung around their necks.

The dusky evening light dipped into darkness. Rufus stroked Albi's forehead and his ears.

Albi burrowed his nose in Rufus's armpit until the boy laughed. Then Albi licked his neck. Rufus smiled at the village children. The boy and girl clapped their hands excitedly.

'Please do it, Rufus Chumnow!'

'Please do it, Glowing Cow Boy!'

Rufus and Albi nodded. Then Albi held his head up high and he began to moo. He mooed a tune that he'd heard the boy play on his sitar, and he and Rufus both glowed as though a light had been switched on inside them.

Dear Reader,

I hope you enjoyed Albi's story. As you might have gathered from it, I, like him, believe that it's better if humans try to stop eating animals and the food that comes from them, to help animals. I also know, from scientific fact, that we can help stop climate change if we change the way we eat, if we all start eating a plant-based diet.

If you want more information about climate change and solutions, along with really nice pictures of calves, interesting facts about cows, games and plant-based recipes please go to the website that I share with Albi: **www.albitheglowingcowboy.com**

Just like Albi, the future is glowing.

Lots of love from me, the author,
Georgia Byng

and

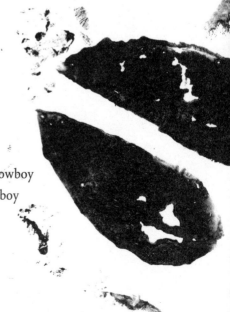

You can also find us on
Instagram: @albitheglowingcowboy
TikTok: @albitheglowingcowboy

If you would like to write to Georgia, please go to the Albi website for the address details.

ACKNOWLEDGMENTS

Albi The Glowing Cow Boy has been a long time in the making. In fact, it's taken twenty-three years. As a result, I have quite a few people to thank.

My first thanks go to my amazing children, Tiger Chadwick, Lucas Quinn and Sky Quinn.

My daughter, the clever and lovely Tiger was nine when I started Albi. I began because she thought it a good idea. She persuaded me to keep going when I was stuck. I wrote the first draft, then, distracted by another book I was writing about a girl called Molly Moon I put it in a bottom drawer. Seventeen years later, my book-loving son, Sky discovered it. He insisted that I bring it up to date and kept badgering me. His judgement and push made me get back to it, even if it was three years later. A year after that, my other brainy son, Lucas helped me with his clear thinking. After long discussions with him, Rufus Chumley was born.

Tiger, Lucas, and Sky have all helped me immensely. I am deeply grateful to them, for being the brilliant, funny people that they are and for putting up with my typing away and burning their suppers.

Also, on the home front, the book wouldn't be the way it is

without Guy Pratt. I have Guy to thank for the mushrooms. If it hadn't been for him the milk mushrooms would have been milk flowers, not half as magical. Thank you, Guy, for making me laugh, for being the best company, a living encyclopaedia/comedy show/newspaper all rolled into one.

My nieces, Grace Wilbur, Fritha Brimble, Ivy Byng, Florence Byng and my nephew, Nathaniel Byng were all Albi guinea pigs, as were Ruby Rainey and Bella Blake. Thank you.

Since the book's beginning, there have been quite a few people who've read versions of it and have encouraged me. My mum, Jennie Bland wise and bright, is as good as mums get, and two people not around anymore, my river-keeper dad, Tom Strafford and my beacon of a stepfather, Christopher Bland. I write children's books because of the happy childhood I had thanks to these people. Thanks to the ever-positive Marc Quinn and friends who've read it, Charlotte Skeen-Catling and Fal Blake, as well as my brother, Archie Bland. Thanks to Elizabeth Sheinkman and to another brother, Jamie Byng for their excellent advice and to the sunny Martina Adamcova, to my dear animal-loving sister, Tara Byng, to Stan Pratt and the influencing vegan, Bonnie Pratt, and to all my supportive friends, including the cows I used to talk to who lived in the field at the bottom of our garden when I was a kid.

But the thanks don't stop here, because there are other hugely important people without whom this book really would not be in your hands. Firstly, there is my agent, Caradoc King. For those of you who don't know, an agent is someone who helps a writer find a publisher. Caradoc is a marvellous agent. He's well-read, which means that he's read barnful's of good books. This makes him extra-knowledgeable when it comes to books. He knows what ingredients work well together in stories. And up there with Caradoc is my other agent, the superb and very sharp Millie Hoskins, with her energy, spot on notes and her instinct that found the perfect publisher for Albi. But before I move onto the publishers, a thanks to Becky Percival too.

For those of you who don't know, publishing houses are the companies that turn authors' manuscripts into the proper books that you see in the shops. Publishing companies are a bit like stables, with the books being the horses that live there. Hazel Holmes is the publisher who runs UCLan Publishing. UCLan's logo is the fox on the spine of the book.

You might be reading a copy of this book in a different language, in which case a publisher from your country will have got Albi translated, and the fox won't be there, but the book's first publisher was Hazel. She is a beaming powerhouse who really cares about children reading. Luckily, she loved Albi and his story and took him on. She asked the splendid Becky Chilcott to design the book. Becky did all the lettering and put mushrooms everywhere and made it look cool and she worked with the gifted illustrators, Levi Pinfold who painted the mesmerising cover and Angela Cogo whose great, atmospheric pictures adorn the book's pages. I love the illustrations. They lift the book up. And thanks to the whizz-kid musician/web-designer, Steve Jones, whose company, Code With Feeling, made Albi's cool website. And thank you, Finn Mackay!

A huge thank you to all these people who have helped bring Albi into the light.

And lastly, but in a way firstly as she is so *very* important, an auroch-sized thank you to my editor, Emma Roberts. The funny thing is she will be even editing these very sentences about her. Perhaps some people reading this won't know what an editor is or what they do. Well, when they are good, an editor is a bit like a very special, inspiring teacher who reads and thinks about what you have written, and then puts constructive notes at the side, with big ticks and congratulatory remarks when the writing deserves them and kind notes when it needs attention, suggesting how it might be improved. Emma is as talented as editors get. She is forensic in her work – she spies problems like a keen gardener who has an eye for rusted leaves or mouldy flowers, who points to all of them with her scissors. I will be forever grateful to her for all the time she has taken in Albi's world, for all her painstaking notes that, like the milk mushrooms have helped Albi glow. Without her, the book would be in some places thin on the bone and in others, flabby. And full of spullung mustookes.

IF YOU LIKED THIS,
YOU'LL LOVE ...

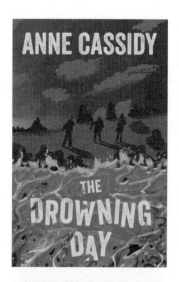